IAN WATSON was born on Tyneside in 19.. .. .. .died
English at Balliol Col........................... in
Tanzania and Tokyo, ... vere
stimulated by his thre.......................... *Roof
Garden Under Saturn,* .... *New
Worlds* and since then .... ous
magazines and antholog............................ *thly*
and *New Writings in Si*....

His first novel, *The Embedding*, was published in 1973 to
enormous critical acclaim and was later to be nominated as one
of the two 'runners-up' for the John W. Campbell Award. In
1974, Ian Watson became a member of the governing council
of the Science Fiction Foundation and has been features
editor of the journal *Foundation* since 1975. However, it was
with his second novel, *The Jonah Kit* (1975), that Ian Watson
really established his position in the front rank of British contemporary writers and in 1976 *The Jonah Kit* became a British
Science Fiction Award winner.

Also by Ian Watson

The Embedding
The Jonah Kit

Ian Watson

The Martian Inca

PANTHER
GRANADA PUBLISHING
London Toronto Sydney New York

Published by Granada Publishing Limited
in Panther Books 1978

ISBN 0 586 04773 5

First published in Great Britain by
Victor Gollancz Ltd 1977

Granada Publishing Limited
Frogmore, St Albans, Herts AL2 2NF
and
3 Upper James Street, London W1R 4BP
1221 Avenue of the Americas, New York, NY 10020, USA
117 York Street, Sydney, NSW 2000, Australia
100 Skyway Avenue, Toronto, Ontario, Canada M9W 3A6
Trio City, Coventry Street, Johannesburg 2001, South Africa
CML Centre, Queen & Wyndham, Auckland 1, New Zealand

Made and printed in Great Britain by
Richard Clay (The Chaucer Press) Ltd
Bungay, Suffolk
Set in Linotype Plantin

To
Sheila

Before me floats an image, man or shade,
Shade more than man, more image than a shade;
For Hades' bobbin bound in mummy-cloth
May unwind the winding path;
A mouth that has no moisture and no breath
Breathless mouths may summon;
I hail the superhuman;
I call it death-in-life and life-in-death.

W. B. Yeats: *Byzantium*

CONTENTS

Prologue

Thirty thousand kilometres out in space, the returning probe *Zayits* raced towards re-entry. The robot 'Hare' was to land softly in the snowfields of Kazakhstan. Its red drogue parachutes would open at six thousand metres. At four thousand metres the main orange parachute would unfurl to spread its bright mark upon the Russian snow, where the violence of winter was spent but the earth was still white and crisply cushioning.

Briefly a small plume of burning oxygen and metal chaff burst from the side of the 'Hare'. In the Tyuratam control centre the telemetry watchers, despairing, reported the failure of the final major course correction. The Hare was wounded. They had no way to trim the craft. Perversely, the angle of dip was still the same; the vehicle could still re-enter without burning up. However, the Hare was now racing towards a strip of atmosphere a few degrees south of the equator and towards the wrong country.

The main parachute should still open out automatically at four thousand metres. However, the Andes reach higher than that. Even the populated high plain that they enclose – the Bolivian Altiplano – lies at that height, in the thin air next door to space ...

Part One

MUMMY-CLOTH

ONE

The village of Apusquiy clung to the base of a double mountain on the edge of the interminable yellow-brown flatland.

Apusquiy was all of slanting steps and shelves. Even its central plaza was two-tiered; and on the upper tier a rectangular marquee of poles and kaleidoscopic woollen blankets had just been erected.

Julio Capac surveyed it with satisfaction. His dozen helpers sat around drinking from some of the hundred bottles of watered cane alcohol stored inside.

This was the first carnival fiesta he had sponsored; the first real rung on the ladder of village life. Military service the previous year made him a fully-fledged man, but the fiesta would make him a respected, prestigious individual, someone whose advice was sought and carried weight. Some day in the future, after sponsoring more fiestas, he would be a *mallku*, headman.

Even this minor fiesta cost all the wages he had saved during three months' labour in the tin mines. Alcohol, cigarettes and coca; several hundred kilos of potatoes, peas, beans, and barley. Money! Life was never cheap or simple if you wanted your voice to be heard. But he would be a great speaker, a great maestro of life's etiquette, a great giver of celebrations.

He blew a kiss to the Sun, for luck.

Like other Apusquenos, he was short and dark, his skin almost chocolate brown apart from his cheeks, which bulged out in glowing red apples, chapped and swollen by sun and wind.

Cheeks also were swollen by chewing coca. His helpers had all been munching spinachy green quids as they laboured on the marquee, making the labour seem timeless and painless.

Spent wads dried to lichenous crusts on the ground. But only lifelong adolescents became *prisoners* of coca, with stinking, shaking lips.

'Christobal!' Julio shouted. 'Is someone watching? Has he a rocket?'

Of course. A boy was up at the cemetery. But a real organizer kept every string in his grasp, however long the string. It was a good idea to give each string a tug now and then. Christobal Pinco, Julio's majordomo for the fiesta, shouted confirmation.

People were arriving now: from neighbouring Quepa, and from the more distant Aymara-speaking village of Santa Rosa. The Santa Rosans were easily distinguished by the floppy style of their knitted caps, earflaps hanging down like grey baggy old women's udders. Those people were a nuisance. They never managed to speak Quechua properly. Always you had to talk to them in their own Aymara. When their clumsy tongues did attempt Quechua, as like as not they turned a *gentleman* into a *lake of grease*.

Still, they brought vegetables and bottles of beer with them – though it was hard to see how you could fit *them* into the web of presents and obligations! A problem for Christobal. He already had his notebook and pencil out, was jotting down details.

A Santa Rosan man who had worked with Julio in the mines greeted him boisterously in incoherent Quechua. After other slovenly greetings the Santa Rosan contingent settled down on the southern side of the lower half of the plaza. The native Apusquenos found their time-honoured sites in the upper half. Bottles began to pass from the marquee. Donations passed inward – though less frequently. Christobal scribbled away. Smells of steamed dough and potato soup drifted out.

Up in the jumbled cemetery above the village, a boy sat on top of a small grave-hut of sods, staring out along the thin line of the road to San Rafael. Only the boy's mouth moved slightly, munching garlic. Before him the Altiplano stretched flat as a table to the westward, achieving a kind of infinity: for the distant Western Cordilleras pushed up their white-tipped wall from a base far below the horizon itself, as though built out on a platform beyond the rim of the world. Yet there was nothing vague about that other, far mountain chain. The peaks looked as sharp as the teeth on a saw. Visibility on the Altiplano was the visibility of Space. The plain's thin frigid air was drenched with light by a near equatorial sun that yielded hardly any heat, but an abundance of pure light.

As a distant dot became a tiny truck, the boy snapped out of his trance and scrambled down to where a rocket was propped in a bottle half buried in the dirt. Laid out on a stone were a few matches and twists of paper. While the truck crawled forward the boy kneaded his hands together patiently, restoring life to them.

A solitary tree grew in the graveyard: a dark twisted *kenua* which stooped like an ancient grandmother twisted by arthritis. Or rather, it never *grew*, but never died either – like the village.

The boy bent and plucked some velvety yellow gentian blooms and hid them under the llama-hide flap of his cap. A certain girl had teased him with her provocations at the last fiesta ...

Now he could make out pasengers on the truck: mites on a beetle. He struck a match, lit a paper spill.

Erupting from the bottle, the rocket left a blue milky ghost boiling angrily within unbroken glass. A good sign. The boy dropped one flower down the bottleneck, whispering a quick prayer, for luck.

And then the rocket burst high over Apusquiy, showering it with orange daylight stars.

'Baltasar Quispe is returning to us from the army!' Julio bellowed at the crowd. However it was still too early to start his speech. He ordered the youth in charge of rockets in the plaza to fire one. At his signal, the church bell began tolling too; for this wasn't just a welcoming-home fiesta, it was the third day of March as well. Holy Cross. Cleverly, Julio sponsored two-in-one.

When green stars rained over the plaza, the band struck

up, their cane pan-pipes fluting up and down the scale, drums banging.

Julio sat, excited, upon the single stone bench, place of honour adjacent to his marquee. He needed all his energy. He had no wife to carry him home when drunk. That was a problem to be faced soon. But for Angelina Sonco's curious perversity in undertaking a trial marriage with Martin Checa it would have been dealt with already – decisively, delightfully. Plucking leaves from the pouch under his poncho, Julio stuffed them into his mouth, peeling the stalks through his teeth. From a little gourd on the thong, he added lime powder to the moist ball in his mouth. He sucked and chewed and spat saliva. The coca taste was bitter, fragrant, numbing. Inhaling, he filled his lungs with its savour.

Another twenty minutes elapsed before the Mercedes truck ground into the plaza, bearing a corral of people and beasts behind the cab. Most passengers were Apusqueños coming back from trading potatoes, llama and mutton in the nearest big town, San Rafael. Baltasar Quispe sat in front with the driver, as befitted his far longer journey.

Jumping down, Baltasar hugged his mother and father and sister. He looked something of a stranger, dressed in his grey military fatigues, till Julio strode over, pulled off his own bright *chullu* cap and jammed it down on Baltasar's crewcut skull. Everybody burst out laughing. Baltasar began unloading his gifts: a cage of scuttling guinea pigs, a box of dried fish, a case of canned trout, and tropical fruits hardly ever seen here. He passed out bananas, oranges and papayas almost too fast for Christobal to keep a record of who received what.

The most important gift he reserved for Julio – even though only Julio Capac could be shown it. Baltasar pressed a bundle of sacking on him, and whispered in his ear.

An automatic rifle with sights.

'Now we can shoot vicuna,' chuckled Baltasar, deftly including himself back in co-ownership of the gift. 'We'll go up Apup-Chaypi – to our secret place, where we saw them, eh? You'll grow rich on the skins? Then you'll be able to take on the Saint Peter feast.'

'My dear friend!' breathed Julio.

'But ... *pacta*, take care!'

Julio nodded, glancing at the Santa Rosans. Hunting vicuna was one of those strange illegal things; and ever since the Government made Santa Rosa the county capital, Santa Rosans tended to put on airs and throw their weight about. It wouldn't do to have them knowing. Obviously absurd laws were made to be used, not to use you. In this case they simply made a few vicuna skins very valuable – enough to pay for a whole fiesta! Still, *pacta*, as Baltasar had observed ... Julio rushed into the marquee and bundled the sacking away behind piles of potatoes.

Returning, he climbed on to the stone bench.

'*Rimanaymi!*' he shouted. 'I am about to speak ...' He raised one hand, palm outwards, and patted his ear. The crowd and the band fell silent; after a moment, the church bell too.

'Now, six months' military service is no small thing. A service to society! That's what they say in La Paz, those *mallku* soldiers who want to stick a finger in everyone's affairs and leave nobody's strip of land alone. Well, they should know. They're all true Bolivians.'

Mockingly he rubbed his finger across his upper lip, and the crowd laughed appreciatively. Facial hair was a sure sign of European ancestry.

'But who is this working class they serve? Is it the people of Apusquiy or any of our sort? No, it means a few tin miners. A few factory workers. Now, I've been a tin miner myself. When I had enough money for this fiesta I came straight back here, and I tell you I didn't see many tin mines on the way home. I wouldn't have had to go so far otherwise. I only saw *campesinos* like you and me. I think maybe the Common Man, for whom our *mallku* soldiers are making this revolution, aren't so common! It was a hard thing and doubly burdensome for Baltasar Quispe to give service in these circumstances. He had to shoot at cousins who speak our language, not Spanish. This is no feud that we choose. Though we fight feuds when we do choose! It's a war and a revolution for the miners and the labour unions –

so that they can tell us how to farm our own land to feed them!'

He exaggerated slightly. The border feud with Peru and the Chilean blockade hardly amounted to a war. Still, the crowd growled agreement.

'Baltasar has been a brave soldier notwithstanding! Baltasar has had to listen, the same as me last year, to hours of their talk. Their "indoctrination" – without even a cheekful of coca to numb the boredom. He's had to pull the flaps of his *chullu* down over his ears. Or he wouldn't have come back here, the same Baltasar!'

Julio spoke much more to this effect. His Quechua words were sweet. His speech, a song. He put words together in new ways to describe the complexity of Baltasar's service to the State; and he was admired for his coinages. His words weren't stone statues, cut to one shape to stand for one thing only; but drops of mercury free to combine and recombine. They cast magnetic nets out into the Unknown. They drew the iron filings of the world into fresh and forceful shapes. Throughout all his speech throbbed the pulse of Man's life; and the life of birds, beasts and mountains. The Government of the People's Revolution co-existed with Puma and Condor: as another psychic beast that affected people's spirits, while happening to occur in the real world too. His particular skill as an orator, several senior Apusquenos remarked that afternoon, was to put their Government in its proper place. Julio wasn't worried that the Santa Rosa contingent would report him to the Government judge in their home village. He felt safe in his language, shielded. What other rampart had the Inca people possessed through all these years?

Finally, the crowd cheered Julio Capac as much as Baltasar Quispe.

The band played again. The people laughed. Women's wide bright skirts spun round them, striped shawls flapping and tinkling with silver medallions, felt bowler hats turning like fat black potatoes on plates. Many of the men wore the knee breeches of courtiers naturalized from a world far away across a sea, four hundred years ago. They danced with arms linked. Then they danced in lines facing one another. Finally they danced as separate couples: and Julio Capac, flushed with success, was dancing with Angelina Sonco, whom he had chased up the mountainside after just such a dance, till he caught her and loved her, till she sighed and cried for him ... But what use had that been!

'How long will you live with that man Martin?' he whispered. 'It's only *sirvinacuy*, not a full marriage. No children coming? You can still break with him. You know, it's *you* who is stopping me from being sponsor of Saint Peter's feast. I have to marry first. But who do I want to marry? Only you. Without you by my side it would be such a hollow fiesta!'

But all she said, with a regretful humorous smile, was:

'Love if you have anyone to love, Julio.'

'But that's you.'

'We're too close in blood.'

'Nonsense.'

'Too close,' she repeated, her teeth flashing teasingly. Whereupon the dance of couples was at an end.

Beautiful was his Angelina. A vicuna he had chased in the mountain clefts and trapped for an hour, touching soft skin, taking soft flesh with his own flesh, losing his soul in exchange. But she was lost to him. She was the Hummingbird who flies straight through the Condor's mouth and out again, escaping. Why?

The truck driver wandered over with a bottle of beer and accosted Julio in angry, tipsy Spanish. From his broad, dour features Julio knew him for an Aymara; but he had given up all his Indian culture to ape the European way.

The man spat out a froth of beer and coca juice.

'One of your admirers explained your pretty speech. You're the world's biggest reactionaries, you people, you know? How much do you spend on these fiestas? Everything! You work to burn money. And where do you think the profit goes? To the rich in the towns who sell you your liquor and fireworks and take your potatoes for a song! Do you ever get angry with *them*? No, only with the Revolution – just to keep every damned furrow separate from the next, to grow your own private potatoes to buy fireworks! That's all your villages are

– separate furrows fighting to stay weak, and bleeding themselves dry for pride.'

'Why drink our beer, if you hate the fiesta?' demanded Julio, incensed. 'Is it as a fee for your advice? We can do without it. And what are you talking about? Baltasar and I fought for this Revolution of yours.'

'You always fight against it in your hearts! We won't win or lose on the borders. They're just thorns stuck in our sides by the Americans. All the people have to fight together, in their minds. Miners, truck drivers, *campesinos*. The lot. A mine union isn't enough. An army isn't enough. Yet you make a speech like that! You carrion.'

The driver seized hold of Julio's poncho. Being a tall man, he pulled Julio up on tiptoes. Who knows how much of their alcohol he'd been drinking? What choice did he give Julio now but to fight him? Yet to start a fight on the occasion of this fiesta would be a poor thing. Besides, the man was Aymara. The Santa Rosans might join in.

Baltasar Quispe caught Julio's shoulder and whirled him away.

'Julio, the sky!'

Other people were shouting and pointing now. The truck driver staggered back indecisively, bemused by the sudden commotion. Up in the sky, a trio of red birds were carrying a bright basket down in their claws and failing. As the birds tore loose one by one, the shining burden fell faster, over the village towards the mountainside. An orange sail broke free: then the thing had vanished behind the church, and they heard a thump.

Julio ran back into the marquee to recover the bundle with his gun in it. He wasn't leaving that for anyone to pick up.

Already the crowd were moving out of the plaza by the main road, to see what they could pick up on the hillside; everyone getting in everyone's way.

Julio and Baltasar took a zigzag side street, steep as a flight of steps, to bring them out ahead of the others.

'Aircraft?' panted Julio.

'Too small!'

'But made of metal—' A piece of fine metal would always

18

find a multitude of uses. Most families still sheared their llamas with clippers of pounded, sharpened tin cans.

They waded through the *tola* bushes fringing the graveyard just as the vanguard of the crowd appeared.

Torn orange silk spread over two grave-huts. A third hut was destroyed by the impact of a steel sphere with sprouting fins and unreadable letters on its side.

The sphere had ruptured into three sections. A fire had started but fizzled out for lack of oxygen. Gruelly reddish sand spilled from the centre of the machine.

Julio touched the metal cautiously. Warm, but not too hot. Tugging a broken panel aside, he scooped red sand away to free the parachute silk trapped inside. Fine, tough silk. He bundled it up while Baltasar gathered the cleaner silk from the grave-huts.

As soon as the other Apusquenos arrived and failed to man-handle sufficiently large chunks of metal loose, an argument broke out about sharing the silk. Julio spoke up promptly with a compromise.

'We can't go to Santa Rosa to ask the judge, or it'll all be taken away! So listen to me: we'll call a council to settle it. But we can't do that today, during a fiesta. I think we should let Baltasar Quispe, whom we are honouring, be custodian of that silk he picked up over there to stop any wind blowing it away. As for this silk that I found inside—' He spotted Angelina in the crowd. 'A big bundle! A big responsibility. I suggest the Sonco household. You all know I have no links with the Soncos, or with Martin Checa who lives there.'

Wadding the silk in his sandy hands, Julio pressed it upon Angelina, who turned away, embarrassed but amused, hiding her face in the silk until she sneezed convulsively; and sneezed again.

'The metal will have to stay here till tomorrow. Lift it if you can!'

A few men tried again abortively; then everyone set off downhill to resume the celebrations.

Back in the plaza, one voice suggesting – in Aymara – that

they ought to report the crashed machine to Santa Rosa was shouted down angrily. It was broken up. No use but for scrap. Where had it come from anyway? There were only nonsense letters written on it, from some foreign country.

The fiesta gathered intensity. More rockets exploded in the sky. A small brass band took over from the pipes and drums. The men started drinking in earnest. The disillusioned truck driver changed his mind about staying the night and drove off for San Rafael, carrying only one or two passengers.

Julio and Baltasar drank till they were pleasantly tipsy and Julio chewed more coca than usual to keep himself awake. Because of this he didn't feel particularly hungry, though there were platefuls of steaming *quinua* dough and hot chestnutty potato soup and hot pasties available to tempt him. They talked about Baltasar's months in the Army, then about hunting vicuna and the cave they knew where they would skin the animals and hide the remains.

Perhaps Julio drank more than he realized. He began feeling sick. Not sick in the stomach, exactly. His whole body tingled as though electrified, then shivered and felt like lead.

His head buzzed.

His body wasn't sure whether it was hot or cold, full of energy or exhausted. It seemed to take a whole minute to drawl out a word. The next minute he was chattering nineteen to the dozen.

Then a man fainted in the midst of a dance. His cheeks burned, but his hands were blocks of ice. Lying there in a faint, his body made dream movements, his knees drawing up to meet his chin. His wife and younger brother straightened him out, to carry him home; but he might have been dead and stiff for ten days, except that his head burned as hotly as if all the fire of his body had fled there.

Soon others were complaining of violent headaches or aching limbs. Others fainted.

There was illness – an illness unlike any typhus or whooping cough or pneumonia that anyone was familiar with. It pounced suddenly as hail, striking people at random in the plaza.

'There was poison in that machine in the graveyard,' a voice cried out.

'No, germs! It was a weapon. These things exist. Germ machines in the sky!'

Maybe it's true, thought Julio, as he saw his fiesta become a turmoil of helping and hindering and hysteria. Remembering his hands scooping through a tide of red germs, he thought of his new rifle too.

He stuffed his mouth full of more coca leaves than he'd ever chewed before, to banish the aching of head and bones, and stumbled away with the sack bundle clutched in his arms.

The village was spinning, droning behind him; but he forced himself to climb. Ahead rose the dome of Tullpanpi-Apup, Pretender Peak. To its right, tapering backward in a long pyramid, was the real chief, Apup-Chaypi. It was around the side of Apup-Chaypi that the cave lay. If he died, which the spirits forbid, Baltasar would know where to look for their gun.

He tramped on, using the parcel as a crutch. The white flood of stars lit his way well enough, casting a milky veil upon the soil.

By now his limbs were stumps of ice.

TWO

Frontiersman was fifty million kilometres and five months distant from Earth when the Communications Officer in Houston pressed his King Switch, to call the spacecraft.

Two and a half minutes later, a yellow light flashed on *Frontiersman*'s radio and a loud beeping sounded around the doughnut of the living quarters.

Not loudly enough to wake the Commander Jim Weaver,

who drifted in a flimsy sleepsack tethered to the bunk in his privacy cubicle, wearing earmuffs.

Pilot Wally Oates and Scientist Astronaut Eugene Silverman glanced up from the magnetic Go board but didn't immediately answer the call. The two men were locked in an impasse of black and white discs. Each held the other in check. If neither quit and moved elsewhere, a process of take and retake could go on for the next hour without producing any changes, till all their pieces were used and the game ran out of fuel.

'I'll see,' shrugged Silverman finally.

Wally Oates continued staring at the board. He wasn't in the least bit mesmerized by the pattern of discs; whereas he fancied that Silverman was. Patterns of Go-discs were child's play for someone who'd sat for hours at a stretch before TV consoles in remote-control combat at Mach 1.5 with Viet-khmer remote piloted vehicles. Not to mention his being the only jet jockey in the whole Air Force to have flown a manned F-15 down the tail of three of these teledynes after the first encounters during the defence of the Isthmus of Kra ten years before. He'd taken 7 gees without misreading instruments, for all the spots before his eyes.

'*Frontiersman* to Houston, we're listening,' said Silverman, and waited.

And waited. Two and a half minutes was too long to wait. Time enough almost to boil an egg. Indeed, Wally Oates had brought along an egg-timer among his personal gear; he meant to fill it with Martian sand, if he could find sand not too finely ground or oxidized to flow, even with the glass bulbs rid of air. Silverman suggested flippantly they should use it for their radio calls. Real dialogue with Earth had long since broken down. Chunks of words usurped the place of conversation now. They felt they were secretaries taking dictation and reading back.

'*Frontiersman*, this is CAPCOM Houston. An hour ago the Russians radioed to tell us they lost guidance on *Zayits*. They can't bring it down to a soft landing in Russia. There was probably a blow-out on board as they were charging it up for re-entry, but they're not saying. Deep Space Tracking estimate it's going to come down somewhere over central South America. If the chutes deploy okay it might still come down in one piece—'

'Well, we're hardly beaten to the punch, even so!' broke in Silverman. 'What are a few scoopfuls of soil compared with a manned expedition? I don't know why they bothered sending *Zayits*. Sour grapes?'

The radio voice carried on, unaware of his interruption.

'What sort of co-operation they get recovering it really depends on which country it comes down in. If it's Bolivia they won't get any more help than we got with our own training programme—'

'*Zayits* should feel quite at home in Bolivia. Too bad we never got to train there.' Silverman undulated from side to side in a slow belly dance as he spoke.

'Christ, be quiet,' frowned Oates. 'They can't hear you yet. You're talking at cross purposes.'

Silverman smiled slyly and moved his hand aside. The SEND switch still stood at OFF. None of his words were being sent.

'If you missed any, we'll play it back.'

'Goddam.' Oates had more respect for the integrity of instruments than to play such a damn fool trick. He'd never wholly appreciated Silverman's quirky sense of humour – though to a greater degree than Jim Weaver did, no doubt!

'Roger,' radioed Silverman. 'We read you. *Zayits* is off course. It's the Russians' own fault, calling it a Hare in the first place. People oughtn't to make jokes about Aesop's Fables. Tortoises always come in first. Over.'

Oates played a white disc, far removed from either of the two current theatres of combat, and assumed a poker face. Now, if Silverman took more than three turns to invade *both* check positions – which he would have to, if he wished to consolidate both of them – Oates would have the groundwork for a 'running ladder' ten moves later as Silverman advanced. He'd frogmarch a whole zigzag of Silverman's stones right off the board into captivity.

'CAPCOM to *Frontiersman*. We'll keep you informed on the Hare. But now we want some figures on Chlorella density in the tanks. Bleed off a c.c. and run it through the counter, will you? We haven't had a report for a week. And we want more figures on Methane, CO and CO_2 levels in the cabin air. Call us when you have them. Over and out.'

Oates shoved himself up from the velcroed stool, with the usual tearing sensation of sticky tape unpeeling.

'I've made my move, Gene. If you check the Chlorella, I'll see to the air.' He pushed himself around the torus as Silverman drifted over to the trio of sixty litre cylinders that broke down the crew's urea, renewing oxygen and water.

Eugene Silverman, at thirty-eight, was the youngest of the three crew members. His eyes were an unusually vivid blue as though he was wearing blue contact lenses. Indeed, he might have been dubbed the blue-eyed boy of space science but for his premature baldness and a broken, badly reset nose – which gave him a cruel look at times, counteracting blue innocence. A nervous action of sweeping hands over thinning hair, combined with a curious side-stepping gait perfected during public lectures, lent his movements a frustrated stylized elegance, midway between effeteness and the hindered violence of a pacing zoo animal. Each movement was trimmed and orchestrated, yet suggested flight, fierce bursts of activity. Had he broken his nose in some impetuous dash, before he learned the trick of infectious enthusiasm and intellectual grace? In a sense. For he broke it in a childhood fight with other kids at high school in New York City, who resented his scornful lack of reliance on the obligatory pocket calculator. At least this was the version that he told his wife Renata; and naturally enough, being a sculptress, Renata believed him. Hadn't Michelangelo's nose been broken by some jealous, dim-witted apprentice? But perhaps it had been a fight, pure and simple. One that Silverman provoked, before he learnt grace and displacement rituals.

Silverman did graduate work at Cornell's Planetary Studies Laboratory, developing new ways of explaining and even in theory engineering major climate changes on other worlds. As he jokingly put it, ways to get rid of the smog on Venus, if you couldn't get rid of it at home. By the time he had organized the International Colloquium on Terraforming Worlds at Cal Tech, he had set his sights firmly on Mars as the second world for Man – in opposition to the Russian faith in Venus. Working quietly and brilliantly, deducing for NASA the surface features of the Outer Planets from the weather patterns, his increasing public appearances and proselytism on behalf of terraforming Mars – not in fifty decades but in one, and not at a price tag of a trillion dollars but a mere one thousandth of this – became a budgetary bonus for NASA. But for the half-promise that Mars could be made habitable by the mid 21st Century, would funds have ever been available, even for a three-man expedition?

Oates drifted to the radio and pushed the SEND switch.

'CAPCOM, Methane and CO are holding steady but CO_2 is up by six percent. Hang on ... Gene says the Chlorella density in tanks one and two is 850 million cells, but tank three is up to a thousand. Over.'

Waiting his two and a half minutes, Oates gazed along the curve of the doughnut. Beyond the Chlorella tanks was the only privacy cubicle which all three men shared, popularly known as 'The Can', from which their waste was sucked into the guts of the Ecological System – urea anticlockwise to the Chlorella tanks, solid matter, homogenized, granulated and oxygenized, clockwise through bark fibres from Californian Redwoods into two tanks of scavenger fish, constantly flickering with life and light like TV sets. A thin pipe led off to the first adjoining greenhouse. Here his view was cut off by the curve of the wall.

With a doughnut shape, there was always somewhere ahead of you, somewhere behind you; always somewhere hidden from view. Always a certain mystery, a certain sense of extension and limitlessness ... In theory.

Vegetables hovered vaguely beyond. Doubtless the sweet potatoes and fungi tasted better than the homogenized paste of fish, snails and water-fleas sucked from the tanks. Yet in some personal, magical sense, which grew stronger week by week, the fish appealed much more to Oates. They could turn and fly down each other's tails all right! He would far rather incorporate such twisting, darting creatures into the cells of his body than slothful vegetables: even cultured fungi that sprang up in thick red clusters overnight. Fortunately there were freeze-dried stews and goulashes too, to alternate.

The hole in the doughnut was occupied by the great cone of the landing module *Flagstaff*, upside down, sealed off and depressurized.

'CAPCOM to *Frontiersman*. Flight Surgeon asks will you check the cartridges in the air filters? He doesn't like six per-cent up on CO_2. Now the Chlorella. It's getting too rich in there. Overbreeding. Switch out one UV lamp in Tank Three. But you can't keep the UV switched off too long. We think there could be unbalanced solar warming from outside. We want to rerun your thermal roll through the computers. Can you give us the exact figures? Over.'

Is it just to keep us busy? wondered Oates. Damn it, they were in the middle of a game of Go. Still, they hadn't noticed the small buildup of carbon dioxide on board or the small population surge among the Chlorella.

It was this damned vegetable existence thrust on them, when all three men were really fish: quicksilver beings!

'Roger. We'll call back. Out!' Oates pushed himself away towards the gyro gimbals.

Earth and Mars were both mentally very distant now. Curiously, each seemed to be getting further away simul-taneously. The idea of Mars stayed locked to Earth, and receded accordingly. A disbelief in their destination haunted him. It wasn't the real alien world of Mars they were heading towards any more, but a vision of Mars remade as Second Earth.

Time had lost its meaning too. The thermal roll of the craft brought a fresh sunrise, a fresh flood of light falling upon the automatically compensating electro-optic windows every twenty minutes. Three days from dawn to dusk were com-pressed into each hour. Forty-eight dawns into every waking day. The only accurate stretch of time was the eight hours each man spent in his privacy cubicle.

Two men always were awake; and one asleep. Oates and Silverman; then Silverman and Weaver; then Weaver and Oates. The crew thus changed its composition without actually changing. The three men formed three separate intersecting crews by now, with separate personalities. Each felt himself undergoing a distinct personality shift half way through his sixteen hours, as one partner vanished off to sleep and the other hidden partner emerged – without encountering one another.

Without discussing it in so many words, each man felt that the fourth, phantom crew – all three awake simultaneously – would add an undue dimension of complexity, threatening this balance of alternating personalities. No one mentioned how many hours he actually spent asleep in his cubicle; nobody enquired. The cubicles were taboo. If someone was emerging or entering you averted your gaze. And expected the same courtesy yourself. Just a tacit convention, but a strong one. No one discussed it yet the arrangement was regularized with a military precision now.

Curiously, no graffiti whatever had appeared on the walls of the public, yet private 'Can'. Perhaps this was as odd as the mystery of the Dog That Did Not Bark; yet no one remarked on the fact either; and as month drew into month no one had scribbled the first joke, the first obscenity.

Finally they returned to the Go board, sticking themselves back on the adhesive stools as neatly as postage stamps. Flying his backside down to a pinpoint landing, Oates reminded, with an air of negligence:

'Your move.'

Silverman invaded both the check points.

Silverman reinforced both his newly won salients.

Ten minutes later, as predicted, Oates was flying down his tail – chasing a running ladder of black discs to oblivion.

Ruefully, Silverman rubbed his palms across his scalp, at once gracefully and fretfully.

The trouble with Silverman's game was that he viewed the Go board as a quasi-living thing. Perhaps the influence of that sculptress he was married to. Undue intuition. Oates saw the board as a perfect mathematical machine, with exact vectors and trajectories.

A wispy hair drifted away from Silverman's head in his direction. Intercepting it, Oates stuck it to a velcro refuse tab on the wall, specimen on a slide.

They'd set off from Earth orbit shaven-headed and beardless, gigantic foetuses, and watched their hair grow back again till they began to look like hirsute Victorian explorers. As little shaving and tonsuring as possible on such a long journey was the idea. Till Mars, hairs and bristles were safest fastened to the body.

Silverman watched the regrowth more anxiously than did the other two, as though he feared that nothing might grow back at all, or alternatively hoped that everything lost throughout the previous decade might re-emerge. However his hair had grown back wispy, flying and receding just as before. The real genetic joker proved to be his beard. It was ginger. The unexpectedly bright splash of colour made the rest of his face look milkier than it was.

Oates' beard grew out thick and brown, covering up the line of moles to the right of his lip. This looked like a service scar, but wasn't. He'd consulted a plastic surgeon tentatively about having them removed, thinking them a disfigurement ... but now that Milly-Kim habitually followed the line of those moles with her lips, towards his lips, he wouldn't dream of erasing her pathway. That would be like erasing Milly-Kim herself.

Oates thought about Milly-Kim far more often than he thought about his wife Kathy and the kids. True, Milly-Kim's photograph wasn't stuck on the wall of his cubicle as were Kathy's, Neil's and Beth's; he hadn't even brought one. Didn't need to. She had burned herself into his nervous system and his memory. Secretly, he had brought a second egg-timer. He would fill it with Martian sand for her, in memory of breakfasts spent together after nights more important than any others. In a sense he was going to Mars to fill this egg-timer for her. The voyage was privately dedicated to her. The first egg-timer – for Kathy – could end up in the Smithsonian or be auctioned for Multiple Sclerosis sufferers, for all he cared. But Milly-Kim's was going to end up on the shelf of the kitchen in her L.A. apartment. Every time she boiled an egg, she would see Martian dust timing it; and know.

No question of divorce. He wasn't mad. Kathy and the kids were family. He simply dedicated his journey to Mars, in deepest secret, to a woman called Milly-Kim. He felt like a Knight of Courtly Love, away crusading for his Lady, as unmarriageable as she was adored.

'I said, Wally, it really is a shame the Bolivians wouldn't let us in there.'

'Let us in?'

'To train! It's almost like Mars will be, after we've switched the climate. When the icecap and the permafrost melt and the flashfloods flow. Same dry, thin, freezing air. What a shame. Damned politics!'

'Three months of Alaska and Patagonia were okay by me.'

'Really, Bolivia would have been perfect. It's as though nature fitted out the Altiplano as a model of what Mars could be. Tell you one thing, Wally. Those Indians in the high Andes are the best adapted humans to colonize Mars. Even better than Sherpas, I'd say. It could be the salvation of them. Isn't much of a life they lead, by all accounts.'

'You're forgetting who's paying the tab for Mars. And just in case you don't realize it, your idea sounds slightly reminiscent of a slave trade!' Oates clicked down a white disc; but play was desultory, since the running ladder. Obviously he had won.

'Slavery? God, Wally, I'm an *idealist*. I know we'll get to the stars. And the first step has to be Mars. We're unbelievably lucky. Think of it: so large a Moon, to draw us out. Then Mars as a second, unused world with that CO_2 reservoir so close to sublimation point, trapped under the water ice.'

'Assuming we can free it.' Oates nodded vaguely below decks in the direction of the main payload, more massive by far than the small *Flagstaff* landing craft.

'As for seeding Venus, that'll take the Russians far longer ... But they'll do it too. We'll soon be on two other worlds, home and safe. Future generations will wonder why we ever hesitated on the threshold. What happens to an ingrowing toenail? It goes septic. Same with society.'

'I agree with you, Gene. It's my whole life too.'

'But you said *assuming* we can do it,' frowned Silverman. He clicked a black stone down with apparent glee, as though detecting a fatal flaw in Oates' position.

'I agree we have to try to switch Mars on. I just can't know for sure. Any more than anyone actually knew *for sure* what would happen at Alamagordo when they switched that first bomb on. Anyhow, I'm not a climate scientist. You're ... carrying on your advocate role too much. That's all over. No need for it. You've won. I win the game, you win the argument, right? What the hell, there isn't any argument—'

The time for Oates' departure and Weaver's reveille was approaching rapidly, bringing nervousness and instability. Aware of this, Oates abstracted himself. The image of Milly-Kim flowed almost as sharply as his consciousness of sitting with Silverman. However there could be no coming together of the two streams, any more than two F-13s flying wing-tip to wing-tip could come together without destroying each other.

Time to be by himself.

He departed without a word, while Silverman tidied the Go discs back into separate boxes.

After Oates' departure, Silverman was only left alone for a matter of minutes before Jim Weaver emerged from privacy to join him. The interval felt quite blank. Not a personal time; a public time, he was on duty – only, there was no public. During this pause he withdrew into his snail's shell, retracting one set of horns to present a different set of horns for Weaver. Blunter, stubbier, less playful horns.

'Good morning!'

Weaver took slow underwater steps: a kind of flatfooted tiptoeing. Really it was so much easier to float about, since the velcro on their shoes was only sufficient to hold the wearer still to do tasks, and a tiny thrust set one free. Quite hard to take normal steps; yet Weaver did so on principle. Likewise he said 'Good Morning', though it might be any time. Silverman felt he ought to say something about how this behaviour might be straining the muscles in Weaver's feet, damaging his arches. Equally, he knew that he couldn't say anything. Weaver's walk conveyed a message; it wouldn't do to criticicize it.

Watching his approach, Silverman wondered briefly how

Oates had metamorphosed so strangely into this new crew-man. A conjuror had turned a rabbit into an egg inside that secret cubicle! Then his horns locked with Weaver's; his mental gears shifted.

'Hullo, Jim. Houston called us. We had to check the Chlor-ella and the air and the gyros, but the main news is that the Russians lost *Zayits*. Something went wrong with the guidance.'

'I'm sorry, that's a shame.' Always the diplomat, even deep in space, Weaver rubbed his nose to erase the implication that one could feel any sense of satisfaction in the Russian failure. He had such a small snub nose for such a strapping frame. Having gangled up from childhood and filled out sturdily, his nose remained forever beset by childishness. Whenever Weaver was puzzled or embarrassed he rubbed this soft button, like the eraser on the end of a pencil, rubbing out whatever offended him. Yet otherwise he was so substantial. His shoulders hardly needed padding for college football to conform to stereotype.

'Sheer pointless upstaging,' retorted Silverman. 'They didn't have to send a probe to Mars just a few months before us! We'll be bringing back enough soil to go round. Loading it before we do anything to the climate. They just want in on the action, if only by token.'

'You're reacting too emotionally, Gene. Neither side is going to "own" a world. That's been agreed a dozen times. Still ... I think it's really a blessing that the world *is* split. If East and West weren't continually involved in races of one sort and another where would we be? Maybe your reaction's healthy.'

'I don't follow you.'

'Well, take the arms race. Maybe we had to be driven to develop nuclear weapons, if only to spur us outwards and scare us away from this risky nonsense of an Only One World philosophy? Can't risk all our eggs in one basket any more ... It's really the old bugaboo of God and the Devil. If we're to be free creative people, God has to let the Devil work among us – then twist the Devil's work to bring Goodness. Suppose this "twist" is programmed into the nature of the

31

world by God. But you have to have the Evil first, to twist against. So Nuclear War is the Devil we twist against in this case, and the twist sends us out here, and the Soviets right in the other direction towards Venus.'

'Venus is in the opposite direction to Mars? First I've heard of it!'

'No really, Venus is inwards towards the Sun mentally. Towards the source of power. Communism looks inwards too, because it's centralized – it bottles its people in. Yet it isn't "inward". It denies the inward soul of Man. Whereas naturally we head outward, towards Mars: then towards the Stars, the Heavens, the mysterious hidden things rather than the sunlit "facts". It's queer how long the Russians have been aiming inwards, towards Venus, the Sun.'

'You're joking. Their early Venus probes were just a way of leapfrogging over our Apollo success. They went out on a limb and it happened to pay off with the chance of terra-forming Venus.'

'No, Gene, it's deeper. A reflection of their whole society: inwards, but not inward. The Soviets believed in Venus even at a time when nobody dreamed of terraforming it. It was their faith. But for us the Inward is out there, in the darkness between the stars out beyond Mars.'

'Actually it's us who are out on the limb right now, so far as they're concerned. Changing Venus with rocketloads of blue-green algae simply takes ... lots of rockets. Changing Mars takes *finesse*. Like skimming milk, from orbit.'

'True. They send bulldozers where we send butterflies.' Weaver looked unaccustomedly bitter. 'I tell you, it's a damned shame we have to go in for weight-lifting too! Having to land and lift off as well as haul *Warming Pan* there. We could have brought a bigger *Warming Pan*.'

'I never heard you opposing our landing, Jim.'

'I wanted to come. Obviously I didn't argue against it. But let's be honest, *Frontiersman*'s a compromise mission. *Warming Pan* says we stay in space. Yet after sending us all this way, the people back home just have to see an American set foot on Mars. Okay, so there's a lot of real work to do on the surface. Biology. Met work. But there ought to be ten of us if we're going to land – and we can't fit ten people in plus *Warming Pan*.'

'We'll do it all. Just three of us. It proves we can do more with less. The Russians,' Silverman smiled, 'haven't dared land on Venus yet. By the time they can it'll tie them up for the next century. They'll have to pour in a damn sight more capital than we will into Mars. They'll end up with *less*, for much more.'

'Still, the algae seeding's certain. I just wish we had more material for *Warming Pan*, instead of *Flagstaff* ... Also, we'd have looked fools if we came all this way, didn't land, and *Warming Pan* didn't work either. So we're a compromise.'

'It'll *work*, don't worry. We'll warm that icecap, Jim. We'll burn off enough water. The storm we start will blow enough dust on the pole to soak up more heat. The buried CO_2 will sublimate. We'll have Mars under control before the Russsians have half way finished cooling Venus down. We'll be visibly living there.'

THREE

The first death occurred shortly before the arrival of a medical team from San Rafael in two jeeps accompanied by a truck with a dozen soldiers under the deputy police chief of San Rafael. The Santa Rosa doctor had already given up his task as hopeless and called for more help. The first act of this medical team was to order all sick bodies to be transported from their homes to one central improvised hospital of tents in the main plaza. The fiesta marquee, still undismantled, became their office once the piles of potatoes and stacks of bottles had been cleaned out and the marquee disinfected.

The bundle of parachute silk appropriated by Baltasar

Quispe and found beneath the potatoes was loaded on the truck sealed up in plastic. As for the smaller wad of silk entrusted to the Sonco household, the president of Apusquiy town council, now embroiled in a bitter dispute over jurisdiction with the canton head from Santa Rosa, merely asked Martin Checa, being Angelina Sonco's common law husband and a resident in the Sonco house, to confirm that there was none still there, and then swore that all silk had been surrendered. That missing man Julio Capac had suggested bringing *all* the parachute material here to stop it from blowing away, the council president affirmed; for he had no intention of talking about informal distribution of what was now State property.

The deputy police chief announced that everyone must keep to their houses from now on, and imposed a curfew. Meanwhile the doctors performed their first autopsy on the man who died.

What killed him was inflammation of the brain and spinal column. And yet his limbs were as stiff as if rigor mortis had set in days, not hours, before. This, with the rapid onset of the disease, then its failure to spread further, were strange factors. Obviously this was meningitis of some sort; so the rest of the population must be regarded as potential carriers. Curfew would have to play the role of prophylaxis temporarily, since there was insufficient penicillin and sulfadiazine in the jeeps' mobile laboratory to supply the whole potential carrier population of two villages – three, indeed, since Santa Rosa must be included for safety. How could a dozen soldiers possibly oversee the curfew of three villages and the guarding of the graveyard? The deputy police chief sent the truck back to San Rafael along with the silk with a call for a full platoon of soldiers ...

Meanwhile, what sort of meningitis was it? The doctors debated.

Meningitis could be caused by bacteria, protozoa, viruses, yeasts or fungi. The autopsy showed pronounced cerebral edema: a lethal pooling of liquid under pressure inside the skull. This liquid was purulent, rotten with pus.

So the doctors took smears and began culturing them inside

the fiesta tent in nutrient broth and on blood agar plates they'd brought from the San Rafael hospital. The responsible organism needn't be present in the brain fluid in any great multitude for it to wreak devastation. It might be quite scarce. They would need to breed it.

Perversely, when they took samples of cerebrospinal fluid from the other victims these seemed perfectly benign, without pus or purulence. The fluid was rich in protein, as though it was itself a nutrient rather than a discharge; the sugar level was inordinately high – as high as the blood sugar level in the rest of the body was low. These samples too they cultured, in normal air as well as in airtight jars with reduced oxygen content and high carbon dioxide produced by burning a candle in them. The samples in these jars simply festered; yielded no evidence of organisms.

Puzzled, the doctors divided the twenty-nine remaining victims into four groups to apply four different forms of treatment.

The first group they dosed massively with sulfadiazine and with penicillin; and hooked up to dextrose drips to boost the body's blood sugar.

The second group they injected with corticosteroids to stimulate the adrenal cortex, hoping that the brain might re-order its biochemistry.

The third they injected with adrenal cortical suppressants.

The fourth they treated by cerebrospinal drainage to release the pent-up pressure in the skull; and coupled this with massive boosts of fluids – dextrose and electrolytes.

Deaths began.

The limbs of the people in Group One grew flexible again. Tone returned to the muscles. Skin softened to suède. Body temperature rose to normal.

Then one by one their fingers and their toes grew gangrenous. The gangrene spread rapidly up the flesh on their wrists and ankles to their elbows and knees. One of the men woke up in high delirium. He talked dreams, he talked madness. Sedating him with barbital and morphine they watched him die. They made no attempt to amputate. An Andean villager with stumps for arms and legs was an

35

impossibility. No one argued about that assessment, brutal though they knew it to be.

One by one those whom the doctors had injected with corticosteroids began to die. Their limbs became rather less rigid: like stiff gristle. They began twitching and trembling as though minute electric shocks were being applied at random all over the body. The twitching became a continuous wobble of uncoordinated activity.

At this point half of the group were injected with anti-convulsants; and the doctors saw them die of shock, eyes bulging wide and blank. The remainder continued quivering stiffly for several more hours before succumbing to exhaustion; before their hearts gave out.

'It's like trying to start a frozen jeep,' one of the three doctors commented bitterly. 'You try to start it, you try to start it. In the end the battery goes flat.'

Meanwhile, the cultures were producing no results. Eyes grew weary with peering through the microscope. One doctor recalled a documentary about American military nerve gases. Perhaps this was some new sort of 'binary' weapon that had gone astray. Only, instead of two individually harmless chemicals uniting on impact to produce a lethal mix, in this case one chemical simply induced a deep coma – and every attempt to cope with the symptoms added the second component, producing this variety of horrifying deaths.

'That would be the ultimate in demoralizing blackmail weapons,' declared the doctor angrily. 'They could put whole cities into coma, and only they would have the key to unlock it again!'

'But we know it's a Russian spacecraft, not a weapon.'

'How do we know? It's perfectly possible to put a weapon into space with any name printed on its side. Russian, American. Who knows? They're both capable.'

'But this only affected thirty people. It can't be a weapon.'

'Something stopped it from spreading further. What was it? The quality of the air here? Low oxygen? Look at the effect of oxygen reduction on the cultures. They fester. Till

36

we know what the link is between the air and this red dirt, nobody's safe.'

'All dead bodies should be burnt,' announced the San Rafael police chief who had listened to the conversation carefully. He had arrived with the new influx of soldiers and taken over from his deputy. Nominally these soldiers were under the command of a young major; however, the major accepted suggestions from the civilian police chief. He would carry them out; so long as he agreed with them. Yet the police chief knew that any false move he made could well result in the militarization of the whole San Rafael area. He wasn't particularly in favour of the Young Turks of the People's Revolution – and this major had not decided to come all the way to this little village with a relative handful of troops purely for the experience. His visit to Apusquiy was surely a pretext ... for interfering, overruling, militarizing. The major's reputation, when he took up his command in San Rafael province, was of a power behind the military throne, a subtle fixer. He paid more visits to La Paz than one would expect of a provincial commander.

What if the machine was a Russian weapon gone astray? Bolivia could denounce Russia once again, reassert the independence of the Revolution, win some slackening of the American blockade. On the other hand the machine might indeed be an American weapon dressed up as something Russian, dropped here to cause trouble. A mechanical *agent provocateur*. Secretly the police chief counted himself pro-American; however, he was only too keenly aware how one little spot of trouble might flare into a raging fire. It had happened enough times. A football match erupted into a revolution – or a counter-revolution. So many discontents were always precariously stacked against each other; so many different hands were always tugging at the steering wheel of State. Any suggestion of outside intervention even in the form of a crashed aircraft or spacecraft might become a pretext for Left or Right. Pretexts were all that people sought. Now he found himself sitting on a possible pretext. An epidemic was never just an epidemic. It was a reflection on the health of Government. He wished it would go away.

'All bodies have to be burnt,' he repeated flatly.

'Autopsies first,' reminded one of the doctors.

'Yes, then you can sign proper death certificates. Quick autopsies.'

'But it's a spacecraft,' sighed another. 'A Russian one. We should ask the Russians.'

'Impossible! You know that we can't ask Russians to send experts into our country. The Revolution only survives so long as it steers clear of foreign support. Cubans, Chinese, Russians. That would be far too provocative. It may be what the Americans are hoping for. We slip some Russians through their *cordon sanitaire*. They cry "the thin edge of the wedge". They invade. The People's Revolution, Doctor, only exists *on tolerance*.'

'In that case—'

'The Americans themselves?' The police chief laughed drolly. If he advised the major that they should appeal for any form of assistance from East or West, or any supposedly international agency, he would be putting his neck on somebody's chopping block. The main thing was for the military presence to disappear from Santa Rosa county, for the village to settle back into apathy after its tragedy, for the tragedy not to become some national scandal or *cause célèbre*. But neither should the major take the initiative out of his hands, or he'd be seen as a weakling; worse still, as a possible internal enemy sabotaging through inertia. A passive resister.

'Burn all the bodies right after the autopsies. Tell the villagers that it's a disease. That'll do. They know all about disease.'

'But what do *we* know about it!'

He leered into this doctor's face.

'You know that it kills. You know that you may well be killing these people yourselves by treating what you don't understand! Responsible for their deaths? That doesn't look good on anyone's records. You don't want the matter to become a scandal. It's safer for all concerned to burn their bodies as they die. Meanwhile, carry on trying to cure the survivors.'

'But what's wrong with them? Maybe we should stop "curing" them!'

'*No*. I insist. Use all your skill to cure them. That's a doctor's duty. If you fail, then we burn your *mistakes*. Do you follow me?' The police chief strode out of the tent feeling he had successfully walked a tightrope. He went in search of the major to organize a squad of his men to burn corpses outside town.

Politically the major, a professional soldier, was neither of the Left nor of the Right; but a staunch advocate of the unity of the armed forces. Thus he made himself necessary to both sides of the perpetual seesaw of military power which currently held the left wing of the army in ascendancy. This seesaw had afflicted the country for decades before the Revolution, and afflicted it still, People's Revolution notwithstanding. Mediator figures such as this major stood constantly between the country and civil war, ensuring that the seesaw would continue tipping this way and that beneath the sacred banner of army unity: the one true constant.

Having no pretensions to political power this major therefore accrued a personal power of his own, one of the still points round which the wheel of power swung perpetually, Left to Right, Right to Left. In his very inertia lay a force. He even remained a major, by choice, declining further gazetting for the present, lest a colonelship be seen as stemming from any single individual's influence.

Sitting at the wheel of his jeep he heard the police chief out, gazing past him into the distance where the mountains fell off the edge of the world.

'Yes, burn the bodies,' he nodded. 'Quite right. If they all die burn them all. As for the spacecraft ... We could say that it crashed into the village and killed all these people. It's true enough as it goes. It tells no lies. Its parachutes failed and it crashed in the midst of a fiesta. I've already been in touch with La Paz by radio to ask what the space powers say about it publicly. All that business about a weapon is nonsense. The thing was just meant to bring back some soil from Mars. The Rusisans admit they lost control of it. But neither the Russians nor the Americans know where it came down. The Guyana Consulate enquired on behalf of the Russians; but it isn't convenient to answer them. Our answer is that the Andes are vast, people are scarce. My men will remove the machine and the soil from the cemetery. Take it elsewhere. Nothing will have happened here. Just a sad accident. Though, in this case, the People's Government will compensate the victims' families at the same rate as we compensate the deaths of miners. That'll be your responsibility, to distribute the money. And see that there isn't much gossip about the matter.'

'I'll make that clear to them, Major. But discreetly. They'll receive the money ... on that understanding.'

'Frankly, just between you and me,' remarked the major into the air, 'there's a suggestion we should "sell" the machine to America, in exchange for a loosening of the blockade. Americans have some men on their way to Mars. They'll want to examine this soil and its strange effects on Man. You see how important this machine may become? The centre of much secret wrangling?'

The police chief rubbed his hands together warming them.

'I thought as much, Major.'

'I'll need all the autopsy reports. But there's no need to inoculate everybody as carriers. It's obviously not that sort of thing.'

'Some people might still recover.'

'Well and good. I'm not suggesting it's a good thing that people die. Let's be on the side of survival, eh? That's my philosophy. A simple one.'

The police chief grinned. He knew exactly what the major meant. He too was a survivor; a delicate matter.

A woman in the fourth treatment group – those from whom brain fluid was being drained, into whom dextrose and electrolytes were being pumped – suffered a stroke on the morning of the fifth day. It was not spotted immediately since the woman was already in a coma resembling a stroke condition. Only when she suffered a second more violent stroke in mid-afternoon did the fluid being drawn off grow visibly bloody.

Her brain was bleeding, maybe in many places. Even if she lived she would be speechless and paralysed.

The doctors discontinued treatment and the woman died early in the evening.

Wearily they performed yet another autopsy.

All the lesions in her brain occurred where the white matter interleaved with the grey matter – where the branching nerve fibres, connecting areas together, met the island-like blankets of specialized co-ordinating cells; around the central canal at the root of the brain and at the outer layer beneath the cerebral cortex.

By the same evening all the other members of her group were obviously haemorrhaging similarly ...

A few of the villagers were breaking curfew by night, slipping out of their houses to spy on what was happening, and the rumour passed from home to home that one villager at least was safe from the doctors. One old woman had seen Angelina Sonco falling down at the fiesta, being carried home quickly by her father and Martin Checa. The doctors had not learnt about her; she was not in their tents. Now a Curer, Pablo Capsi, a shrunken fungoid man whose ancient jacket, crammed with herbs and powders, woolspun widdershins and phials of condor blood, was his dispensary, was staying secretly in the Sonco house, breaking rotten eggs underneath her bed, chanting the Seven Sacraments and singing the Benedictus over her. He knew that she and all the stricken villagers were afflicted by *susto*, the fright of the soul; he knew how to woo her soul back from where it wandered. The doctors knew nothing of *susto*; it wasn't written in their books. So their charges perished one by one.

Nightly, now, a truck drove through the shuttered village; and an hour later the sky flickered red out on the plain as the soldiers burnt bodies.

FOUR

The Russians might indeed be about to use heavy technology to bombard Venus; yet once started the algae seeding was a self-perpetuating and entirely natural process. The algae would feast on the carbon dioxide clouds and multiply a billion-fold, freeing oxygen and forming water till the first rains fell, boiled up then fell again, edging their way ever closer to the surface. An organic, earthy process. The American plan for Mars demanded the fine tuning of technology for centuries, or else the climate would relapse. Culture, versus Nature. It took less technology than the Russian plan for Venus. But the technology had to go on working perfectly till that distant day when the eccentricity of Mars could itself be trimmed by moving in an asteroid as an extra, more massive moon. Unfortunately, torque couldn't be applied to fix the precession of the Martian orbit thus to permanent spring for another ten thousand years.

Till then, Mars would have to wear its solar mirrors of cantilevered sails, and wear them well. A simple process; but an artificial one.

Weaver's onset of evangelism irritated and offended Silverman. Not on account of what Weaver actually said. Weaver wasn't against altering the climate of Mars. But the misplaced soulfulness reminded Silverman of quarrels with Renata about machines and the soul of nature . . .

Romantic claptrap, thought Silverman, lying in his bunk. Man's destiny was to modify his environment. To go on modifying it increasingly. Man must become his own environment.

He stared up at the grey ceiling. Though metal, it looked like felt or velvet. It wore the bloom of skin. A picture of Renata smiled down at him, the sculptress in her studio. A full oval face with a brow quite out of proportion; her jeans,

42

rolled up at the ankles, still lapping her sneakers – she was buxom yet squashed, like one of those beatific Japanese *daruma* dolls. Yet this wasn't something you noticed, exactly; she simply seemed taller from a distance, then strangely foreshortened by a joke of perspective when you came close to her.

He met her at the Fuller Concert Dome in San Francisco. She was setting up an exhibition off the lobby, billed as *Transforms & Deforms*. He was due to address an audience on transforming worlds.

A dozen nude female manikins a few centimetres high were enclosed in blocks of clear plastic upon waist-high stands, two to each stand. Every figure was distorted, subtly or grossly. Legs were too long, bodies too fat, breasts too vast, heads acromegalic, nanocephalic. Prehistoric Venuses, they glowed in rose and pearl from lights hidden in the plastic bases; beyond each tiny couple stood an empty dais. Intrigued, he ducked under the rope barrier.

'I'm still setting it up,' she said, turning. 'Oh, Dr Silverman? I'm honoured – stay and look. Actually they're just casts of free space. Caves in the plastic, lit from below. Even the plastic isn't very solid. Feel it.'

When Silverman rested his fingers on a block, it deformed. The imprisoned, illusory figure deformed along with the block. Funnily, each distortion seemed to improve its appearance. There was a queer family likeness between each warped couple. She bent and flicked a switch, and a moment later the empty dais was occupied by a life-size projection of the figure he touched: nude, nacreous, awry.

'Acoustic holograph?' he guessed.

'Right! The ultrasonics pick up the hollow shape in the block and the holograph projects it. Shift your fingers, Dr Silverman, mould it.'

As he did, the figure changed shape. Squeezing cautiously, he tried to play it towards ...

'Normality?' she laughed. 'Or perfection? Which are you aiming for? The snag is, no actual body's perfect. We only have this idea of perfection in our minds. My sculptures diagnose the malady.'

'We all have our own vision of beauty,' he flattered, squeezing the block, producing ugliness, grotesquerie, then surprisingly magnificence.

'You have to use both hands, on both manikins. They'll only deform in certain ways. You bring them together. What you'll discover isn't an ideal body, no! It's the actual person I modelled from.'

Silverman's cheek itched. While he scratched it, the projection held its last shape on the dais.

'How long for?' he asked; already, a shorthand of communication existed . . .

'Thirty seconds – that's for the show. You can vary the time setting.'

Left hand on the white block, he manipulated the pearly nude. Right hand on the other, he evoked a rose nude, interpenetrating the first. Where rose and pearl diverged, slabs of raw flesh bulged loose as though flagellated – with a hovering aura of a multi-limbed Hindu goddess. He finally fused rose and pearl into a single flesh-tinted entity – an authentic human body, even if some diverse shapes *en route* had been more elegant. Raising his hands, he regarded his creation, regarded her.

'You got it in one minute ten. Good. You abandoned perfection for the sake of life.' She sounded like an *I Ching* divination. 'Most people go for perfect symmetry with both shapes. But they won't coincide that way.'

The image vanished from the dais. There were only tiny grotesques left, glowing in their plastic prisons. And her.

'Many commissions? Could be bitter medicine – proving one's not perfect.'

'Oh, it makes a good party piece. Shall a guest flatter his hostess, or unveil the true naked self?'

Initially, the exhibition struck him as a costly gimmick. Yet, as she spoke, suddenly it made sense. After all, even physicists were coming round to the idea that the Universe might well be mathematically perfect, yet that Nature only approximately heeded her own laws. He said so.

The planet Mars, seen by Cro-Magnon eyes, presumably was a blue summer world with air and water. Winter Mars, seen by modern man, a red ice-capped desert. Two Marses coincided briefly in his mind's eye, then rushed apart into endless cycles of Red and Blue ... Human fingers intended to halt Mars at the moment of perfection, and hold a whole world there! But what if this perfection wouldn't correspond with Nature? A false analogy! He dismissed it.

'Suppose that the ideal human body relates to perfect shapes? Artists have often thought so. But suppose it really relates in an imperfect way? Isn't your space-time geometry different from normal geometry, Dr Silverman? A distorting geometry? The presence of an actual body *warps*.'

'Too much Euclid in Art,' he grinned. 'Not enough curved space? Is there a self-portrait of you here, by the way?'

He invited her to dinner after his speech to continue the discussion.

The speech was routine enough. Still, it must always be inspired routine. He started out by remarking on the elegance of the Fuller Dome arching over the auditorium in branching tetrahedra. The building reflected the forms of viruses and crystals, the architecture of the DNA. It reflected Nature. That made it beautiful.

Mankind would reflect Nature too, in a new way, in outer space. Man would reflect the Sun's radiations back on to the Martian pole, raising the temperature just enough to bring about what the eccentric roll-around of the Martian orbit would perform spontaneously in another ten thousand years. Martian climate had two widely differing stable states, just as Earth did: Ice and Heat. Once, it was simply thought that Mars lost its atmosphere to the polar cap; seared by ultra-violet rays, no complex life endured. But the cap was frozen water. Yet atmosphere was trapped there – according to the boring into the cap undertaken by the Rover Series probe, as well as according to an impacting seismological probe – and elsewhere too, in 'clathrate' form, by molecular imprisonment. Ice was the cap on the bottle.

Warming Pan would trigger the flip of climate artificially: a huge mirror, hanging in space. Not a mirror of glass, though. The Pan would consist of a great stretched lattice, a cantilevered sail composed of extremely thin, extrudable moving booms with draw strings to maintain tension.

Silverman couldn't allow himself to say in so many words that the hardware for *Warming Pan* already existed in prototype in Earth orbit – as a Department of Defence scheme for climate modification. Yet there was sufficient vibrancy of Swords Beaten Into Ploughshares about his words to make it obvious that the American military were sure such a system would work. He did hint, though, that it might be a good idea if any Warming Pans in existence were towed far away – say, as far as Mars. The Soviet Union would look favourably upon such a move ...

Russia would certainly go ahead with the transformation of Venus by algae seeding, using a hundred robot probes and a manned orbiting station. Could America let Mars lie fallow, when a single expedition might tip the balance for a world?

Silverman pointed at the Fuller Dome.

'May I quote you a few lines of poetry written by the inventor of this building? Yes, he wrote poetry as well as building it! They're from an *Epic poem on the History of Industrialization*.' He picked up a sheet typed by his secretary, and read:

> '*By Industrialization*
> *and its mechanical extension*
> *you and I are both*
> *mutually and at the same time*
> *New York,*
> *Grand Coulee Dam ...*
> *Route U.S.A. 1, from Maine to Key West,*
> *the stratosphere liners,—*
> *they are our mutual*
> *flesh and blood extensions ...*

'In other words our technological landscape is part of our nervous system now. Part of our very bodies. I agree! Shall Mars not become part of our body too?'

As the audience clapped, Silverman brushed wild locks of hair and wished he was already with Renata Blum: one body

46

melting into another as her holographs melted together, creating something fine and warm and human ...

But first there were the questions.

One Senator in the audience opposed the whole idea on budgetary grounds. Thus it had to be forcibly suggested that the groundwork for *Warming Pan* already existed. That the journey to Mars need not be cripplingly expensive – if only three men went. Finally – and Silverman paused a moment before defiantly committing himself to this secondary role for the mission – this would be the first time that a human being had ever set foot on an alien world.

'Have you already forgotten those ten billion dollars spent to set foot on the Moon – to film footsteps!' demanded the Senator angrily.

'A moon is not a *world*, Sir!'

'Won't you destroy Martian life forms by wrecking the climate?' called out a newsman known for his ecological bias.

'Certainly there's life there. But it's only simple life. The long winter knocks out any other option. Anyway, we're only doing what nature will do in any case ten thousand years from now. Spring will be a little early on Mars this year, that's all.'

'How about the theory that the Martians are all asleep during this long winter? Hibernating under the sand dunes? If you woke a bear up in mid-winter, you'd make it pretty sick.'

'Honestly I don't see anything more sizeable than a mosquito being able to last it out that long.'

'But bears hibernate—'

'For twenty thousand years? Hibernating mammals live on fat reserves, and they still need to breathe. You'd have to halt the process of life entirely – dry right out, lose all moisture, every drop of blood, become like a stone.'

'Well, toads can sit inside a cement block for a hundred years. Then they jump up and hop out.'

'That's one of those "Believe it or Not" stories! Still, I'll grant you a hundred years for your toad. But after one thousand years, let alone ten thousand, I assure you your toad would be a dead lump of leather at best. Only really

47

simple organisms can hibernate for as long as twenty thousand years. What isn't on the surface already can't be very large.'

'Caterpillars hibernate inside chysallises, don't they, Dr Silverman? They form their own stones round themselves.'

'Yes – and all the time life processes are going on inside, or you wouldn't get a butterfly out of it! Change consumes energy. Imagine twenty thousand years' energy consumption. Pretty huge storage batteries, eh?'

Still, objections didn't die. Someone else, calling himself an agriculturalist (and meaning a farmer?) spoke up.

'Fleas' eggs lie around in cracks in boards for years. Decades! Till a bit of vibration triggers them. You just need a trigger, like footsteps.'

'Let's hope we don't catch any Martian sand fleas! But joking apart, there's no way we can conceive of any sort of complicated beast lasting through two thousand centuries of cold. What would it matter if there was? We aren't killing it. We're just waking it up! But alas, there isn't. There can't be. The most complex animal on Mars will be the first chicken we hatch there ... The main technical problem, of course, is stabilizing the orbit so that it affects such a high latitude. So we have a computer system at the heart of the sail to co-ordinate it. A power plant feeds off the lattice's solar input for controlled correction over at least a five-year period till a second expedition gets there with more hardware. If we could pulverize Phobos and spread it thin on the north pole as a heat-soak, that would be great. But the cost of doing it! *Warming Pan* will be quite sophisticated enough ...'

This being indeed the big cost factor in *Warming Pan*: its capacity as a steerable, directional war system; but he could not go into how manipulable and dynamically flexible the system really was; besides, there seemed to be far less interest that night in the technical than in the biological problem – which was essentially a nonsense.

Tethered in his private sleepsack, Silverman looked up at Renata till it seemed that he and she were really standing upright facing one another. Her photograph was a door he could step through ...

48

He'd been so enchanted by her at first, by their conversation, their love making, her perfectly imperfect body.

Once, she mentioned that her mother might have taken some drug during pregnancy affecting the Renata foetus inside her, slightly deforming it, stunting the growth of her legs. But it was only a suspicion on her part.

When Gene and Renata had a daughter a year after they married they called her Gaia for gaiety and as a personification of Planet Earth: the idea of a world as a living being.

Renata watched Gaia grow, by turns brooding and exhilarated. She sculpted Deforms and Transforms of her daughter, who was thus surrounded from early days by transitory playmates that were images of herself, twisted out of true along twin axes of perfection and deformity. It was as though Renata was intent on running through the whole chromosomal gamut of possible daughters she might have had. At times she seemed in danger of losing the knowledge of her own real flesh-and-blood daughter amidst all the range of alternates she evoked.

However when Gaia was three and the expedition only a year away Renata took a revulsion against this whole sort of art. She called it bankrupt, dreary and mechanical. Overexpensive. The technology level was too high. In any case, after a year or so of constant handling, it appeared that her manikin moulds succumbed to plastic fatigue and spawned monstrosities never intended.

She turned to natural shapes: flow patterns of sea and sand, the spirals of shells. She began avidly beachcombing with a holocamera.

Silverman guessed she was rejecting the whole idea of transforming nature – bodies, or worlds – because it was this which would soon hurl him so far away from her. Yet he accepted Renata's rejection gratefully. At least it meant that Gaia was now being reared in a wonderland of nature objects instead of amongst the many simulacra of who she might have been.

He was fairly sure that Renata was having an affair with someone she had met beachcombing. Some other driftwood artist. And he was glad of it. It absolved him of guilt for deserting her. It let him forget about her with a good conscience throughout the intense preparatory year. He almost found it funny that whilst he would be delivering a warming pan to Mars, Renata would have a human one back home in her bed with her. That's all her lover was. Amusement flushed away the uncertainties she was trying to implant in him under the skin about the wholesomeness, the permanence of deforming Mars ...

Of course it would work! Enough water-ice would boil off, fierce enough storms would rage, dumping dust back on the pole, soaking up more heat, with *Warming Pan* sustaining the process. The bottle would be uncapped, the locked-up atmosphere freed, triggering its freeing from the trap of sub-soil ice elsewhere, in turn ...

FIVE

Julio Capac lay in the cold of the cave, frozen yet unaware of the cold, a man embalmed by his own body. His arms and legs were stiff as leather, mummified. His body preserved itself in a half-life of the flesh. Blood pooled round his heart and bore oxygen only to his brain; and his brain dreamed rapidly, feverishly: dreams of the many selves that made up a man.

The jigsaw of his life was taken apart, each picture re-examined. Yet there was really layer upon layer of jigsaws; and whenever his dream moved from one jigsaw piece to the whole jigsaw to know the picture at large, it slipped through the interstices, down to another piece of another jigsaw. Thus Dream turned in on itself and swallowed itself. Yet only in this yearning drive of each jigsaw piece towards all its auxiliaries did he now exist. Only by virtue of this thwarted hunt for the whole picture was his mind powered. And he split into many minds, each dreaming its own jigsaw dream, while his body hunched, tough as cured leather, in a stasis of life ...

In one dream he marched up a road around the mountain to neighbouring Quepa, the partner village, with a band of Apusquenos. The Quepans had caught a condor, netted it, caged it, invited their neighbours to the Fiesta of the Blessing of the Village. Afterwards, the youths would chase girls through the starlight, startling the grazing llamas ...

Angelina stood near him in the crowd lining Quepa plaza. She pretended not to notice him, but whenever he was on the point of turning away she glanced. A barrier of corrugated iron, *tola* bushes and bales of *ichu* grass formed an improvised arena, leaving a single opening to the main street. Only people's bodies held the barrier in place.

In the arena the giant bird, hungry, angry and afraid, ducked its raw head from side to side inside its cage, clicked its beak and stamped its scaly legs.

Julio squeezed closer to Angelina, while the band blew their pipes, whistled their flutes and banged their drums. Bottles of watered cane liquor passed from hand to hand, from mouth to mouth. The air was thick with sweat, excitement, fever. Julio accepted a bottle from Angelina, squeezing her hand. She grinned with those large white teeth as though about to bite him. How he ached. Her cheeks: as amber and round as some tropical fruit, imagined but never tasted.

The men of Quepa chorused:

> '*In storm time*
> *In hail time*
> *Drag me back home!*
>
> '*Who brings storms*
> *And who brings hail?*
> *Who snorts* tunrun
> *In the hills?*
> *Drag me back home!*'

Till the bull was led into the arena by the rope through its nostrils. Then they sang:

> 'Lord Apu, Lord Auki,
> Mountain guardians,
> Your mad animal has escaped!
> His hoofs stamp hail,
> His hoofs rake furrows in stone walls,
> So drag him back home!'

While the bull's keepers strained on the rope, three men pulled the screeching condor from its cage and bound it to the beast's back by the legs. Freed, the bird's wings beat wide open, broad enough to span a narrow street, battering the men's heads.

> 'Lord Apu, Lord Auki,
> See his red packsaddle,
> Packsaddle of blood!
> Send wings,
> Tie angel wings to him,
> To drag him back home!'

When they let their ropes run free, the bull ran across the plaza, bucking and swerving. Tugged along like a giant kite, the bird beat its wings in a fury of flight, trying to leap skywards. Frustrated, it gouged at the bull's back with its talons. Carrion-eater though it was, it tore live flesh from the bull's flinching neck, goading the bull to fury. The beast danced and stabbed at its back with its horns. Unable to rid itself of the condor, it ducked its head and charged into the iron sheets and *ichu* bales. A horn stabbed through thin iron and a human thigh beyond. A man screamed. But the wall of people held – while the bull stabbed again and again, ineffectively now, lacking momentum.

It would kill if it broke through. People would kill each other trying to escape. The barrier would fall. Then they would know that those Lord Apus and Aukis, mountain guardians, crop guardians, who lived on the highest peaks with savage monsters for pets, disdained them that year. The

Lords' haciendas hid high above the snow line of Ulma-sapa, whose head reared to a heaven where only condors could soar. Up there the Lords kept their herds of Ccoa — cat beasts whose spit was lightning, whose eyes shone hailstones; but big as bulls. Those beasts paraded their spirits on Earth in bull bodies, to be mocked by people and to mock them. If the Ccoa bull killed anyone today, men and women would roll on the soil in an ecstasy of misery, begging for a good death this next year.

Time and again the tormented bull charged the barrier, to toss it aside; while the condor tried to rise free of that weight of crazed hide and horns, wings battering, beak tearing.

> '*Packsaddle of blood,*' sang those who swayed behind the bales,
>> '*Angel wings!*
>> *Drag him back home!*'

The bull tired, slavered, gave up charging. Though its eyes were fogged with madness, it bowed beneath its rider's spurs. Broken by the bird, it pawed the ground aimlessly.

The bull handlers zigzagged out again to gather up its nose tethers, crying with joy, hurling insults at the beast and singing the praises of the bird. Unroping the condor from the bloody back, they led the beaten bull away down the main street, each fleck of blood or foam that fell into the dust refreshing the village.

Corrugated iron and bales were pushed to the ground as the villagers danced out over them across the plaza. Flutes and trumpet-horns sang out, drums throbbed a racing heart-beat. They petted the condor, tying wild flowers and bright yellow ribbons round its neck and scaly legs. Holding its beak wide open, they poured cup after cup of fermented *chicha* down its gullet to slake its thirst.

'Little dove,' sang Julio in Angelina's ear, 'let me be your fine condor! Let me carry you off to the mountain!'

'Maybe our Lord Condor can't fly, he's drunk so much.'

'He will fly, *huayra-hina, nina-hina,* quick as wind, fierce as fire!'

She teased. She tantalized.

All the people fell back as the music ceased, and the only sound was a sad, thin dirge of farewell rising from the throats of old folk.

While the old folk wailed at it the condor staggered drunkenly about.

It beat its wings. Its claws bounced off the ground then back again. Then suddenly it soared up from the plaza trailing its ribbons and flowers. It circled twice, gaining height each time, before vanishing into the dusk sky heading for the heights. Rockets chased it up, showering green fire back on Earth.

Angelina squirmed from Julio's grasp and ran away through the crowd out of the plaza. He pursued her, making sure he did not catch her. Other boys were chasing other girls who squealed in fear to let their pursuers know just where they were.

Stars shone out, and brushed the mountainside with milk.

He awoke within the dream. The dream stayed, but now he knew that it was a dream. He watched those phantom stars. They were knots of light tied in the darkness of strings stretching everywhere.

That dream sky was an Inca *quipu*: the ancient knot-string record of the Incas, the key to which was lost, years since...

Julio had seen those quipus in a building in a city where he was a soldier for a while. They called it a museum – for dead things; yet it was full of things that his people used at home. Were his own people dead, then? Had they disappeared into glass cases already? He'd read the printed Spanish captions angrily. (Spanish and Reading were as compulsory for soldiers of the Revolution as Drill and Indoctrination.)

Coloured strings lined with knots were laid out in sun-bursts. Of all the things in the cases only these seemed utterly dead and lost; and these were his own people's heroic memories. Padres had gone about the land burning them. The quipu readers had all died out.

What did they record? Harvests, history, praise songs? Who knew? A baffling code...

As he chased Angelina up the mountainside in dream, the stars shining on their strings arrayed themselves around him. His skull swelled to contain them. They burned within. Memories, his memories. Thoughts, his thoughts. This was the Way of his Thought. It was a huge quipu made of stars, of knots of energy. Yet he could only follow one pathway, not all pathways; his life had printed out the constellations he could follow.

This time the pathway was Angelina. The constellation, her. He ran faster and overtook her, tumbled her.

The sweet tart tang of her hair, shampooed in fermented urine, combed out a hundred times till it hung glossy and smooth as silk or vicuna fur! The firm warmth of her open lips, touch of her tongue, her teeth! He heard her breath thundering in his ears, and at the aching opening of her body to him heard the cry of a hare snared in a gin, its body pierced by wire, followed by a sigh of release. With this fierce knotting of their bodies a fresh knot of energy was tied into his life, a knot which his ideas would always have to flow by way of . . .

Yet he saw how the knot was tied, as he dreamt the tying of it. He saw how all such knots were tied and might be untied, retied in many other ways. He saw how strings might be attached to other strings instead.

How tight and simple was the quipu of his Thinking hitherto.

Yet who was the *he* that saw this? It was a later different person from the dream-boy. That dream-boy had died into him, becoming part of him. Yet suddenly the boy was reborn in dream with awareness as full as the man's. For a moment the dream-boy greeted him. The man greeted this other self and knew the knots that bound the boy within him. Awareness greeted Awareness. Then brusquely the dream-boy was squeezed back down into darkness as the dream broke into jigsaw fragments.

He slipped . . . down into another dream, constantly chasing his own self only to be squeezed away from himself at the moment of discovery.

And some dreams repeated themselves many times, as

though to push him closer and closer to that moment of fusion with other hidden selves within himself.

Much later, in the timeless circuit of the dreams, he became a miner ...

Around the miners' barracks humped huge dumps of tailings containing a fortune in tin if any way could be found to recover it. As much metal lay in Bolivia's dumps as had ever been exported; but no one knew a way.

During the past few years the lowest grades of ore had been hauled out: ore ignored and bypassed in earlier richer years as too poor to bother with. Spent veins were block-caved entire now. The industry would soon be in its death throes.

Rumour said that the Americans knew there were vast new deposits somewhere in the unsurveyed mountains. Satellites could see it from the sky. But the Yanquis wouldn't say where, till the mining union was weak and broken; or the workers overthrew their People's Government and let foreigners and the rich control affairs again. Believing passionately in these unrevealed tin mines, the miners slaved twice as hard to haul out the last spent ore: which the Yanquis in turn kindly let pass through the economic blockade, to be shipped to their shores. And all the while the miners grew poorer, angrier, more frustrated at the People's Government.

Julio, now twenty-one years old, would see miners praying to a hunchbacked home-made idol deep down in the mine – welded together from broken picks and shovels, decked with tinsel and mouldy coca leaves, coins and medallions. The miners would pour cups of alcohol into its twisted steel mouth and shout into its shovel-blade ears, to tell them where the new tin was ...

From the freezing cold of a mountainside tunnel, a lift cage plunged him and fifty other men within ten seconds to the heat of Hell. A hundred degrees hotter, overwhelmed by fever, the miners tore off their leather jackets and trousers; stripped to shorts, gloves, boots and helmets. Half-naked, they rode an ore train into the boiling, booming tunnels. Explosions thundered through caverns and galleries as dynamiters blasted in the distance. Each detonation echoed a dozen times. On Saturdays when the workers got drunk they hurled lighted sticks in the air and laughed. Their ears were almost deaf to any other tickle of sound. When they spoke it was in bellowing shouts.

Echoes turned speech into a mush of noise. Julio's shouted questions beat back around his ears like startled bats, becoming bestial and nonsensical – an idiocy of sound. Was he a speaker of human language? The mine mocked his words. It allowed only work, and slavery.

As the men leapt off the train in a jagged, dripping hall, a pack of demons with single eyes of light in their brows began packing it with what looked to be – nowadays almost was – pure rock. He trotted away with half-a-dozen other men alongside a straining conveyor belt to a place where a wreckage of blocks and boulders marked the latest dynamiting. A demon was already driving a mechanical shovel into this shattered wall, reversing, dumping great rocks for them to drill apart. Water hoses snaked about amongst their legs, powering the drills and dousing the dust. Hot water spurted back at their faces from the burning drill bits.

Chewing coca, Julio drilled and spat and thought of the fine fiesta he would buy.

When he felt about to die after twenty minutes, the overseer sprayed all the miners with jets of freezing water, shocking them alive again.

Hours later, the lift hurled his shift of miners skywards, out of the boiling stone guts, to blink in amazement at a sunlight which delineated every single fragment in the dumps with fierce clarity. Dragging their leather jackets about them, they trembled in the cold of day as trucks lurched back through the stone tips to the barracks town.

At nightfall they lit a bonfire between these barracks and stove in the ribs of a white llama with an axe. Wrenching its heart free, they roasted it and bore it through the streets, singing and drinking, to the church. The priest had already withdrawn. His church wouldn't be his own that night. Still, far better that the church was there, a focus for their mania, than not there at all!

This was the beginning of a whole night and day of

Diablada when the Devils danced free, before the Earth swallowed them again.

Inside the whitewashed church, a Virgin of Poverty stood above the altar: carved wooden statue with a broad Indian face, mongolian eyes and drooping lower lip. A hundred years of candle smoke had stained the Virgin a waxy Indian brown. She wore a ragged woollen shift with scores of silver discs sewn to it. Her incense was burnt coca leaves.

They offered the burnt llama heart to her upon the altar, begging her too to show them tin, or they would all die ...

Somebody else stood beside Julio in the church. Somebody who wasn't another person in the crowd. Somebody immaterial, dissolved throughout it.

Julio grew conscious of himself within this larger Being – who was also, strangely, himself: Julio Capac. For a moment he imagined that the Virgin was granting him a revelation. But no, that wooden doll was equally part of this larger presence.

Though the Virgin was only wooden, sometimes bloody sweat would break out on her brow and ooze as she listened to their tales of sorrow. At such times God, Christ and Inti the Sun suffused through her wood, animating her. He too, miner Julio, was only a doll consciousness like her, animated.

They said that God gave life to Man so that Man could struggle to behold Him, so that Man could speak His name ...

Yet the name of God this day was: Julio Capac. It was Julio Capac who suffused throughout the church, through the Virgin too, through all the miners and through the body of the miner-doll who thought he was Julio Capac. The miner-doll began to realize this. He struggled to know who he really was; who this larger, enclosing self was. While the adoration of the Virgin went on around him in the dream, he began waking up within it. Yet the swaying bodies pressed him cruelly, squeezing him back into himself. They squeezed this dawning understanding down.

For the hundredth time, forbidden Fullness, he slipped into another dream ...

Yet he didn't slip so far this time.

Next morning, drunk on alcohol from the commissary, deafened by dynamite and drums, he stood with an Aymara acquaintance from Santa Rosa watching as a three-headed nightmare danced through the streets in a whirlwind of dust. This was the God called Trinity. Bull's horns and a bull's muzzle swayed atop the dancer's left shoulder, with glaring glass eyes and splintered mirrors for teeth: God the Father. On his right shoulder bounced a fat evil toad wearing a judge's wig made of tufts from oxen tails: the Holy Ghost. Squeezed between, set on the dancer's own head, was seated God the Son: a giant parrot bristling with green feathers.

The priest officiated at the dance, having crept back to his church and cleared the heap of offal from his altar. Various officials of the State Mines Administration, Comibol, were there too, laughing at the way the dance mocked the religious superstitions that stood in the way of Revolution. Yet the Diablada paid fearful reverence, too, to the triple God that had been forced down upon this people like a lid upon a boiling pot.

Next, dancers mocked and mimed the Incas. The old rulers of the land danced past wearing bald red-beaked heads of condors. Adorned with haloes, they were all dead and slaughtered into Heaven or Hell. Strings of false gold coins clashed round their legs.

Llama-masked men capered past: the *llameros* who once brought golden gifts to the rulers. The Moon swung past wailing with grief for the death of Atahualpa who paid the Spaniards a ransom of a roomful of gold, to no avail. Lucifer and Archangel Michael sprang out at one another sparring with knife and axe. Lucifer's skull was iron and wore a shark's fin crest. Michael's face was a silver pan with two eye holes; he reflected the image of evil back upon itself, whilst angel wings of blue gauze blew from his shoulders.

Spangles, beads and broken mirrors glittered under the bright sun, transforming the street into a cascade of shattered light.

As Julio watched the dancers try to trap Lucifer by weaving invisible magic strings to bind him tight, he realized what miner Julio had never realized: that here were strings which a man might pull to make the whole scene fall apart – this whole uneasy co-existence of Workers' Unions, People's Government, Army, Church ... together with an Indian past that filled the heart of the country yet existed in a limbo far removed, forgotten except in the words of the people.

This Julio who stood drunk and deafened saw no such contradictions. Yet he was awakening from his drunkenness, too. In the shapes that the green-capped, pink-masked and moustachioed magicians were dancing to trap Lucifer he saw how to untie and retie knots. All the dance steps and dancers too were thoughts dancing in his mind.

Suddenly the mirror of Michael pranced before him, and he saw his own face in reflection. Michael was *himself*. He realized that the Trinity dancer with three heads was himself too. Those three heads were his own head, divided against itself!

For one head was a condor head; and he saw through its mask to the condor boy who had chased a girl away up into the mountains. He knew that boy so well. Who else was it, but himself? Young Julio Capac capered before his eyes – a part of himself, yet forced away from him.

And who else was that giant parrot, but himself: Julio *Rimac*, Speaker of Words?

Who else was that bewigged toad, but another deeper, more ancient, reptilian self – the root-ghost of his being?

He grew aware; this time the awareness could not slip away.

He began to see how to enter this dream; how to alter it; how to take over the action and replay it in other ways with other outcomes. This wasn't dreaming any longer. The past ran through his mind – a past that tied its knots around him in knots such as trapped Lucifer. Even as the dream pulled puppet-Julio to and fro, lolling on the dusty street, gawping at Inca devils, he saw the strings and he became his own puppet-master.

He was all the people in that street. He was the street too. Although he could only see through a single puppet's eyes at any one moment he could shift his vision from one puppet to another. He could see through Inca eyes, through the eyes

60

of the condor with the halo. Seeing, he spoke to all the gathered miners in Quechua, Speech of Man. He called back the Inca State, to bring back Indian dignity, to recall the banished Apus and Aukis from their hidden haciendas in the high hills, to bring back Human Speech as the language of the land. He changed the past. The drunken miners suddenly sobered at the sight of their old Inca rulers mocked, and joined in mourning sincerely for slain Atahualpa.

Shifting to the eyes of the Aymara puppet from Santa Rosa, drinking companion of the dream, he felt a bitter resentment at this Inca resurgence; and knew how to neutralize this.

Shifting to Julio-Lucifer, he faced the Condor-Inca, blessed him by tearing off his halo then throwing it into the air as a hoop to catch the Sun. Now Lucifer was Inti the Sun God again. All along he had only been *masquerading* as a Christian fallen angel.

Julio-Inca accepted Julio-Lucifer's blessing. Julio-Inca gazed into the crowd to locate Julio the miner once more. But that miner was nowhere. His place was empty. Momentarily, Julio panicked as though he had just seen his own death. Then he knew that he no longer needed that puppet. Miner-Julio had only been the keyhole to look through, before he turned the key.

He sent the miners away with their dynamite to blast the mine shafts. No more agonies underground! Riches lay in the rubbish heaps. Surely he, the Son of the Sun, the Inti, must know how to smelt them out!

All the masked monsters danced together now; each monstrous because each was only the homunculus of a partial knowledge – each, only a jigsaw fragment of awareness.

They all saw one another. Knew one another. Quipu stings bound all together now; and the Julio personality lingered momentarily in each of them. As his awareness moved from one to the next he was a spider darting across a mind-web, still aware of each tug, each tension of the web, even when he wasn't everywhere at once.

And Julio Capac woke to the real world.

His limbs felt as stiff as a corpse's. Yet he lay on a bed of flame. Blood flooded back into his furthest veins, wires of molten gold drawing themselves throughout his whole body: fingers, toes, intestines, penis. Every soft organ blazed awakening. His head sent signals to flay him, to massage him back to life.

Pain unlocked his tongue.

'*Chayapuni! Rimani!*' he cried from a mouth dry as stone, with vocal chords of leather. 'I return to speak to you! I am reborn. I am the Son of the Sun. The Inca.'

Voices from the cave mouth answered him.

'*Ma-chaicaa?* How is this! It's a miracle!'

'Julio? My friend Julio!'

Pain began to mellow as the hoop of flame through which he had passed dwindled till it was no more than a distant bonfire, far away. It didn't wholly die out; for a while longer he lived in a rawness of the flesh, sensing all the strings that bound his body to his brain. Buried deep in all the cells, below the knowledge even of his toad-brain, was this root stimulus, this first goad: the pain of awareness.

'It's Christobal and Baltasar. Can you see? We have food and drink. We knew you'd be here. We haven't betrayed you to the soldiers in the village.'

'*What soldiers?*' he cried angrily.

SIX

Jim Weaver sat in his underwear pedalling the exercise bike till he clocked up two kilometres of imaginary travel. He always visualized a real route back on Earth while he pedalled. The route was always the same. It was that which he had pedalled as a boy delivering newspapers to the doorsteps of neat little houses surrounded by neat little lawns in Cleveland's Lakewood suburb. The Weavers needed every dollar to stay in a neat clean neighbourhood away from the ghettos and troubles of the city.

Lakewood was a board layout of identical basic unit homes with white wooden walls, picture windows and green-tiled pitched roofs. Lawns might have been all cut from the same large sheet of felt. The same basic family sat in each house complaining about their taxes and clipping coupons for grocery offers.

Jim biked across the lawns and paths tossing wads of news to the Bunches, to the Kellers, the Hubbards, the Martinos; riding past the church, also of white horizontal boarding, where families met every Sunday, and past the bowling alley where wives met every Saturday night he turned right, ticking off each house family by family. The interiors were transparent through their picture windows; and no secrets lurked below ground level in their basements either, only different models of freezers.

He reached another corner, spotted the white needle of the Sprint missile in its wire compound, vying with the church spire in his mirror. The neighbourhood committee opposed the siting of the missile here at first; then it dawned on them that if the missile had to be specially protected, so did their streets too. They would get something back for their federal taxes this time: peace of mind about the tone of their neighbourhood, a clean sweep of strangers, militants, undesirables. The missile was enthusiastically voted for.

Weaver's feet felt uncomfortably swollen and dropsical, as if he was carrying pools of fluid round in them; but he carried on cycling dutifully till he arrived back home again and the bike clock read two thousand metres. Only then did he undo the buckles holding him to the seat and swing down. Velcro took gentle hold of the deck; however, his feet still felt like balloon tyres. He had lost the precision of contact with the metal surface. He rocked on podgy feet instead of standing firm at brace. It was a free-fall problem they'd been forewarned of: blood pooling in the feet. But he'd exercised his feet, unlike the other two. He'd tried to keep the tone in them.

Life was unfair. His father often said so; without ever losing faith in justice, though.

Well, this business of the feet was only a tiny injustice. In every other respect life had been very just to him because he'd been polite, honest and worked darned hard since he was ten years old. Indeed, because of his bright success his parents felt more sanguine about God, Government and justice nowadays.

Stepping carefully past the fish tanks and plant houses to the medical locker Weaver issued himself two pressure stockings, swung out a stool, pulled the stockings up to his knees and pumped them up.

'Are you okay, Jim?' asked Silverman.

'My circulation needs a little tuning. Like Mars does,' he grinned.

He'd long since learned not to show irritation. It was one of the main reasons why he was mission commander now. His moods were as tidy and scrutable as the homes of Lakewood. Nothing in his basement but hobby tools and a freezer full of groceries. Light flooded it at the touch of a switch. Everything in its place, neat, decent, well-earned.

While Weaver tuned his circulation, Wally Oates was lying in his cubicle with his eyes shut, unable to sleep, intent on the remembrance of Milly-Kim ...

Milly-Kim didn't belong in the photograph album side of his life. That was where he enshrined Graduation Day, Wedding Day, Christenings, Family Christmasses and the Presentation of the Highest Combat Award. Frozen moments in gilt rectangles. Milly-Kim belonged on the negative side of life among undeveloped snapshots stored in sealed compartments where the sun couldn't get at them, nor prying eyes.

One of these negatives was of a childish face in a Penang brothel: some Malaysian waif of war whom Wally would dearly have loved to adopt and take home to the States with him, except that he could never explain where he met her. Besides, he knew how loving he would be to her. Sooner or later he'd tiptoe into her bedroom. Sooner, probably. It was as a child that she enchanted him.

He'd paid the Madam for exclusive rights on her; actually set her up as though she was in a foster home.

But she would grow up and denounce him, damn her ! She would run away from home at sixteen leaving him with a wrecked life.

The arrival of the swarm of remote piloted vehicles from the Communist North, the imminent collapse of the Isthmus of Kra and the boiling out of the jungles of the 'Red Ant' insurgents solved the problem for him.

The Malaysian girl had been innocent; hadn't known what she was doing, she was so innocent about it. She must have come from some hill tribe where this was how they entertained strangers ! And the war drove her from the hills into his arms.

Undoubtedly she would have turned out wicked if he took her to America. Because he would have had to teach her Good and Evil in his home – Good and Evil spelled out in heirloom needlework, framed in gilt.

You couldn't be good *and* enjoy yourself. Not to the hilt, anyway. Children enjoyed themselves. Personally, he hadn't particularly enjoyed himself as a child. Still, that was untypical. Psychologists called children polymorphous perverts, didn't they? Kids enjoyed their bodies. They were free. Everything was still fresh to be explored. Really, some Asians looked just like children when they were already seventeen or eighteen ...

Yes, then you found them smuggling a grenade on to base, right into your bed !

At home, romping with Neil and Beth, Wally Oates thought of himself as still a big child who never really grew up. Equally, he had never really been a child in the first place! Golden childhood passed him by locked in photographs.

A photograph of Summer Camp was stuck above his head in the cubicle. Opening one eye he flicked on the light and squinted at it.

A place called Hickory Falls. A mixed camp: which is to say that there were boys and girls, rather than Blacks and Whites. Boys' and girls' huts were strictly separate, though. Monitors slept by the locked doors. The windows all had mosquito netting bolted over them; not that there were any

65

mosquitoes, but this provision soothed parents' worries and effectively prevented anyone from climbing in or out at night.

At a time when city ghettos were ablaze and college kids were rioting, burning the flag, tripping on drugs and writhing around nude in the mud at rock festivals, Hickory Falls was a very old fashioned, healthy, gracious, polite camp. A slice of Louisa M. Alcott; with its own little men and women. So why did he think he'd had no real childhood? Hickory Falls was childhood writ large – the whole idyllic adventure of growing up. Kids were given silver stars and gold stars for merit. They learnt dancing and woodcraft. Afternoons, in the limpid lake, they practised swimming ...

Hickory Lake had been drained, filtered and chlorinated. In effect it was just one huge safe swimming pool. Yet an old boathouse stood on piles, boarded up and disused, the board-walk collapsed. You could enter the boathouse from under-water, though, if you could hold your breath long enough; which was enough to deter the nine- and ten-year-olds. Thus it wasn't until his second year at camp that he even heard about the secret place inside the boathouse where the little men and women met, and he was eleven by the time he braved the suffocating water and the darkness.

He'd clambered up panting through broken boards into the Dark Room, water blocking one ear with a buzzing burr. Car-peting the Dark Room he felt torn blankets, old clothes, leaves and grass which stank faintly of mould and mice.

Laughter tinkled faintly from the lake far away.

Negatives of faces and of naked bodies shone ever so faintly as his eyes adjusted, flesh picked out by light trickling through knots and empty nail holes.

A girl's face loomed. He could only tell she was a girl from the long drip of her hair. He'd never be able to recognize her outside. Smaller than him, she knew so much more about his body than he did himself ...

At her hands, in this dusky foetid underworld above the slap of chlorinated water, he experienced his first bubbling orgasm outside of dreams, from which he'd always woken guiltily and too late. Those were dreams he wanted yet dared not want. Figures hovered in them treacherously, pretending

66

to be one thing – a well-costumed dance partner or a fellow boy – then suddenly changing, becoming ambiguously smooth and naked, rubbing themselves against him. He tried to avoid the dreams. But the dream figures were cleverer than he was. They could always don a disguise to distract him, then suddenly shuck it off and stick to him like a tar baby to Brer Rabbit. This girl did the same to him, awake, then slipped away giggling, leaving him with no response. No words. No kisses. He had to return through the water, excited, incomplete.

Outside, everything was still the same. The little men and little women read stories aloud, danced decorously, sang camp-fire songs, said their prayers.

He watched the water for an hour from the bank; but so many swimmers were ducking and diving about he had no way of telling when one extra swimmer emerged from underwater. No idea who the girl in the Dark Room was. She remained a negative he could never develop.

There must have been some mould or fungus in the boat-shed where he'd stood, which the chlorine failed to wash from a cut on his toe. The toe began pulsating during the night. Next morning it throbbed and burned and swelled like a saus-age. The following night he hunched up in bed in a tent of arms and legs, one ankle resting across the other so that his toe would touch nothing, terrified that it would burst and spatter his bed sheets, telling everyone what he had done.

Finally the camp nurse had to lance it and bind it tightly in white bandages. He spent two delirious days in a sick child's bed while the nurse encouraged him to be a brave little man.

When he could walk comfortably again he still wasn't al-lowed to swim. He could only sit watching laughing bodies slapping the water and seeing the dark boarded boathouse. He didn't dare go too near the boathouse. *They* would know, inside.

Camp ended and he had a whole year to think about it. But when he came back to Hickory Falls the next year they had knocked the boathouse down to make room for a proper little marina of yachts and rowing boats. There was such emptiness, such a sense of physical loss that Wally drifted through the weeks of camp like a robot.

They chose Wally Oates for *Frontiersman* not only because he'd once been the best jet jockey but because as a military astronaut he knew exactly how *Warming Pan* could best be used in a Cold War situation where climate modification might be called for. Even before commencins his training for *Frontiersman* he'd spent time in the Air Force weapons simulators deploying the proto-*Warming Pan* in a mock Earth orbit.

It had become increasingly obvious as development of the original *Warming Pan* went along that it could only be used against a low-technology enemy who had no means of knocking it down. Yet low-technology enemies generally had high-technology friends. Bolivia was exceptional in this. For a while it seemed that the Bolivian situation might best be dealt with by switching on a Warming Pan. This was when the last large sums of money were appropriated. Yet in the end the Air Force was left with an expensive embarrassment, the very presence of which in space became more and more inexplicable as the months went by and no use was made of it.

Providentially, Eugene Silverman had been campaigning for several years within the ranks of NASA for exactly such a device to warm the Martian north pole, free the hidden carbon dioxide, set up a greenhouse effect on the red planet . . .

Wally met Milly-Kim in Los Angeles only a year before *Frontiersman* was due to fly while at Vandenburg working with the weapons simulators, this time practising upon a simulated Mars.

Milly-Kim was a Korean negress, small, pert and lithe. Her eyes were oriental almonds. Indeed, her whole face was oriental. Yet her colouring was ebony. She was the negative of an oriental: the negative of that girl in the Penang brothel, transplanted to America, matured, independent.

He had met her in a nightclub called The Plush Scene on the Strip, where she was one of the hostesses. That evening he was with three other officers from Vandenburg. She came to their table accompanied by a blonde bosomy Viking girl. Two of the officers preferred the Viking, but the third burly officer set his cap at Milly-Kim, squeezing her and lifting her off the ground while they danced and whispering drunken invitations in her ear. Wally hated him bitterly and snubbed him thereafter for ever. He himself danced with Milly-Kim in a formal detached way that was almost a parody of decorum, precipitated back into those dancing lessons beside Hickory Lake, but he said very little to her apart from confirming her name. He felt contaminated by his friends. Couldn't talk decently.

Next day he sent her yellow roses and orange ones the day after.

Whereupon he presented himself at the club alone, apologizing for the crudity of his colleagues and for his own tongue-tied state. Now that he'd found his tongue again might he invite her to dinner? She agreed, amused by this bustling coyness. But she wanted to eat at a Korean barbecue. During the course of the meal, as she laid the strips of raw meat on the table brazier and carbonized them, he detected the hint of a snub. She was saying that she wasn't American; she just happened to live in America. Yet obviously she wasn't Korean either though she spoke the language. He noticed how derisively the waiters served her: a subtle thing but detectable in the tones of their voices. He realized that she'd actually brought him here to snub *them*, to flaunt her indifference to their disapproval of her colour. He relaxed. She had nothing against *him*.

Thereafter there were other dinners. She relented about venue and allowed him to drive her out to the Point to eat broiled lobsters and steaks. Her story emerged, and Wally listened intoxicatedly.

She talked in a quiet, sing-song yet clipped style, as if her voice was tape-recorded then spliced, discarding the resonance of every word.

Her father was an unknown Black serviceman, of course, and her Korean mother had dumped her on the door of an orphanage aged one month old.

As she grew up she noticed that only ugly, deformed or crippled girls stayed on beyond the ages of ten or eleven. Brothel madams were buying the other girls as guaranteed virgins. When she reached seven scandal blew up about the fate of the girls. A religious charity intervened, promising higher bids from authentic adoptive parents in America and Scandinavia. All the girls were photographed by the Charity, even the ugly ones, and the photographs airmailed abroad.

Six months later a bid came for Milly-Kim from a family in San Diego, to whom she was packed off knowing little except her price, one thousand dollars; arriving bewildered and alien in a rich ad-bejewelled stage-set squeezed between desert and sea, a world of patios, pant-suits, swimming pools and blue-rinsed ladies with the faces of flabby vultures.

Her new family already had three children, all of them older than her. This new arrival was a superlative, exotic Barbie doll to be dressed up, taught to speak and swim and wash the family cars.

Wally knew! Yes, he knew!

Her new father, a middle-aged unglamorous golf professional whose idea of lunch was three martinis in the club house, increasingly found himself custodian of rich old ladies who settled in San Diego for the climate; while a younger pro escorted the glamour round the greens. When Milly-Kim was thirteen, while the house was empty . . .

'I understand!' soothed Wally, blessing fate.

After that it happened every three or four months.

The golf pro would treat her with a mixture of sternness and bribery with little presents for several weeks after each episode before he reached emotional equilibrium again and his fear of being denounced had died away. Throughout the following weeks the plateau of normality would slowly tilt and tilt again till it slid him down it back into her bed . . .

She remembered him saying how beautiful it was, and reading her stories by some Roman poet called Ovid about fathers and daughters who fell in love. He kept the dust cover of some famous golfer's autobiography wrapped around the book so that she never actually saw the title.

The moment she was sixteen she ran.

Exactly! thought Wally. It would have happened to him too. Betrayal. Abandonment. However, Milly-Kim had been through it all by now. She was clear. Free. She could free him too. Rage and excitement filled him. His eyes shone with such sincere and bitter adoration that Milly-Kim was startled. It was the first time in her life she had been so adored.

After these dinner dates – soon, after nights spent in Milly-Kim's Atenely Avenue apartment, easily explained as call of duty – Wally returned home to Kathy and the kids feeling purged, harmonious as never before.

He opened his eyes and winked in a friendly paternal way at the picture of Kathy, Neil and Beth before dousing the light and dozing. Yet just before he slept he prayed to dark child goddess in his soul.

SEVEN

'I am my own ancestor,' declared Julio. 'I have given birth, to *myself*. Surely this was how our Incas suddenly woke up hundreds of years ago, unfolding the Inca Empire across the whole of the Andes as their thoughts unfolded!'

Baltasar Quispe and Christobal Pinco sat on their haunches listening alertly. They believed, almost.

The Indians of these Highlands were the only civilization ever to make the Andes truly habitable by man, through the force of their thinking, their words, their society! The Incas were torn down and betrayed by Whites who brought only desolation, but Indians still remained true masters of these heights, even in their vilest poverty. What did they know of the Inca past, though? Nothing! They were all asleep. Yet they still had their language, which the Incas had called *Runa Simi*, Speech of Man – because it was so strong, so flexible, so fine. Why, the early priests had been scared to catechize their Indian flocks in it – and their God-sayings in Spanish and Latin were the ignorant mumblings of barbarian conquerors beside it. With that tool alone, the Incas hadn't needed wheels or horses, jeeps or aircraft to make the Andes human ...

Julio rubbed his limbs and flexed them.

He saw all the contradictions of the State: the tiny loop of private wealth which held power even over the army; the paternal aid which the Revolution bestowed on the bankrupt mines, which in turn, like birds with broken wings, supported the Revolution; then the great limbo of Indians living outside the money world, despising money, squandering it on the fiestas that cemented their society. In poverty and exclusion lay salvation.

And a few bribes could wreck the State.

Such as a bribe of tin. He could glean vast wealth from the waste tips ...

Puppets danced before him as he talked, in and out of his two friends. He could juggle these puppets: see what thoughts were possible, the true muscles of Thought, which ways they pulled. What walls hemmed it in, what roads it could run along, what hills climb, what views discover.

However far his arguments stretched, he never lost track. The double vision of the coma, the sense of himself as at once boy and man, remained – in the guise of himself as puppet and puppeteer. World and image-world, superimposed. Reality, and the puppet actors from the theatre of Thought.

Baltasar Quispe rubbed his chin.

'It affected thirty people. They fell down and seemed to die like you. Their bodies were leather, their brains on fire. Then the doctors came and really killed them. The soldiers burned their bodies so that nobody would know!'

'One doctor's still there packing up his poisons, and the soldiers are paying money for the dead.'

'What language do these soldiers speak, is it ours or Aymara?'

'Some order us about in Quechua, some in Spanish. But don't worry, they're going.'

'I shall speak to them before they go.'

Julio stood up. Pain still danced along his nerves. He grunted.

'Unwrap my rifle, will you, Baltasar?'

'Aah—' sighed Baltasar. 'You mustn't do that.'

'I said I shall *speak* to them.'

'But they're going, Julio. They'll only kill you, or take you with them to find out why you didn't die.'

'No one was meant to die. They could all have been Incas.'

Julio reviewed the quipus in the museum cases of that barracks town. Those were the true shapes of Inca thought. Museum cases stood around him in puppet ectoplasm, solid as the walls of the cave, while Baltasar and Christobal shuffled in the interstices of his double vision, blind to it. Engravings and relics of Inca rule glowed in the cases, messages from the past.

'In the very old days, in the true days, Baltasar, the new Inca was crowned on his throne sitting right next to a mummy of the dead Inca. What so we call a mummy, Baltasar? *Malqui*, is it not? *The tree that bears fruit!* What a queer word – unless Man's life is really only a springtime. What follows a springtime? The falling of the petals. But then comes fruit! What fruit ever comes for *us*? All through our lives the petals fall, till none are left, then we're buried and we rot. However many fiestas we pay for, we've only been springtime adolescents all our lives. We never alter. But the first Inca must have altered. He must have shed his petals, become a mummy – as I did! – and borne fruit from that mummy! He must have given birth to himself. That's the meaning in *malqui*. I'm not the first, my friends. Just the first for a very long time.'

Time! Years measured themselves out, congealing into flowing jelly-like strings, running through his fingers as he touched the quipus in their cases. For four hundred years the Inca Empire had slumbered, submerged in people's words. For two hundred years before that, the memory of the transformation of the first Inca, from adolescent man through mummy into man reborn, had slumbered on in the ritual adoration of the mummy of the ruler.

'Now' was only a flicker of the eyelid of Time. The first reborn mummy was only yesterday; was almost Julio Capac's own parent – who now anointed him.

Years flowed ever faster though his fingers, melting into Giant Years that sang of an ancient monkey-past, before Man; these Giant Years in turn melted into Star Years, which hummed the song of a toad-past: that toad cemented into the top

73

notch of his spine ... Star Years were chains of toad spawn. Slowly, time untied its message knots from the spawn of life as time ran backwards, till he reached the first ageless tying of the first knot, which was simply: life itself. Whereupon, time reversed and flowed back through his grasp. Knots grew ever tighter, tinier, more intricate. Rippling through his fingers, their vibrations sang him into being – wove the very fingers which now touched and tried in vain to read them.

Some knots in this spawn that generated Man had not yet expressed themselves in Man. They lurked within, tightly knotted, awaiting the pull to untie them.

Those who did not die 'before they died', as the caterpillar dies into the moth, reborn, should not rule themselves. They did not know how to! They had no idea how to pull the strings which pulled them.

Museum walls faded into cave walls again; reality supervened.

'No wonder they pinned the lips of mummies with thorns!' laughed Julio. 'So that they should not wake up and speak! Or a whole world would be overthrown. Now, will you unwrap that rifle? We have a world to remake. The Inca has been waiting all this time – in me.'

An hour later, one-time aspiring orator and sponsor of fiestas Julio Capac walked down into Apusquiy right into the centre of the plaza. Baltasar Quispe, rifle-bearer, was his army. Christobal Pinco, recorder of donations of coca and potatoes, his scribe.

They both suspected that Julio was crazy. Yet both believed in his madness. He was a man of magic now; he had been struck by lightning. Hatred of the interfering, murdering Government gripped their hearts.

Curfew was ended. The epidemic was officially cured, stamped out. The major had already sent off the wreck of the Russian spacecraft wrapped in tarpaulins, along with red soil packed in two oil drums sealed with wax. The grave where the spacecraft had crashed, indeed most of the cemetery, had been sterilized with blazing kerosene. Two of the three doctors had left for San Rafael along with the spacecraft to report by radio to the Minister of Health while their colleague stayed to pack the agar cultures and jars of cerebrospinal fluid. Soldiers were still busy questioning the relatives of the dead to prove their identities to the reasonable satisfaction of the police chief before paying out Government funds.

Julio walked through the midst of a bitter argument about burnt bodies and paper money. He climbed on to the stone bench.

'*Huañuscam cani! Chayapuscam cani!*' he cried out. 'I have died, I have returned.'

'It's true,' called a voice. As Julio finished, the Curer Pablo Capsi sprouted out of the crowd. He stood there, chthonic and primaeval, his face wearing many wrinkles radiating tattoo-like around both eyes as far as his ears and hairline, and round a puckered but still toothy mouth. He rubbed his brow wrinkles fiercely, as though grating a vegetable; for he read in Julio Capac's face what he read in Angelina's when she also woke and spoke on that seventh day: a person reborn within their own life. More *animos*, more souls than Pablo Capsi had ever dreamed existed had flocked together like the feathers of a bird, setting the whole soul soaring. Angelina Sonco saw with a double vision now: a second landscape illuminating, clarifying and redesigning this world every moment. Julio Capac only repeated what she had said.

This was how it had to be if you were reborn a God. In the beginning Viracocha, Spirit of Rain, first appointer of the Incas, made several statues and brought them all to life inside a cave, whence they emerged: the human race. Angelina spoke of dolls and statues brought to life before her eyes, of memory dolls that showed her how the world was put together . . .

'Now listen to me, I'm the Curer!' shouted Pablo Capsi. 'With all my skill I stopped Angelina Sonco from being killed. Yes, she's alive – exactly like Julio Capac! In secret, with my prayers and my sacrifices I was the channel for the power of the Old. Despite doctors. Despite soldiers. Why did they cut open the heads of the others and poison their bodies and burn them if they didn't fear the Old Gods coming back?'

Christobal and Baltasar had indeed guessed that Angelina

might be lying sick in her own home. Evading the curfew themselves to discover where Julio was, they had noticed Pablo Capsi creeping to and from the Sonco house. Later, the rumour reached their ears, confirming this. However, they hadn't mentioned the possibility of Angelina's survival to Julio. He was so different when he woke up, so much larger a man. Perhaps he didn't care about love any longer, only about the sinews of his vision. And then again, Martin Checa remained alive and well.

'So she's changed!' laughed Julio. 'Bring her to me, Maestro. Tell her that the dolls dance before my eyes too. You cured well, by protecting her. Just as my friends Christobal and Baltasar protected me.' He pointed violently at the fiesta marquee where the remaining doctor was talking urgently to the police chief and the major. 'Does this government of soldiers watch over anybody, except some miners and city workers and themselves? Do they save anybody? But I can save you all, dear friends, all Indians of the Andes, from this desert of the soul. I can save you from the coming desert of collectivization: common labour to feed the worn-out mines and buy jeeps and bullets to keep us fastened in this prison they call our "country". I can save the mines too! I've the key to wealth as great as the silver mountain of Potosi. But that's another matter.

'Listen, why is the name *Indian* banned from the language of the State? Is it from guilt at our condition? From repentance? The wish to repay? Oh no, it's out of fear. They fear Indians – for we Indians are the true rulers of these high places, and as long as there are *Indians* rather than *Workers* there can be Incas again! We can refound the great society of the Andes. We in the Andes will be the successful ones while the rest of the world fails and starves. While their factories die for lack of tin and electricity, while their cities go to waste. They will beg us for our Inca way of life then!'

The doctor approached with the police chief, major and a band of soldiers.

He said, in Spanish:

'I'm afraid you're a carrier of this illness. This Angelina woman must be too. Do you know the word "carrier"? You're safe, yourself. Immune. But you're probably bearing this illness in you wherever you go now. So you see, you mustn't mix with people. You must come with us, let us find out what we can about it. Whatever it is, it's very like one of the worst fevers that can kill your children. It's a miracle that your children aren't all dead, only some adults instead—'

'*Only?*' echoed Julio sarcastically in the doctor's language.

'I'm sorry, that's a bad way to put it ... This fever is very like something we call "cerebro-spinal meningitis". It can kill children by the thousands. There are epidemics every few years – and fevers mutate, they change in the body. They lie asleep, then they wake up every few years. It's very serious. We don't understand this strain of fever yet. Whatever set it free came from the planet Mars. Will you help us? We'll drive you to the hospital in San Rafael and bring you back afterwards. You see, we really can't risk leaving a carrier of ... whatever it is.'

'Of course I shall go to San Rafael! In my own time— for my own very good Inca reasons. This came from Mars? Well, maybe it came from the Sun? You fool, I am *Inti*, the Son of the Sun. I know it.'

Several soldiers pointed rifles at him.

Superimposed on the scene, interpenetrating it, Julio saw a second scenery of capering dolls acting out models of what might happen. He only needed the right words to bring the right deeds into being.

Showing no concern for their levelled guns he spoke out in Quechua to those Quechuan soldiers, knowing them to be so from the set of their faces, and continued his speech – denouncing the unreality of their Revolution, exposing the sacred unity of the armed forces that bound reaction and revolution, revolution and reaction into the same choking rosary of power ...

The major was brought up bilingually from the cradle by a Quechua nursemaid. He listened, bemused by this peasant's sudden insight into his very own speciality: the permanent government behind the Government, the state behind the State, ever-oscillating, currently revolutionary. He listened for far too long. The Indian's voice vibrated the political tight-rope till he felt he could no longer keep his balance on it. Had this *campesino* really experienced such a leap of understanding on his own in that cave? *Cambo letrao es cambo fregao*, he'd often heard said over dinner tables. An educated Indian spells trouble. The only hope for the faceless Indian mass was somehow to intermarry and mix their blood and enter the economy. He'd heard this from the Right, in nervous tones. He'd heard it from the Left, voiced enthusiastically. The Right craved consumers. The Left yearned for producers, within a modern collective state. But really it amounted to the same thing; captivity. He had always supported the policy, faint-heartedly, since it amounted to the same safe thing.

Now this troublesome Indian risen from his deathbed made him pause, mainly in surprise.

He paused too long, of course. His pause gave consent to the Indian's words. Power passed into the Indian's hands. The soldiers let their guns droop.

Why not? wondered the major. *Why not indeed?* Try something new; try something different from the endless switches and swerves of power ...

The several Aymara speakers under his command looked wary and resentful as though some subtle treachery was being acted out. The Quechua speakers, however, relaxed and hovered towards affability. The police chief stood by, bewildered. It certainly wasn't his place to usurp the major's authority or even remind him of it in his presence. If only the major was somewhere else. Then this upstart Indian would be under arrest fast enough. Unfortunately the major was here. Perhaps a major saw further than a simple police chief? Perhaps he saw political advantage? Consequently the police chief did nothing either.

'But he might be a carrier,' the doctor nagged. 'We can make vaccine from him—'

'Yes,' the major nodded. But he gave no orders, mesmerized by the possibility of Something Else. Truly, he had loved his Indian nurse who taught him her tongue. He remembered that now. Really, this was why he had always sought to be a still point round which the wheel of power swung: because the Indians were the still point of this land, round whose lives the wheel of State swung clockwise, anti-clockwise, for ever.

How ridiculous to imagine that this *campesino* emerging from nowhere could outface the labour leaders in the towns or the leading families currently biding their time.

However, the major did not give the People's Government more than another year or eighteen months before the families and the army's right wing officers spun the wheel rightward once more. And this time there would be civil war. The People's Government wouldn't resign. Almost certainly they would retire to the forested Yungas where the high world fell away to the Amazon, along with *their* army.

The pattern of troop movements and relocations during the past few weeks betrayed the first hints of preparations of an impregnable rearguard for their faltering revolution, far away from the capital.

Simple logic told him that to let this self-styled Inca loose among the Indians would be the most reactionary thing he could do. It could pull the rug from under the Revolution. Already the man was pouring scorn on the Revolution with typical Indian resentment and peasant petty-mindedness ...

Yet his interference would do this a full year before the People's Government could possibly have predicted. The Government wouldn't have time to set up its jungle bastions. There would be no long civil war. No prolonged slaughter, no wreckage of the poor torn land. The upshot would just be a few deaths, a few exiles. Another switch of power as before: from Left to Right this time.

For if these Indians rose up and defined themselves as 'The People', then where would the People's Revolution be and all its urban supporters? This would be no engineered thing, paid for and fomented by the Families. It would be authentic. Left and Right would soon have to compromise over it; and with it. Life could go on. America would relax its strangling blockade.

'You,' he said roughly but tolerantly to Julio in Quechua while his Aymara soldiers looked askance, 'how do you propose to make a fortune from empty mines?'

Julio Capac smiled and told him.

The major listened – amused, then bemused.

What was it that the Inca Huayna-Capac was reported to have said? 'If you can't find anything else for the people to do, get them to shift a mountain'?

So this new Inca would institute a new system of labour and a new technology on the Inca style ... It almost sounded plausible, the way this Indian described his plan. It almost sounded like a humane liberating endeavour ...

What nonsense! The man didn't know what he was talking about. It sounded just like those Chinese with their backyard blast furnaces producing rubbish that couldn't be used. From militant workers into mining peasants! He laughed inwardly. Laws of supply and demand and the whole wage and labour relation were a complete mystery to this Inca.

And yet ... it sounded beautiful. If the people believed it ...

Impatiently the doctor cleared his throat.

'Major!'

The major vacillated.

Julio Capac stood there on the stone bench overtopping him, grinning in a brotherly encouraging way.

The doctor plucked the police chief's sleeve but the police chief shrugged him off impotently.

Julio reached out his hand to Baltasar for their one and only rifle, held it idly shoulder high pointing at the sky.

'You soldiers have so many rifles, Major,' he said politely. 'So let me fire the first shot in this campaign, killing no one at all? There has to be a beginning. So this is it. This moment. Now I am the Inca.'

He pulled the trigger. The gun banged, the echo of it returning a moment later from Apup-Chaypi.

Tun-rún, the mountain muttered.

The major glanced at his watch, noting that it was 3.15 in the afternoon.

The villagers noted something else: that one man calling himself an Inca had fired one single gun – with impunity! – in the face of the army that had recently patrolled their streets and burnt their relatives' bodies. And this army was frozen. Without a doubt Julio was the Indians' spokesman now. Egged on by Baltasar and Christobal, the Apusquenos began to chorus approval. Even the Quechua conscripts grudgingly approved.

Yet the rifle shot did hit one target. It severed the strings pulling to and fro that prevented the major from reaching a decision. He must be mad to think he could play such games. There were limits. Armed miners were bad enough. But armed *campesinos*! Abruptly a civil war seemed closer rather than more remote. In a reproachful voice, suggesting laxness on the part of the civil authority, he told the police chief in Spanish:

'Arrest him. We can't waste any more time. He has to go to hospital.'

Yet the soldiers were still heeding their cradle tongue. They did not hear the major's words, and when the police chief repeated them in Spanish why should they obey him? While they hesitated Julio, who did hear, lowered his rifle. The major stood transfixed. He did not care! he realized. He had been at the still point for so long that whatever happened, it did not matter! He actually waited for the bullet as Julio aimed the gun.

'This is for all the burnt bodies!' Julio cried, discharging it at the major, catching him in the chest and blowing him backwards. 'Now we will all burn yours! This is for our Dead, who could have been Gods and Incas!'

The police chief scrambled into the one nearby jeep which was parked facing the main exit street. Ducking over the wheel, his mind swirling with the *campesino*'s mad talk of double vision and mind-dolls, and the impossible sight he had seen, of the major inviting death, he gunned the vehicle away, abandoning the soldiers who had refused to obey him. He was, after all, a survivor; the very fact of his escape, to report these crazy events, should exonerate him from any blame ...

'Did you ever really belong with his army, *allyu-cuna*, my kin?' Julio demanded of the shocked, paralysed soldiery. 'Now I am your major. But better than a major! I am an Inca. Together we'll restore the world that majors and conquistadores destroyed. Won't your families respect you far more for this!'

The smaller number of Aymara soldiers were slinking together meanwhile, back across the plaza – protectively, poking their guns outward like quills of a porcupine, yet not daring actually to aim them. They had no idea what had happened. What anyone had said, except for one order blatantly disregarded. Why their major had stood there to be shot. Slowly the quills rose, not pointing at Julio Capac or the villagers so much as at those other Quechua soldiers who were shouting and arguing but taking no action to punish their major's death – though at the same time they were becoming increasingly intermingled with the villagers. Instead of leaping down into the shelter of the crowd Julio stayed right where he was: above the line of fire which he foresaw crackling from those soldier dolls, in a rekindled memory of soldiering days. The first Aymara soldier fired a moment later, purely out of fear – bringing about what the man most feared. In the crowd an old woman fell down screaming, tripping one of the Quechua soldiers, who dropped his gun. Baltasar seized hold of it. Blood roused, he pushed it out of a knot of soldiers and fired at the Aymaras, who were too tightly grouped for him to miss his target. Seeing themselves fired on by their own Aymara comrades and apparently hearing themselves retaliate, the other Quechua soldiers swung round and fired back.

The porcupine only loosed a few shots before all its members were lying on the plaza, killed by their own friends: who could be no friends of the army, whether they liked it or not, any more.

The doctor nursed a shattered wrist which had caught a bullet from one side or the other. He could only stand by as the villagers moved forward, ransacking the fiesta tent, destroying the sample bottles and slides. Julio surveyed the scene jubilantly. Now he had the nucleus of his army: eager recruits – who had no choice but to join. Now he had a truck and a jeep. He calmed the soldiers, wedding them in to the people of Apusquiy; whereby the people of Apusquiy also became soldiers.

When Pablo Capsi reappeared with Angelina and Martin Checa, Angelina swiftly left Martin's side and walked through the milling crowd, through the dolls of her own double vision, to Julio.

'Now,' grinned Julio to everyone, 'we shall really begin to alter the world. This Inca takes a queen.'

Amazingly, far from appearing jealous or embittered, or trying to prevent it in any way, Martin Checa nodded his approval. (Angelina had spoken to him privately when she awoke, about her own dreams in the coma state and what she had learnt from them about her hidden self, in particular about one episode when she was just a child, and how this had made her regard all men, including Martin Checa; hearing which, Martin was quite glad to let her go . . .)

As Julio proclaimed the new Inca Empire, Angelina saw the dolls of Julio's own past capering around him, overlaying him in a stiff fog. She knew that these were not his own personal insight dolls; they were her own images of him culled from memory, over the years – dolls of pride and prestige, low cunning, rhetoric and braggadocio, as well as of tenderness and bravery. Wearing gaudy distorted masks, out danced Friendship, Valour, Adoration; yet also Ambition, Boastfulness and Bumptiousness. Why couldn't he see these all himself? She was anxious. He really seemed to think he was a God.

'I am my own Ancestor,' he smiled at her while the people wrecked the medical equipment and trampled it like potato mulch, as though making *chuno* to last through the winter. 'So are you too, *huarmillay*, dear wife. The Incas have come back!'

'But we aren't Gods,' she whispered urgently. 'You didn't wake up a God! You woke up a human being – or what human beings might be if they had this double vision we have of the World and the Thought-World. The dolls of memory caper out of yourself, Julio – not out of Heaven or the Sun or Viracocha's bosom. Even if you have to call yourself an Inca, to express your wonder at the change!'

'We have to be some kind of Gods, Angelina,' explained Julio wryly. 'Or they won't follow me bravely enough, or for long enough, will they? We'll be destroyed. That's why I must become the Inca even if I'm not him yet. Don't worry, I can see how.' Still, he seemed to confuse the excuse and the ambition, self-defence and the will to power, quite happily.

The doctor ran to Christobal Pinco, as more reasonable looking than the rest. Hitherto the villagers had ignored him,

83

venting their anger on medical instruments; yet eyes were glancing from the slain major to him and back again. His wrist raged.

'Someone was hurt. I can hear she's in pain. Let me fix my wrist, then I'll help.'

Christobal laughed and thrust him away. 'Help? Did you help before?'

'We didn't understand . . . what went wrong with the brain. But this is a hurt body. I can heal bodies.'

'I already looked. She's dying.'

Christobal shoved him away harder, spinning him round as he sheltered his wrist. As bravely as he could the doctor faced the crowd.

They flocked on him like condors on offal.

In a moment of horror Angelina saw Julio suffering such a death because he was different. And herself! He was right! She thrust her doubts aside. They had to be Gods to save themselves. The very least they could be was an Inca and his Queen!

Shortly, Baltasar and Christobal began pairing every trained soldier with two villagers, to organize them. They would expand these initial triples into companies of ten later on, Julio ordained. And then one hundred. One thousand.

Part Two

THE WINDING PATH

EIGHT

'We haven't heard any more about *The Hare*,' observed Silverman. 'Three weeks now. Houston haven't told us anything.'

'More like four weeks,' Weaver corrected.

'Well, that's good news. Time's still capable of passing. Say, what do you know? You just broke my dream. I had this dream last night about how I invented a time machine. But it was a very slow time machine.'

What a breach of etiquette. Dreams took place in the privacy cubicles. They should stay there. Didn't Gene realize that other people's dreams are always very boring? Even the most amazing of them. (Why was it? If you told a dream and said it was some Polynesian legend it sounded interesting. As soon as the listeners knew it was a dream the shutters of interest slammed down ...)

'The only way I could travel forwards in time was by travelling backwards, accumulating time-potential on the way. This was my big discovery. Real mad professor stuff. I'd worked out that there were "quanta" of time – basic units that depend on the total age of the Universe. They get larger the older the Universe is, you see. So to jump forward twenty years required crawling backwards downhill for twenty years first of all. I could build a reversing chamber all right, which would take me backwards at a snail's pace. That's to say, at the pace of real life, but lived backwards. So here was I shut up in this metal box with a single window to look out of, no bigger than a suitcase ... When I got back into the past, was I cramped and crazy! But it was only way back then, that I could push the button and make the quantum jump through time twenty years ahead of my starting point. And that's when I woke up, damn it! I spent the whole dream locked in this steel suitcase, crawling backwards.'

You couldn't pay much attention to other people's dreams. Stupid excursions into ill-organized basements!

'But there might really be such a thing as a quantum of time, Jim, that's the strange thing. I never thought of it before—'

He wasn't really talking about time machines at all. That was only a pretext. He was talking about his damned privacy cubicle and what went on inside it!

The Weaver basement in Lakewood had been just as confined as the doughnut torus of *Frontiersman*, yet Weaver spent his happiest hours there making models of jets and spacecraft to the background hum of the freezer. He wasn't scared of being locked in. And his father would never have locked him down there to punish him if he thought that Jim would damage instead of getting on with some useful work. It was always more a pleasure than a punishment.

'We never heard about *Zayits*,' he said, blandly changing the subject, 'because there's nothing to hear. *Zayits* burnt up. Hit the Andes. Nobody found anything. They're still looking.'

Weaver's feet were no longer blood-laden. Unfortunately his system had bounced right back, making the sort of idiotic quantum jump that Silverman's time machine indulged in. Blood was pooling in his chest around his heart now. He realized this, though he felt fine, because he was hardly drinking anything. Dehydration – a sure sign! He had stepped up his intake of drinks promptly, forcing himself to take in fluid. He had commenced a new cycle of exercises to centrifuge the blood out and around his body.

It was a damn sight better to have a few minor physical glitches than start dreaming about being locked in suitcases and feeling you had to justify yourself out loud.

Conceivably heavy ionized nuclei from space could be bombarding Gene in his privacy cubicle, sparking off these odd warning dreams as they carved their tracks through his brain. The liquid hydrogen tanks were supposed to act as shielding; but suppose it was inadequate in Gene's case?

'I think it's time we checked the cosmic ray counters.'

In the conference room at Mission Control sat Spike Thorne, flight director for the *Frontiersman* mission, Charles Klein, director of manned spaceflight, Dr Albrecht, their flight surgeon – and the man responsible for the meeting, a freckled curly-haired Central Intelligence officer called Inskip who introduced himself as chief of the western hemisphere division. He had arrived from Washington within the hour. The telephone call preceding him only hinted at something urgent concerning the flight to Mars to be discussed in extreme secrecy.

Charles Klein had been closeted with Inskip since his arrival; he brought him to the conference room. If the head of public affairs had been summoned too, Thorne and Albrecht realized, this might have had something to do with the past of one of the three astronauts; plainly it didn't.

'I'm sorry about the short notice, gentlemen,' smiled Inskip. 'To coin a phrase "Houston, we've got a problem".' Inskip was in his early forties but boyish with all the freckles of a compact fifteen-year-old and not much taller than one. His voice had a quality of tough-minded whimsy about it: a small guy's wounded pride, grit and determination, a dewy-eyed moment, a flare of temper. Life was tough, but it was fun; he'd always bounce back grinning, no matter how many times the opposition knocked him down. And yet he seemed like some sort of ingenious robot acting this role synthetically. On the whole he synchronized neatly with his environment. But on occasions he lagged, or leapt ahead incongruously – responding to some programmed version of reality that wasn't actually there. Or not there yet. His whimsy was the Emperor's New Clothes of the reformed soft agency; his lag and leap the agency's continued faith in foreseeing the future and manipulating it, softly, to bring it into line with what they saw.

'It's about this Soviet Mars probe *Zayits*. It came down in Bolivia near some godforsaken village called Apusquiy.' He dipped in his briefcase. 'I marked it on this map. You know the current political complexion of Bolivia?'

'We weren't allowed to train our crew there,' shrugged Thorne.

'Oh yes, I remember.'

Albrecht raised an eyebrow.

'I remember if from a briefing. That's what I mean.' Inskip said it with such a boyish disarming grin. Albrecht saw there was little difference between real memory and an intelligence report in Inskip's eyes. If anything, the latter was more trustworthy.

The present administration in La Paz is highly antipathetic to America. That won't last forever. Meanwhile we're having to use some gentle economic muscle against Bolivia. Which is a pity, it's a poor country, needs all its exports and imports. Well then, La Paz recovered the Soviet probe from the mountains. They kept it secret. They aren't exactly on speaking terms with the Soviets either. Really xenophobic revolution, this one! Personally I'd prefer direct Soviet or Chinese influence. At least there's something solid to kick out! La Paz is offering to trade us the probe for economic good will.'

'A heap of junk. That's all it'll be,' said Thorne dismissively. 'You want us to risk our relations with the Russians—?' Utter anathema to Thorne was the idea of failing to return even the tiniest piece of space debris.

'That isn't the point,' cut in Inskip. '*Zayits* brought back some Martian soil which started an epidemic in the village. About thirty people died, who'd touched the soil. Of a kind of meningitis. Brain inflammation. La Paz has the soil and the autopsy reports. As we're sending people all the way to Mars hadn't we better know about this soil? About it being lethal. That's what they're really offering.' He looked pensive. 'Can't guarantee a sterile craft, can you? They're bound to tread some soil in. It's an awful lot of money and reputation to write off. But the bigger worry is, what if Mars is unusable because of Whatever-It-Is?'

'Thirty deaths, then it stopped?' sneered Thorne. 'Do you call that an epidemic?'

'I call it an epidemic if you have a total population of three on a world and they all get it! But that's not all either. Item, there was no treatment they tried that worked. They'll tell us what they tried. They know a lot of negative information about how not to treat it if our men get it. Item, two survivors pulled through.'

'Who'll have immunity,' mused Albrecht.

'That isn't all they have. Those two Indians have had brainstorms about the state of the nation. This is where our information gets muzzy – because now they're leading a rebellion. They called the Inca Empire back into being a month ago from their crumby little village: with themselves as reincarnated Incas. Apparently it's snowballing. People believe it. Some units of the army joined them. Poor bastards, can't blame them for wanting the People's Government off their backs! Well, we finally managed to get a report on roughly *how* the two Indians were affected. A local police chief got away just as the killing started. We have a contact in the *Control Politico*, in the Panoptico prison in Sucre – *that's confidential.*'

And Inskip told them all he knew about the speech that Julio Capac had made – about becoming a mummy, and re-dreaming his life, then waking up with enhanced perception of the workings of his own mind; and how 'mind-dolls' danced in a double-vision in the real world, redirecting his thought processes, making him a God ...

'Suppose this Martian bug is some parasite controlling these two Indians? Is that what's waiting for us on Mars?'

Albrecht shook his head.

'I really don't see a parasite from Mars taking over a human brain. You need a certain size of creature before you get intelligence. You need brain weight. You can't have microbes hatching up plans.'

'I don't know about that. A lot of data can be packed into a human sperm. Suppose it's that sort of intelligence? Tied up in a virus. It gets into a body, a host—'

'No, no, no.'

'A sperm's a biological machine for passing on data.'

'Anything as complex as a sperm would be destroyed by the ultraviolet on Mars.'

'So what accounts for these two Indians' success, Doctor?'

'You said yourself that you wouldn't blame anyone for rebelling against the People's Government.'

'No, I'm sure it's related – the Martian dirt and the brain-storm. The victims all died of inflammation of the brain. They went stiff as leather. These two survivors go through this same process and promptly declare they're Incas with enhanced perception, almost double minds if we're to believe it! Did you know that the old Incas practised trepanning? They cut skulls open in a highly sophisticated operation by the standards of those days. They inserted gold plates to enlarge skull size. What for? Supposition: the very first Incas underwent some kind of brain change. Believe me, it took brains to set up their empire in the time it took, in that terrain!'

'Then it could hardly have been the fault of some *Martian* parasite.'

'Precisely.' Inskip had an infuriatingly endearing way of agreeing with a statement that someone had just made contradicting him; as though he had only tossed his supposition into the arena to tease the truth from reluctant or bumbling lips.

'Item: the Incas practised mummification. The mummy of the dead Inca sat on the throne beside the new Inca at his coronation. These mummies would have felt just as these sick Indians are reported in their comas. Stiff as leather, unquote. Obviously this brain-change, or whatever it is, only happened to the very first Incas – then this all degenerated into ritual. But something happened in Peru at the start of the Inca Empire. A new strength of mind. Pressure on the skull. Comas.'

'Mr Inskip, the ancient Egyptians had mummies and so did half-a-dozen other peoples I can think of. You have to dispose of dead bodies somehow. The way is quite likely to blend elementary hygiene with religious rites based on survival. Mummification, in a word.'

'Right. Those Egyptians practised it. It's widespread. Now *why* is it widespread? What's it a memory of? That "stiff as leather" business worries me when it coincides with a trepanning situation plus Inca rebellion *that works*, led by a revived mummy—'

'A man in a coma isn't a mummy!'

'He just seems like one. Same thing to a primitive mind. Final item which worries me: all this results from a shipload of Martian soil. Well, we don't want our astronauts having messianic brainstorms up on Mars any more than we want them falling down dead. That's a pretty powerful weapons system they have up there.'

'Actually,' intervened Charles Klein, moderately, '*Frontiersman* can't physically return to Earth without first jettisoning *Warming Pan*.'

'So there's just their health to worry about. *And* the investment in Mars. On the Bolivian precedent they're certainly at risk.'

'We'll voice up a warning to them, and I suppose we'll have to examine this soil somehow,' Klein conceded.

Inskip frowned.

'The Bolivian medics burnt all the corpses, then apparently the rebels destroyed any actual blood or tissue samples … Pity.'

'It doesn't sound as though the Bolivians are offering very much!'

'Exactly. The only way we can really *know* is by bringing out this Inca or his queen intact. I assure you *that* will not appeal to La Paz at all, no matter how much nuisance he's causing. So, playing for time, we should negotiate for *Zayits* and the soil. That gives us a foot in the Bolivian door. How long is it till *Frontiersman* gets to Mars? Eighteen weeks, if I remember. Do we have a secure code for talking to the spacecraft?'

'Of course not.' Thorne shook his head. 'Absolutely no need for codes in space.'

'Oh? The present situation indicates otherwise. It's irresponsible not having a code for emergencies. Suppose we meet extraterrestials?'

'We *try* to keep paranoia out of space, Mr Inskip.'

'Which seems to be what our Inca is suffering from! We can have *Zayits* itself and the soil in two to three weeks, depending on negotiations. Obviously you need every scrap of evidence. But equally, we can't have the Russians knowing we've borrowed their spacecraft—'

'Christ, no,' begged Thorne.

'We're the soul of discretion, believe you me. Very quiet Americans. Gone are the old barnstorming days. But you can still safely radio a warning to your boys in plain language – describing the "Inca" incident, without saying anything about obtaining *Zayits*. Base it on our intelligence reports and that police chief's description. Tell them that *Zayits* was destroyed by the rebels, and that this is *all* we have to go on. In fact, I'd say it's vital that you do tell *Frontiersman* this much, or the

Russians will get damned suspicious. They can't actually do anything very active in that part of the continent. Bolivia's too well contained. All the neighbouring countries are what they are pleased to describe as fascist dictatorships. Peru, Chile, Paraguay, Brazil, Argentina ... to one degree or another. Their agents are pretty well all flushed out by now and their diplomats are fairly strictly restricted. Meanwhile we'll work on the problem. It's delicate, but I think we can swing it – what we really need is that Inca himself. Or herself. *That's* something we can't announce out loud till it's a *fait accompli;* and preferably not even then. Dr Albrecht, if your presence isn't needed here on an hour-by-hour basis, will you join us on the Potomac? Obviously we can't bring *Zayits* and the soil here.'

'No,' said Klein flatly. 'I don't see our flight surgeon visiting your headquarters in any circumstances.'

'I agree with you,' nodded Inskip. 'We'd better keep intelligence and space travel apart. So we'll report our findings to you by secure courier as they come up. Now, the *Zayits* negotiations are all in strict confidence, understand. Nobody outside this room is to know. Not your wives, not your most trusted colleagues.'

Albrecht noted the order of precedence wryly. Maybe Inskip only echoed the order of precedence among astronauts; spoke the lines he thought appropriate to a space centre? As Albrecht studied him, Inskip's eyes unfocused temporarily and the man seemed to stare right through the doctor into the wall beyond – as though Albrecht was not merely transparent, all his opinions X-rayed and recorded, but as though he had physically dissolved, leaving the walls of the room a movie screen with the foreordained film of Albrecht, Klein and Thorne momentarily off its sprockets in Inskip's head and nothing showing on the screen. Then Inskip was his grinning, freckled, boy-scout self again. Contemporary reality bounced back, after that momentary sag.

Shortly after Inskip had departed, Spike Thorne went upstairs to radio the news about the Martian soil, the deaths and the Inca 'double vision' to the spacecraft.

When he did so, he read from a script they had all agreed

on. Nothing would be said to anger or alert the Russians; or the Bolivians. In time, a formula would be worked out – for whatever was in the soil; and a political formula too. But that would not be till *Frontiersman* was much nearer Mars.

NINE

A week later, Silverman was still speculating eagerly about the news from Houston. If only the Inca rebellion hadn't wiped out so much vital evidence! As it was, the nature and the true effect of the Martian soil was anyone's guess. No doubt this accounted for Houston's subsequent reticence on the subject. Houston were trying to find out more; but without success, as yet. Obviously Houston couldn't give vent to wild public speculations over the radio. There'd be instant pressure from the former opponents of *Frontiersman* to abort the Mars landing and maybe even *Warming Pan* itself on the grounds that not enough was known.

Silverman found himself drawn closer to Jim Weaver, for a while, by the news. Wally Oates seemed curiously uninterested in the implications, dismissing the whole enigma of the soil as a decontamination problem, to be dealt with by sterile care and hygiene. Yet Jim Weaver's ears had pricked up at the rumour of God, even in Inca form. His recent red-neck religiosity burgeoned even more till he became nearly intolerable to talk to about it; yet at the same time he was the only person with whom Silverman could unburden himself about the implications of the 'God illness' as he saw them.

'I can't comprehend how you can talk about God and illness in the same breath,' protested Weaver. 'Next thing, you'll be saying that when Jesus was taken down from the Cross he was only in one of these comas—'

'I don't think Jesus comes into this. Mystic, reformer, Jewish freedom fighter who deliberately got himself crucified; whatever he was.'

'Gene, I realize you never even were a Christian, but that's not merely disrespectful; it's downright diminishing. Of *yourself*.'

'I only mean that the crucifixion was a normal physical punishment. Nails, spears, the Cross ... It wasn't something programmed into the brain.'

'Well, *that's* debatable. Christ did *know* it was going to happen; even when it had to happen. Do we have to talk about his mission as though it was a computer programme?'

'We're getting off the tracks. Look, this Bolivian peasant becomes an Inca and a God by contracting a brain fever – which I'll bet he had no inkling of, beforehand. He goes through a mummy phase, becomes like a chrysalis, and emerges as something different, something exalted, his consciousness, as they put it, "doubled". Two vital clues there, Jim: the mummy-chrysalis stage, and the doubling of consciousness. Suppose that this illness triggered off something genetically laid down in Man, which had only expressed itself so far during human history in a few rare instances. In ancient Egypt. Even as long ago as Neolithic times. But just to one or two individuals – and the memory of this transfiguration of a man or woman, through the "chrysalis coma", is preserved in all the mumbo-jumbo of mummy rituals. From Neolithic times till now is only a puny few seconds on the evolutionary clock. By and large, we're still all contemporaries, genetically.'

'How can you have a dormant mutation being triggered halfway through somebody's life? Either it's dormant, in which case it's passed on in the DNA and doesn't have any effect upon the person carrying it, right? Whether haemophilia or,' he nodded significantly at Silverman's ginger beard, 'red hair. Or else it shows up from birth onwards.'

'Really? Puberty only sets in at a certain age. If I'd had red pubic hair and I'd died when I was six years old, no one would ever have known about it! There are inherited illnesses – Huntington's chorea is one – that only "clock in" when you're about sixty. The programme's all there. It just has time-switches built into it. And this "Inca" programme is one that hardly ever gets switched on. One or two neolithic men who become shamans afterwards. One or two ancient Egyptians like Akhenaton. One or two 14th Century Peruvians who founded the Inca Empire. The Incas were just one trivial mountain tribe among many up to a hundred years before the Spaniards got there; then they exploded like a supernova, from Bolivia to Ecuador ... Why shouldn't you have a mutation that never expresses itself – till triggered?'

'No, Gene. Martians never landed on the Earth in ancient Egypt or Peru, spraying Martian soil around, whatever the "God was an Astronaut" brigade may think. Jesus Christ was simply God born as Man – as an ordinary man; that's the miracle.'

'I didn't say Martians did, damn it! That's preposterous. I say that there's something evolved in the DNA which *can* bring about this coma, then rebirth on to a higher consciousness level ... which naturally an Indian peasant describes as becoming God. The Martian soil contains a catalyst. A speeder-upper. Yet the same thing *can* happen spontaneously too. It's written into our evolutionary programme. Only, it hardly ever happens at our present state of development.'

'Programmes, programmes! Man isn't a computer, Gene, you insist on forgetting the soul.'

'On the contrary! I admit I'm not a life sciences man, Jim, I'm on the physical side. So I think in terms of systems analysis, programmes ... But I do know that a whole lot of research into the nature of mind and consciousness has been going on for decades now using systems approaches. It produces far clearer insights than mysticism ever has. This is exactly where this Inca's talk of "double-vision" links up with, say, John Lilly's approach to the mind as a biocomputer.'

'That dolphin man, who freaked out on drugs?'

'The dolpin man who decided we can't understand dolphins till we understand our own minds. I'd prefer to put it that way. Lilly saw the mind as a computer partly programmed genetically, in the form of the available circuitry; then partly by experience, particularly those domineering survival programmes we lay down in infancy which programme the way

95

we use the circuitry. Lastly, and most importantly, there's a capacity for self-programming which we can get access to.'

'Through LSD?' sneered Weaver. 'Opium of agnostics.'

'Through drugs, meditation, hypnosis, sense deprivation – whatever extreme state of mind. Mainly, the consciousness programmes operate below the awareness threshold. They're not visibly operational. And when ordinary perception space, as Lilly calls it, gets flooded with the cognitive process – whether it's due to drugs or black-room isolation or whatever – and when we *see* the programmes governing how we think, we often think we're in contact with beings other than ourselves. Higher beings. Gods. Actually we're in contact with our own metaprogrammes – the programmes that govern our own thinking programmes. This must be what the Inca is seeing. He's aware of his own mind programmes as visible entities, which he can manipulate too, in real life situations – the way that researchers have only been able to do in lab situations. In Lilly's jargon, he can metaprogramme his mind. I need hardly add that that's a highly desirable state. It means that the human race really is biologically capable of higher awareness because of the very way our biocomputer has evolved. Of course, there's always the risk of assuming that there are real Gods at large in the world, or that you're one yourself, and in not realizing just how overriding and intransigent some of the survival metaprogrammes are : how much like Holy Writ they can seem.'

'All you're saying is that God is within us; and we go *out there* to find Him. I've been saying this all along. Exploring space is the opening up of a whole new plane of religious proof. Thus our own outward urge versus the Russians' inward urge. Metaprogrammes? Words, Gene, just words. You refuse to feel the wonder of the void.'

'I'm the dogmatist, am I? You amuse me.'

'You are, and I'm sorry for you.'

'The real wonder is that the human mind should evolve along lines so that it can *know* itself. That's huge enough for now. We can worry about "God" when we're really on our way—'

'—to being Gods ourselves? I'm surprised you fall into that materialistic trap!'

'I was going to say: when we're on our way to knowing the metaprogrammes of the universe we're in. To knowing how a universe programmes itself so that life evolves in it, which *then* evolves consciousness that can examine the hidden programmes that form the basis for it.'

'Must I say the obvious, that the programmer is God? That we're simply in His hands? That would be too callow for you. Not enough hardware.'

'How about dreams, if you don't like computer analogies? Years ago a Dutch doctor called van Eeden found that he could wake up in his dreams and consciously direct them. He had this same impression of other superintelligent beings being present. Some very slippery demons indeed! Instead of "metaprogramme" let's say the subconscious mind, the dream mind; instead of "programme" let's say the awake mind. Well, the awake mind *can* enter and examine the unconscious mind, even modify it. This sort of training has been going on in California for ages now.'

'All cooky ideas come to roost in California. California's not a state of the union, it a state of mind. Nutsville, USA.'

'A psychologist called Charles Tart started it. He got the same kind of effect by "rapport-hypnosis", where one hypnotized subject hypnotizes a second subject. Subject, object; object, subject. The effect was of consciousness and subconsciousness – or programme and metaprogramme – alternating between two separate individuals, who each felt sure they were passing through each other, interpenetrating each other mentally ... I suppose this was one reason I fell in love with Renata, really.'

'Because you wanted to interpenetrate?' laughed Weaver frostily. For all his talk of programmes and hardware, Silverman was becoming all too intimate, too cloying, clammy. Damned materialist. He had no real spirituality. He spoke as though human destiny was for man's mind to *copulate* with itself! Writhing around inside the head. Weaver wasn't interested in the colour of Silverman's pubic hair – a quite gratuitous piece of familiarity, that! – or his writhings with his wife, masquerading as spirit made flesh. He must end these discussions. Cool them off. They were going the wrong way. Wally's attitude to the soil and the illness was the right one. Ignore it. He'd been a fool to be drawn into these conversations – to have his own wonder exploited by Silverman's sticky spider's web. He must back out; but diplomatically. Without causing offence. He was a mission commander, not a missionary.

'Because of the sort of art she felt bound to create, out of whom she was. She was working right at this frontier. On the one side, perfection, the idea of the perfect human body; on the other side, actual imperfect bodies in the real world. Her art mirrored the whole idea of underlying forms – metaprogrammes – and the real, imperfect structures – the programmes they give rise to. Renata wanted to get back across the divide from the one to the other. To find how a real world body could seize control of its own shaping, reshape itself . . . That's why I loved her. I see that now. I knew about this consciousness research. It fascinated me, but I was too far into the hard sciences. Well, Renata built hard solid . . . machines, that I could operate and understand – even when they just generated dreams, illusions . . . This is what's happening in Bolivia now, Jim; someone has woken up to himself. He's got back across the divide. It's a very human thing that he should, no matter if some Martian soil did switch him on. The capacity's been there all along. Our biocomputer is built to rewire itself this way—'

Shrugging, Weaver walked past him to check instruments.

Several tens of millions of kilometres away from the speeding spacecraft, Inskip was cruising into the car park at headquarters, humming to himself as he hunted out his own parking space two lanes east and one lane north. Till the previous month all directors and deputy directors of sections and offices had had a space reserved for them by their acronym stencilled on the gridded tarmac. Inskip's space had been DWH: director western hemisphere. Then somebody decided that this was a security risk, since it printed out the whole administrative structure for any passing plane or orbiting satellite to photograph – as though it wasn't public knowledge already! But much could be gleaned from the absence of a car from its proper place, or from its prolonged presence. Consequently all the stencilled letters were blackened out, to the chagrin of the acronym-holders. Yet senior staff still sought their way to the old familiar, if now anonymous places; and by tacit consent any black smeared space was left vacant by employees below acronym level. Parking wantonly on one of these black blotches would signal a naïve newcomer or a deliberate personal challenge. It was always possible to trace which interloper owned which number plates!

Inskip let his finger tips pilot him automatically to his proper place, which was vacant, while his lips emitted a tuneless hum – the hum of his own mental engine purring smoothly. The hum cut him off from disturbances. It blanketed the cawing of crows in the woods, a radio commenting a ball game, a light plane overhead.

White noise. He liked it; it liked him.

Once, long ago, the hum had been a hymn. Now and then a few bars still poked their backbone above the white smother and the hum took on a deeper organ drone.

He slotted his turbine in among the other small powerful turbines patronized by employees of the refurbished 'Company': discreet, clean vehicles, polite and ecological, with one hell of a boost in them. Apart from a few contrails unravelling into frayed woollen cords and the general haze eastwards towards Washington, the sky was serenely blue. He strode humming though the cars into the Honeycomb, as they dubbed headquarters. While his pass was being screened the humming died; his mind brightened with Bolivian scenarios.

Elevator to the sixth floor, then a walk westwards for exactly five minutes. He pushed the door of 692. The Bolivian desk officer Ted Ferguson sat drinking scalding aromatic coffee, flipping through folders. His secretary Sylvia Herrera was typing something for John Wenner, nominal head of station in La Paz, forced to work from the Lima embassy these days, when he wasn't in Washington.

'This Inca is an ideal wrecker for their revolution,' Wenner said to Inskip. 'A genuine populist uprising against the collective state. What better could we hope for? We should be filtering aid to him. He sees La Paz as a foreign government. On the other hand America is too far away to mean much to him. Whatever propaganda he hears from the Government radios we're remote. So we could easily befriend him. Airdrops of arms over the Chilean border—'

'Arms, up to a point,' frowned Inskip. 'We can't actually let him win. He's too much of a wild card. An Inca on an Andean throne would stimulate all kinds of ethnic balkanization. You know how it is these days. Mohawks, Sioux, Cree, Eskimos, Basques. God knows who next.'

'But the People's Government itself expects to fall some time this year or next. They're already starting to shift their power base to the north and east of the country where nobody will be able to blast them out. And next time around they mean to make the revolution stick.'

'Which means a full scale civil war?'

'Right. The Left will win it too, given time. The next pro-American régime will be far too busy trying to keep hold on the urban economy. Okay, so we'll end the embargo and boost aid to them. But they'll still have to manage the miners and workers. They just can't handle a rival government as well, fully organized and well ensconced. However much we support the new régime, given our present guidelines, it'll fall apart if the Left have established a firm rearguard within the next few months. What can stop them? Peru and Chile refuse to escalate beyond nuisance value ... You see, this Inca could fatally divert strength just at the time when they're trying to redeploy. We have to assist him. We can't just lift him straight out as you seem to want.'

'Hmm. Houston need to know in seventeen weeks at the latest. Well, it could take two weeks to pull him out and analyse him. Can our Inca do enough damage in fifteen weeks?'

'I think so. His people only control the country right now. The acid test is when he tries to mobilize miners. That'll stir La Paz. They'll have to do something. At the moment one-half of the officers on the army council think it's more vital to shore up the rearguard for the second, decisive revolution. The others want to use the army to root him out. Any success for Inca power in a mining area should tip the balance.'

'You could actually get the People's Government attacking a mining community and occupying it?' pondered Inskip. 'A black mark on their revolutionary record!' He accepted a cup of coffee from Sylvia Herrera and thought a while. 'Okay, I see it this way. Our Inca causes trouble in the mining areas up to about fifteen weeks from now. He alienates the miners from the Government and stops the Leftists from redeploying. Then the army neutralizes him. But we whisk him off to safety having first won his trust. So we need a pincers strategy. Aid for the Inca in discreet moderation, plus somebody planted with him. Then the Bolivians get to him in approximately fifteen weeks, and we have someone reliable with them too. Meanwhile we buy *Zayits* and that soil and loosen the embargo to make La Paz think we're playing ball. What operations do we have, Ted?'

Ted Ferguson scanned the folders.

'BOLSHOY. That's our standing watch in the armed forces movement – a Colonel Pomona who really hates the unions and is scared shitless of Indian populism. But he keeps his manias to himself. The army see him as loyal even though we did train him in Panama. After all, scores of Bolivian officers passed through Panama.'

'Can he get in charge of neutralizing the Inca?'

'Probably. He already spoke out against this Inca strongly as a menace to the revolution. Naturally that's because he's pushing for holding on to power in La Paz rather than falling back.'

'To abort the fall-back?'

'Right.'

'Well, he's our man for the second arm of the pincers. How about the Inca arm?'

'I think we'll have to send in a penetration agent direct from Chile, with the arms drop.'

'That's fine so long as he's Chilean. No Americans in the field, remember. And only enough weapons to last a few weeks!'

Angelina Sonco was saved from the fate of other sick villagers because her father kept her illness secret. Yet his true reason for called in a Curer instead of doctors was a guilty one stretching back years to when Angelina was only eleven years old. She didn't know any of this till she woke up from her dreams; however, simply by telling Martin Checa what she dreamt she easily broke her false *sirvinacuy* marriage with him. Now that the Inca had captured San Rafael and was ready to push against the first mining settlements, and now that she was pregnant by him (for her bleeding was late) she told him too, to change his mind, if she could, about the value of the Inca Conquest.

They lay together, having made love that was still a freshness and a wonder, in a grand antique four-poster bed bescrolled with knotty gilded carvings, its cornice a frieze of cherubs and cupids, in the commandeered home of the former Prefect of San Rafael, now their palace.

'Remember Justina, Julio? In Apusquiy, ten years ago?'

Angelina's best friend, her beloved, an older girl called Justina lived on the outskirts of Apusquiy in a less handsome house than the Soncos' two-storey tin-roofed adobe dwelling with its courtyard for chickens, goats and pig. Justina's father was a Curer; but when Justina was born she bore a mulberry birthmark on her shoulder shaped like a hummingbird, and she was born with her eyes wide open – *Beloved of God*. She would only stay on Earth a brief while to carry some message back to Heaven ...

'I remember. But I wasn't there, when they killed her.'

'I know. I was there.'

'You!'

'Oh yes, I watched it all.'

For days after Justina's birth the Curer bathed his daughter in prophylactics and rubbed sticky paste on the hummingbird to hold it still and bandaged and rebandaged it with black llama wool so that it couldn't see to fly. He tossed rotten eggs up the mountain at the cemetery, to fool the Spirit of Death. He danced round his house, whipping the walls to chase away any other spying spirits. Then he searched the village for whatever the hummingbird was supposed to report – which he found in the llama herd of Damian Oquendo, richest of the Apusquenos. Twin milk-white llamas with identical black saddle markings had been born. Men do not ride llamas. Who could ride them? Only children, dead children.

'Martin Checa helped kill her. He was a male of that pack. The smear of his scent protected me from *that* fate, so I married him—'

'You told him *that*? So that was why—'

'I only realized it after I woke up. I told him before Pablo Capsi came to tell me you were still alive, changed like me. One must be sincere, after such a change. Anyway, I was only being cruel to be kind. It would have been unmanning for Martin to realize the difference between us as the days and weeks went by.'

'And dangerous, if he thought that a witch had come home to roost!'

'That too, I suppose ... though I wasn't thinking that way.' She regretted her concession, as it passed her lips; it buoyed up Julio's drive for a position of strength. 'I only wanted honesty,' she qualified.

All the village knew that Damian Oquendo's daughter was being groomed for marriage to a prosperous old roué in distant San Rafael. The old roué had heard enough tales of country girls sleeping like monkeys with any and every boyfriend. He insisted on guarantees. The village priest of Apusquiy was coaching Oquendo's daughter in etiquette, Spanish and morality ...

Justina's father deduced from the sign of the llama foals that the Oquendo girl had got herself pregnant and rid herself of the embarrassment – buried it, or them, in the house or the yard where no one would know about it. The white llamas were born to carry those misdemeanours away. When Damian Oquendo refused to pay heed, a spirit hummingbird alighted where its message was sure to be read.

Justina's father arrived at the Oquendo home, cracking

his whip, screaming at the house, accusing the Oquendos volubly. Justina's life was in peril, so long as Oquendo kept his secret. She might die any time to carry back news of what she saw with her wide open eyes. After ten minutes they scurried him inside.

The Curer had been right about the abortion, though Damian Oquendo believed not a word about the spirit messages; Justina's father was just a snooper and eavesdropper who haunted people's windows at night listening and peering – a poor man out to make a miserable little profit, heedless if he ruined a girl's marriage prospects.

Still, Oquendo bottled up his rage, promising coca and alcohol and coins and even his llama foals for slaughter in exchange for the stealthy removal of the box with the (single) foetus in it to be burnt up on the mountain.

They agreed on secrecy, and night-time; but, flushed with success, Justina's father carried out his rituals of disinterment, spirit-whipping, sacrifice and cremation with such caterwauling and prancing, such scolding and whipping, that one quarter of Apusquiy knew all about the scandal for certain by dawn and the rest of the village by the evening. The Oquendo girl stopped visiting the Priest for lessons in Spanish and etiquette and morality ...

For years thereafter Justina's father kept a magical regimen around his only daughter, till herbs and medicines became second nature to her. This was Justina's only education; along with the tale of how her father saved her at birth by braving the richest man in the village – which explained why their little family was a sort of pariah nowadays, albeit in demand whenever there were stillbirths or other anomalies to exorcise, or birth cords to dispose of.

When the Curer died, vainly trying to cure himself with expectorants and vomitary agents, Justina's mother swore there was slow poison in some grape juice that her husband received from a relative of the Oquendos. After that Justina and her mother lived alone; the girl an outcast, who *knew things*. The girl grew up aloof, distant, the spirits of the earth and her own passions for companions.

'My father saw the mark of Justina on my brow one day,

Julio. I was only eleven, she was five years older, but she had become my friend. My lover? Yes, I loved her. I worshipped her. She knew so much more than me. She wanted to teach secrets to a "decent" child of the village. We walked in the hills together, we caressed, we kissed. My father saw it and hated it. Because it was unnatural? Maybe a little of that. But more because he was afraid that I would die of it. My brother, my infant sister, my youngest brother too all died of the scarlet fever within twelve months. A curse might have been pointed at our family! But, wrapped up in love, I grieved too little for them.'

'Why are you telling me all this?'

'Because I want you to know how my dreams cleared my mind instead of obsessing me with power, like you, Julio.'

Child of magic, Justina had never known a boy. The village youths eyed her with greedy desire and fright that their souls might be snatched away. That secret mark of spirits on her flesh! A dangerous feat to woo her or love her. Only venturable as a dare; but no one dared.

'She undressed in the hills to show me her hummingbird mark. She made me touch it, kiss it. I wasn't unwilling. Her breasts, her body. At night I dreamt about the magic mark; waking up, I still dreamt about it – till finally a little mulberry mark appeared on my own skin too. A star on my brow. Nothing much. A rash. Still, that was her mark. I'd willed it there. When my father saw it, he knew who had sent diseases on our family, to make me an only child like herself – without any friends but her. Now she sent disease upon me too, to have my body near her in the graveyard . . .'

A pack of village men burst into the house of Justina and her mother one night, hunting through it for the familiar beast that must be sucking spirit milk from her milkless nipples. Finding none, they hauled Justina out into the full moonlight, past the bloody foetus of a llama drying on a line, to tear the clothes from her body and search it for signs of sorcery.

'I saw from the *tola* thickets, Julio . . . I'd watched them daring each other in the plaza, working each other's courage up. I was scared for her, I'd run there. Yet I never connected it all with my father's fears till I dreamt it again. My father was a friend of Damian Oquendo – he used to ask him for advice. What a perfect excuse for revenge! You see, revenge carries on. Oquendo hadn't gorged himself on it yet. In the dream, I was watching it all like a puppet – but a puppet that could *think* about what it saw in ways I couldn't think back then. I knew why I refused your love, Julio, *because* I loved you – because I wouldn't let you become one of those pawing violent men.'

'We made love! Have you forgotten? I was the first one you chose!'

'Yes, I led you up the mountain to that same place where Justina bared herself for me. That was a magic act of love – a branding deep down in me, by you, a man, of what Justina taught me. Oh yes, I chose you to deflower me, with her medicines saturating my flesh when you entered it! She made love to me *through* you. But a brand doesn't only mark, it burns out, erases ... So I couldn't enter a *sirvinacuy* marriage with you. Society likes *sirvinacuy*; it approves. Society's approval, turned upside down, was what destroyed Justina! I had to tease and refuse.'

The males pawed Justina under the blinding moon. Hauling her to and fro, they blundered into the drying line, setting the moon-shadow of that foetus sprinting back and forth across the ground. The shadow alighted briefly upon Justina's birthmark, then leapt off, and the men cried out at the escaping shadow in fear and triumph as it danced into the side of the house and out again. Yet as soon as the drying line and the foetus quit cavorting, they grew blind to the shadow and its origin; they were too stunned by proof. At that moment Justina slashed a captor's face with her nails and tore herself free, fleeing half naked up the mountain.

They chased her, baying like hounds, and two of them brought dogs from the village to hunt her. Angelina also raced, stooping, after her beloved, hiding behind hummocks and *tola*. She couldn't reach her.

'I saw them pull the dogs from her skirts. Then the skirts from her legs. She howled like a dog herself while they held her down and raped her one by one. So she knew men at last. What joy. Then they dug a pit with stones for spades. They bundled her down into her grave, throwing the soil down on her while she cried through it for her life. And they danced on it like mad mourners till there was nothing left of her but the bare hillside.

'I was on the wrong side of a chasm. A ravine. If only I could have leapt it, Julio! It was a real chasm, you understand? The dream remembered exactly. But it was a chasm in my soul too, in my thoughts. When I trod on the edge of that dream chasm to cross it – when I tried to take over the puppet-me – the clay and pebbles parted like rotten sponge. I slipped. Down, down.'

'From dream to dream, I know. I also slipped. Again and again. Till I took control. We're both witches of power now, my dove. We see what is and how it is. We'd be naked witches too, like poor Justina, if we didn't use our seeing to guard ourselves! Isn't it so? You had to join me to save yourself.'

'I'd have joined you gladly years ago but for her murder. It fouled men for me. It twisted my life. My dream tried to clear my thoughts. If I could have jumped the chasm, it seemed to me ... But I was squeezed down into another dream where I was as old as Justina – where I'd been elected Queen of the County Carnival for Apusquiy.'

'Ah yes. I spoke for you, I sang your praises to get you elected, didn't I? Eh, that was the first time I really made a mark in public! Then I was your throne-bearer through Santa Rosa. Martin Checa too, I recall.'

'A carnival for you. A nightmare for me, Julio! I never knew why till my dream retold it. That mob of strangers, that rabble of boys crowding round my skirts, yapping at my heels ... I'd crushed the memory of Justina's death like frozen *chuno*. I couldn't understand why this should bother a Queen!'

'Now that you're an *Inca* Queen, it shan't!'

Santa Rosa was hung with decorations, a brass band was playing boisterously; yet Angelina hadn't eyes for buildings or streamers. She sat frozen to her throne – an old armchair hung with bright striped cotton – with her pure white dress draped about her, inclining her head this way and that, wearing an expression of idiot nervous elegance, as crowds began to press, throwing confetti and squirting ether, dizzying her.

Her heart pounded, as if she was racing up a mountain. Her palms bled cold sweat; all the while she smiled and smiled. She *must* be their Queen, or she would be their . . . victim!

Her throne rode second; behind, to louder applause, floated the Queen of Santa Rosa. Yet she couldn't tell how elegant her rival might be, how gracious, how well enthroned, without turning her head to stare – and she couldn't turn her head to stare. All the time the *Oohs* and *Ahs* grew louder till all she knew about was a pack of human voices pursuing her, half a street behind.

'I couldn't look over my shoulder. Yet someone was looking over my shoulder for me. Someone sat by me.'

'Just like me in the Miners' church! The next day I changed all their minds for them and became their Inca!'

'That was my soul perching on my shoulder, my true *animo*.'

'I know. In the church, my true *animo* was everywhere. It *was* the Church, it was everyone in it, including me.'

'But who was *I*? Who was this dream puppet that my *animo* was making ride this throne and smile inanely while it read my thoughts?'

'And among the miners during the *Diablada*, I was everyone!' Julio wouldn't listen. Everything she said only proved how Godlike he was. Still she persisted.

'I wasn't really sitting on this throne. I was only a doll, trapped in a model of the world I'd known once – so perfect a model that it couldn't be told from the real. But as soon as I thought this, you bearers all stumbled.'

'We never did!'

'My throne tipped. I grasped at the cotton covering the chair and it tore. My dress ripped open on a nail as I slid towards the crowd. The whole fabric of the world tore itself wide open and I fell right through, losing myself.'

'We never dropped you!'

'No, the *dream* dropped me. I dropped through the dream. Whatever. I couldn't connect enough things, not yet. Though I was getting closer to my true *animo* because this dream repeated itself again and again, sliding me from my throne, tearing clothes and cotton and tearing veils that hung between me and my other selves. More slowly every time. Two hands

108

held up to save me were Martin's; two were yours. They were puppet hands – the strings that pulled them up to save me were inside myself. "I am the Lover", you recited – I made your lips open to say it. "And I, the Husband", recited Martin – I made his lips open too. Such a ravine, between Husband and Lover! "It's time for love", you sang, nearly catching me. I knew I was in a dream of my own creation now, made from my own world – I knew I could make it be otherwise.'

'Ah, I did just that. The people in this world are just puppets, if you can see their strings.'

'Every time I tried to think how my throne was really just a shape of thoughts that bound me on that day as queen and victim, the throne tipped me off. You see, I couldn't think *what* it was, while I was still in it. But the last time that I fell, ah then, the dream stayed. The knowledge stayed – even though the street split wide open in a chasm, and Santa Rosa and all of you fled far away. It became the same chasm where they killed her. Only, now I was standing over on the other side, where it happened, the soil still soft from their digging. So soft, it let some air through – and a thin voice crying from the earth's bowels. It didn't cry words, but a baby's cry before words have come. Her *animo* was losing the things of the world: being peeled, stripped bare. It cried at me to follow it; and the soil shifted round my toes. The soil *in my mind*, Julio! This time I had the courage to shout farewell to Justina's soul. This time I stamped my feet. I firmed the soil. Then I called all my *animos* together.'

'As I called on Michael and Lucifer and the Parrot and the Condor and the Toad!' Boasting, boasting.

'I was whole, when I woke up. But Julio, all I really saw was what was wrong with me before and how it should never be so again. Justina had been writing my life, and I didn't know it. I found how to rewrite.'

Julio grunted. He disapproved of writing; its dictatorship over people's minds. He would do something about this as a Ruler.

'So I don't think you should do what you're doing; this Conquest. You haven't come to terms.'

'*Reconquest*, please!'

'You think you see the whole truth of the world, yet you're only seeing what your own thoughts are. They needn't be the *right* ones. I too felt clarified. Yet only *within me*. This limited person, me—'

'Weak words.'

'No, strong. Don't you see?'

'Subjective, woman's talk ... Listen, we will both be Justina on that hillside unless I *act*. Anyway, it's started. We've taken San Rafael, haven't we!'

'So you're a prisoner of yourself again. The puppet of your own mind dolls. How sad.'

'How can I be, when they caper for me at will?'

'Your deeds escape you, you can't grip them any longer.'

'Get some sleep, little dove, we've a long way to drive to-morrow. Night's always a dark time to think about the future. You'll feel bolder in the morning.' He whispered lovingly, but sternly. Then he fell asleep, satisfied.

ELEVEN

The two Incas rode in a jeep driven by Baltasar Quispe. A flag fluttered from it: silver condor with wings spread against a golden sun. Julio wore a red fringed headband just as he had seen in a picture in that museum; Angelina's temples were painted with thin vermilion streaks rising above her eyes. He thought she seemed merrier this morning; action was a tonic.

The jeep was closely followed by four trucks of *campesinos* and soldiers. San Rafael lay behind them now, their provisional capital: the new *cuzco*, navel of the four quarters of the world. Their target was the mining centre of Aracayo where the Inca had once worked as an ordinary man. Behind the jeep voices rose in a war song handed down from fiesta to fiesta.

> '*We'll pave the roads*
> *With the enemy's bones!*
> *We'll make his teeth*
> *Into necklaces!*
> *His skin will be drums*
> *And his head a cup*
> *And we shall drink*
> *And we shall sing!*'

'The fever of the Sun!' Julio exclaimed boisterously. 'That's what touched us. Don't its rays cause changes in animals and men? That machine flew right up where there's no air, where the Sun is naked, and drew it down to us. Now we see the rays of the world itself, rays of power leading everywhere. I hear that the Yanquis once dropped an artificial sun upon the sea that changed the shapes of all the fishes. Fishes only have their shapes to change. We have our thoughts. Look at the Sun, Angelina. See how it doubles when you look away. That's the way it is now. Our thoughts double, and dance for us!'

'No machine came down and touched the first Inca, Julio. I'm puzzled.'

'I agree. But he lived closer to the sky than any other people in the world. Soon, I'll build machines to focus the Sun's light on the hills of debris at the mines. Wealth will flow. All the miners will follow us.'

The song of the Inca soldiers shifted to praise of Julio's words which would win the miners' hearts without a fight. They sang of the talk-talk flower, *lima-lima*, which lives high up on the snow line and cures the dumb.

> '*Hey, lima flower, speak to them*
> *The way you speak to us!*
> *Hey, lima flower, you ate the Sun*
> *So speak to them, lima, speak!*
> *And if they thrust a knife at you*
> *We'll trample them all like* chuno
> *We'll grind them all like chili*
> *We'll beat them like jerked mutton!*
> *But speak, lima flower, you only have to speak!*'

Angelina tossed her urine-glossy braids from side to side, black ropes thrashing the chilly air streaming past the jeep.

'Yes, you're the flower they sing about, Julio. But a flower still has its roots in the earth, whatever sunlight soaks it from above. What happened to us must have earth roots too.'

She stared at the sky. She saw a man flying up to Heaven on a condor's back. He carried a lump of mutton along with him to feed the bird while it flew. The condor was so hungry that it soon ate all this meat up. The man had to peel off strips of his own flesh to feed its greedy beak. He unpeeled flesh from both his legs, from his belly, then from his other arm till he only had one arm of flesh and all the rest of his body was raw nerves – raw nerves riding on a condor! With his one flesh arm he strummed on those naked nerves as on the strings of a guitar! That fiery cloak of nerves was her own naked mind, bound to the world by a club of flesh; and their weave was more intricate than the finest poncho. She saw them re-woven even more intricately by the shuttle of the condor's wings. As the condor-rider plucked his strings Thought twanged, woven in red and rose and electric blue, and did not fade; but stayed, bright-threaded. Thought twanged again and did not fade; it overlaid the first thought, woof over warp, in an awareness of awareness.

She was carrying Julio's child within her now – and inside the unfolding seed of son or daughter surely must be a second seed which could only spring to life in the midst of life. A nurse from Santa Rosa once told her that all the children a woman will ever bear are in her at the moment of her birth; are made before her birth. Yet there must be another seed too, a seed of a different sort in people. A seed for giving birth to *one's own self*, somehow, in the midst of life.

Yet this seed could only grow from the soil of ordinary human life. How narrow was their life? How narrow was their knowledge? This was what Julio wouldn't, couldn't see.

'Julio, your dreams didn't show you the gaps and chasms in your life, the ordinary soil, the rifts in it. They only showed you the peaks, the summits.'

'Yes indeed, where the Gods sit in their haciendas!'

'But there are such gaping empty valleys—'

'Aircraft!'

The plane was mosquito size ... fly size ... the size of a humming-bird, though with wide wide wings perfect for flying slowly through thin air.

Standing up in the jeep, Julio called out to the trucks as much with his hands as with his voice.

'Keep driving! Pass the message back! When I say so, we all drive very fast – except for the truck with the machine gun. That one stops and shoots, at where the pilot is. When the plane passes over, fire all your rifles up at the engines.'

As the slow long-winged jet dropped closer, becoming a condor, Julio crooked his arm, palm spread sideways blocking off the sight of it as though in some new kind of salute. As soon as the plane's wingtips emerged beyond his masking fingertips and wrist he shouted, 'Now! Drive fast.' And waved the trucks to follow while the jeep darted ahead. Almost at once the plane banked steeply. Its wingtip nearly touched soil as it turned out of the line of fire. Instead of a horizontal target, it presented a vertical one and was soon swooping upwards on the turn. A rattle of bullets followed it incoherently, ineffectively. Withdrawing high into the sky the aircraft swung round so as to cross the route of the speeding convoy. Six white bundles fell from the belly of the aircraft, blossoming into parachutes when they had dropped too close to the ground to be shot at. The loads jerked briefly backwards in the air then settled heavily astride the road. Six crates. Julio halted the convoy. High overhead the aircraft continued circling.

'They might explode if we go near,' he warned. 'So only two men will go and look in those boxes. Look in all of them. Take metal bars to force the lids.'

He chose two soldiers who had joined him on that first day when the Empire was announced in Apusquiy. They trotted off carrying jack handles.

'Rifles,' the first shouted back. 'New ones. The best.'

'Grenades,' the second shouted.

'Mortars!'

'Bazookas!'

'And ammunition!'

'Whoever sent this, Inca?'

Julio frowned.

'We mustn't overvalue weapons. So many weapons might corrupt us. If they make us rely on strength, not speech and spirit.' He nodded to Angelina, accommodatingly.

'But we need weapons,' protested Baltasar. 'You hardly refused that rifle I gave you!'

'Test them first,' Julio called to the soldiers. 'Try one grenade and one rifle – from the bottoms of the crates.'

So a soldier threw a grenade out across the plain, and it exploded in a single smack of sound without an echo, there being nowhere to echo against. The other soldier sighted on the swirling dust and fired once, twice, thrice into it. Bullets sped off to nowhere.

Julio ordered the crates all loaded on to the rearmost truck, with its passengers dispersed amongst the others. High above the plane still circled.

'It's fine to have these things,' Julio told his soldiers. 'But we need the willingness of the miners, not their deaths. This gift could be an invitation to attack them! It mustn't be that. The miners have to be shown to *live*, not die.' (But that was not what Angelina meant at all. He did not know it. He couldn't understand it.)

'Look up there,' interrupted Christobal, who had just glanced up from itemizing the amazing gift in his notebook to look at its point of origin again. (He itemized in writing, for the time being. Later, would be time enough in Julio's opinion to restore the quipu way of recording life's events, so that men could learn to remember again instead of locking up memories in books of words, making them dead things.)

A seventh blob detached itself from the aircraft's belly, dropping down on a thin cord, a gob of spittle from an old man's lips. It blossomed. A white parachute opened, high up. A man hung below.

That took a crazy sort of courage, when they had greeted their plane with gunfire! Or stupidity. Or blind obedience. Down drifted the white canopy while the parachutist tugged his reins, aiming to land not too far from the jeep, nor too close. Perhaps he fell faster through the thin air than he expected, since he hit the ground hard, stumbling and sprawling. He rose with difficulty and limped towards Julio: a wiry dark-skinned man with black stubble on chin and cheeks. No Indian, he. A soldier relieved him of a knapsack, which contained maps and a small radio transmitter, while he stood there shaking, gasping for breath.

'You *are* the Inca?' the man panted, speaking Spanish.

'Yes indeed. Why the weapons?'

'Inca, you have good friends outside this country. People who admire you – who know that the government of this land is a tumour in the Andes. They want to see it cut out. They'll help you do it.'

A shifty man. Julio read cruelty, subservience, deceit, worship of wealth and power in his face. Arrogance battled with his fear at being abandoned on this plain.

'I'm from across the border, from Chile. You can flee there, if you have to. You'll be looked after. Sanctuary. Only if you need it. We give you weapons, hoping you won't need it. But you have a rearguard now.'

'My rearguard is the people. Their hearts. Their stolen history.'

'Of course,' grinned the visitor, lies in his grins: the greedy deceit of the first Spaniards who cheated and garotted Inca Atahualpa. And that Inca himself danced out on the plain before Julio's eyes in a phantom *diablada*, lamented and reviled.

'I'll show you on the maps, where to go, if you have to.' The parachutist recovered his map and spread it on the jeep hood. 'Here we are, now.' His finger tracked westward. 'You drive across the great Salar – the hard salt lake. Towards these mountains. There's a pass. Marked with ink. That's the way to escape. I promise you'll be protected. Able to rule your own state. Grow strong. Return. Till your final victory. Only if you need it. We hope you'll rule here—'

'So I shall,' agreed Julio. 'How about you?'

The man leant against the jeep weakly. 'To arm you,' he panted. 'To advise you ...'

'I can advise myself.'

The man's face was slowly turning blue beneath the bristles.

'Alvaro's my name ... Really, I *can* advise. I know all about ... how revolutions happen ... what stops them ...'

Julio laughed. 'You can't even breathe properly.'

'Adjust. Needed an oxygen mask for the drop. Had one on the plane. Wasn't one for dropping ... Stupid error.' Then the man's hand crawled to his heart and he stared far away past Julio.

He was gazing at his death. He was seeing Death stride towards him, realized Julio. It was to be this cruel cheating man's one moment of vision – his single chance of seeing the double world: his own mind-doll marching out there in the world, in the shape of Death. Alvaro's face contorted in bewilderment, rage and grief while his hand tore his leather jacket open to chill the pain. In the mirror of Alvaro's eyes were many bodies begging and screaming. Those were what marched towards him now. Alvaro thrust a hand out to fend them off; but Death passed through his outspread hand and entered him. His body sagged and slid.

'Did they drop death in him, to kill us?' faltered Angelina, appalled. 'Don't let them have done that!'

'No, it was the fall: without any air to breathe. His heart wasn't strong enough. Curious, he was a bold man in his way – and such filthy rubbish at the same time. That was a bad tormented death he met. All his own horrors greeted him. Now they have him forever.'

Up above the plane quit circling. It departed westward towards Chile.

At last they reached Aracayo, a place somewhat worse than Hell since its denizens had to pray for its survival. Overhead the white-haired mountain, whose foothills the town climbed in ripples of slag and scree, held aloof; air froze down from it upon barracks and debris, deep underneath which wormed the workaday furnaces of tunnels.

'I've worked here,' Julio told a crowd of miners and wives with rifles. 'How many of you can even breathe properly after a few years? A man forgets that things grow on the surface; and what's at the end of it? Nothing! In five years' time

116

the metal will all be gone and you'll only have hills of dross. I'll show you how to be farmers of that dross *and* become proper farmers too—'

'How do you "glean" tin from the tailings?' a voice jeered. 'With one of your dibbling sticks for poking potato holes?' Laughter jerked at him like hail. It felt harsh; yet the sneerers weren't necessarily the deciders of opinion. He hunted for faces whose voices would be heard when the mockery died away.

That man. That other fellow there. And him over there. Boulders in this human stream. (A stream confined within a square of buildings: fluid in time rather than in space. The jeering was only the jangle of water rippling round these boulders; unconsciously the crowd organized itself in eddies round them.) He spoke to those boulders.

'What's the wealth of these mountains? Metal? That would have seemed madness in the Inca days. Yet those days were *wealthy*. Crops. Llamas. They made these Andes a place where Man could live nobly.'

'The Revolution provides,' growled one craggy boulder. 'Pensions, sickness benefits, you name it.'

'How does your precious Revolution see these Andes? As a useless barren place to be thrown away like last year's newspaper. Aren't they trying to force everyone to move to the lowlands and the jungles? And people still refuse, because this high plain holds their souls. An Indian gets lost in those forests. The heat and the heavy air where the spiders eat the birds and the snakes sting you to death. We Indians know it. Even the name "Indian" is outlawed nowadays so that you'll forget you're children of the Incas—'

Some boulders definitely were leaning his way. Others sunk their butts deeper in a silt of bitterness and blind political dogma.

One of these bellowed, 'Your Incas were exploiters and Conquistadores themselves! Then liars and cheats, because they tore up history and even made a law against writing so they'd seem like saints who had civilized savages!' Such a tiny crag of a man, this heckler. His finger stabbed the air as if to stab out Julio's eyes. A fine orator, terrifying in his tininess; he weighed tons.

'You make me sick, whining about the Revolution opening up the forests to find food for us all. Your Incas forced the people to move up here in the first place to settle the dead mountains. You think they *wanted to come*? That's why we're here today, not for love. The only joy under your Incas was licking handouts of salt cake, like cattle. You even had to eat every damn meal with your door wide open so that everyone knew what everyone was eating. Is that the freedom you like?'

How could a man be a 'revolutionary' yet so rigidly anchored in bedrock? Surely it was an intolerable strain?

'You hate "Capitalism", right?' demanded Julio. 'Well, where did the first Capital come from? Right here in the Andes – *after* the Incas were destroyed. All the metals pouring out into Spain and Europe fuelled the furnaces of Capitalism! What do you think you're doing now, digging metal out and exporting it, but keeping that furnace alight – in America! That's why we have to restore the Inca way. What started here can be stopped here!'

Boulders rocked approvingly, ragged cheers rose from the stream. The leather-jacketed miners swayed like bulls; their women in shabby felt jackets, trilbies and spinning-top skirts clutched their rifles less decisively.

'Señor Inca, if that's what you believe, why bribe us with a new way of gleaning tin? How typical of Inca lies! Besides, all very well to promise!'

Frozen sunlight drenched the hills of tailings, brightening them but leaving them cold as ice. A breeze blew fitfully against Julio's cheeks. Landscape faded to a spotlit engraving, in a museum ...

'In the Inca days,' he sang out, 'what a grand sight it was to see ten thousand clay furnaces burning on those hills! Twenty thousand furnaces fired every dusk! The wind blew all night long through the wind holes. At dawn it fell. The farmers only had to collect the metal before they got on tilling their fields, then set the fires again next dusk—'

'So *this* is the Inca's bribe! How rich we'll all be with one peso's worth of tin a week.'

'That's why these Andes are dying. Pesos! Buying food instead of growing it! No one has to go to death and suffocation underground any more. You'll be farmers. The world will soon be starving for a single grain of tin. The tin you glean will be gold.'

'Rubbish! You're talking about smelting high grade copper or silver. You don't know the first thing about ores.'

'And you've lost the spirit of a man! *Indians*, who has courage? Who'll destroy this Capitalism at its root by planting living roots in the soil?'

The stream swayed two ways at once. To him; and to Stone Finger. That single digit had Julio breaking on it like a reed. Could it be snapped first? Could an instant of violence sway the crowd for him, as in Apusquiy? Two choices. The dolls streamed for him; and against him. He lived, he died. A moment of balance.

Stooping into Baltasar's shadow, he rose with the vicuna rifle.

And fired; and killed. The stone finger broke and fell. Julio felt a surge of sickness before elation cured it.

'I am the true Inca,' he cried, jabbing his own forefinger at each boulder man in turn, transfixing them before they could recoil to carry the stream away with them. 'You five men shall be my lieutenants here, my brothers.' He smiled, astonishing them by knowing them all. Pointing his rifle at the sky, he grinned, tapping his red *borla* headband with the telescopic sights.

A woman who had thrown herself upon Stone Finger's body rose howling, plunging towards Julio. The front rank of miners surged with her, then pulled her back into themselves, comforting and controlling. Squirming, she taunted them, reminding them what their comrade had done for them.

'But it wasn't murder!' protested Julio. Singling out the nearest boulder man, 'What do *you* say, brother? Isn't the present way of life madness and absurdity? Don't we need a new way?'

'I suppose so,' shrugged the man, aware of the wild look in Julio's eyes.

'Louder, brother!'

The man's voice leered back, 'Yes.'

'Tell them to pull the covers off the weapons truck,' Julio whispered to Baltasar. Aloud, 'I had to kill him, or he would have killed me.'

'Coward, he had no gun!'

'But he had all your guns. You would all have shot, for him. Yet I did the thing myself. I didn't get others to do it. Respectfully, there's the difference between the Agitator, and the Leader of Men.' People were filtering out of the rear of the crowd, sneaking off with whispers and glances. Comibol officials, a sixth boulder man whom Julio hadn't spotted till now; he could do nothing yet to stop this attrition.

'That man wanted to keep things the way they are and he called *that* a revolution. Listen, the real revolution is to return to the Old Way.' Julio swung round. Baltasar's message had been passed; blankets were being stripped from the fourth truck. 'See all our guns and bombs? Enough to destroy a city. Did I use them or even threaten to? I stood out alone armed with words. So are you with me, Brothers and Sisters? Or do you want to be written down in some Spanish history book as *Indian* Pizarros who betrayed another Inca?'

The accused boulder man eyed that pile of weaponry with some surprise. They hadn't even been made ready for use! One rifle was nothing beside all those. It was true. This Indian had *coraje*, all right.

'I'm with you,' he applauded.

'Then I proclaim the Inca strength!' cried Julio ecstatically. 'Inca compassion! Inca care for the world and for men. I shoot my second shot, for joy! All of you shoot. Blow the sky apart.' (They had to discharge those guns, they had gripped them so tightly.) When Julio fired, the crowd erupted gunfire. When the last echo died, he found he was still alive; for a long time he breathed out.

'You must dynamite the mine shafts,' he ordered Brother Boulder. 'That's an order of the Inca. Let there be no way back down.'

'There's a shift down the mine.'

'So drink till they come up, to keep warm.' (Drink, with

dynamite in your hands, the more to enjoy the devastation of your hated mine!)

By now, the widow too had slipped away in the wake of those others ...

They waited merrily for the trainload of miners to ride out of the tunnel leading from the shafthead in its cave of rock; but when the train ground out of the tunnel mouth, hauling its long lines of benches, the miners crowding them began shooting at their welcomers. Stone Finger's widow rode at their head, Comibol and union men in their ranks. Warned and propagandized, lied to, armed and primed, the emerging shift fought back ...

When the shooting died away, miners from within had killed fellow miners without as well as some of Julio's men. Really, the shooting only died because the deadman's handle halted the locomotive when the driver was hit by a bullet; injured and scared, the driver had reversed the train back down the slope till the locomotive blocked the tunnel mouth. But now there was no second chance of erupting with surprise. Those within barricaded the archway with boxes of stones piled around the locomotive, leaving sniping holes. Those without pitched sticks of dynamite that fell short. Both sides hated each other bitterly now.

When an anti-tank tube was brought from the weapons truck, the first rocket flew wild, soaring over the tunnel mouth to explode on the hillside, raining scree. A second rocket flew; the barricade erupted and settled back, the locomotive's wheels wrenched from the track, broken boxes spilling stones. The third rocket hit the roof above the barricade, hammering the rubble, forcing a thin gap; and the fourth rocket skipped through this gap to detonate inside. When the attackers rushed the barricade and clawed at it, bright lights blinded them from the far end of the tunnel and shots ricocheted off the rubble; the majority of the miners had fallen back. Yet a truncated thing still flopped about in the settling dust nearby; a living Scream. The scream wailed on and on as shots flicked up and down the tunnel.

'Kill that Pain Thing, Christobal,' moaned Julio. 'If I ever suffer, pray I may suffer for something. May my suffering speak. May it carry me up, not down into such noise!'

Christobal's fourth shot stopped the wail. Julio's soldiers were still trying to douse the floodlights.

'Leave them alight, they'll help us aim our rockets,' Julio grieved. Baltasar was already hauling the bazooka into place.

The fifth rocket flew true down the beam of light and blew it out. Cries shrilled down there, peas rattling in a whistle.

'Enough! Now dynamite the entrance. That'll do.'

'Oh no,' Brother Boulder grinned, at Julio's side. 'The rails are still good beyond. We keep a bogie in a side cut. We'll load our dynamite on. The slope takes it right into the pithead. You said to destroy the mine, eh?'

'Yes, yes, but do it quickly!' (Before any more broken dolls danced out of the tunnel, shrilling armlessly.) Leaving them to wreck their mine, Julio strode back to Angelina, head held high, wishing he could cradle it in his arms.

'The pain,' he mumbled.

'You don't understand pain, because you haven't suffered, Julio! I have! The pain inside me, whose name was Justina, was my awakening. You're causing suffering because you don't know this. When you *do* know it ... Pain can become its opposite then!'

Bewildered, Julio shook his head. 'Shall I tell you how the Incas judged criminal blasphemers against the Gods – men who violated shrines? They let the Gods judge them *through the beasts*. So they put the criminal in a pit with snakes and jaguars and if he was still alive after three nights they set him free. Do you suppose many survived the teeth and stings? So was that a beastly or a Godlike act? Maybe beast and God are both innocent, and only Man is evil – the being in between!'

'Yes, *in between*. Beasts are all absorbed in the world, and humans are separate as soon as they start to think about the world. Humans are opposite – which means that we know the great opposite of all: evil. Because evil is absence, loss and separation, Julio. How Man has thrived on it for years! You can stop it now, if you *see* this. The evil can be left behind. It's just the black thread that tangles with the white thread; the design isn't black or white, it's something else.'

The ground heaved under them, earth rippling like water as the mountain boomed and lurched. A fierce stiff wind slapped at them from the tunnel, knocking a few people off their feet. A jet of flame leapt into the sky from an air vent higher up the slope, staining the rising dust briefly red.

Angelina imagined she had convinced him; but no. Julio's confidence swept back unchallengeably as the miners cheered him, and the village orator spoke to his most enthusiastic crowd since San Rafael.

Part Three

HADES' BOBBIN

TWELVE

Oates, Silverman and Weaver were all up and about together. For the first time in almost eight months their personal days and nights synchronized. The thermal roll had ended; and the Sun stopped rising and setting a hundred times a day. The sense of being perpetually stuck in an elevator just below floor level abated.

The three men watched each other as curiously and jealously as wives introduced to mistresses at an unfortunate cocktail party, or husbands to lovers, eyeing one another carefully for signs of subtle personality shifts in each partner, which a third partner had provoked in secret while they slept. Ghosts of infidelity stalked the torus. Meeting again thus before Mars, they felt shocked by an unexpected access of imagined femininity: a kind of repaired virginity as human beings. None alluded outright to this almost sexual sense of strangeness, for all three sensed that it could spark a bitchy substanceless quarrel.

Recalling tales of brothel girls having plastic surgery to restore their valuable hymens, Oates felt that he himself had just awakened from such an operation, nauseated by anaesthetics.

Silverman was remembering Renata's oscillating, doubled bodies. He felt blurred and falsified by the simultaneous imprint of two men's hands on the two malleable homunculi that formed images of him.

Weaver suspected that Oates and Silverman had been quietly sodomizing while he slept, but he put this idiot idea down to the abstinence of the long voyage. A man got so pent up that the mere fact of the sudden doubling of the human quota, male or female, brought sexual urges boiling to the surface. This astonished him; since he had dutifully used the detensionizer in his privacy cubicle once a week, always running a chemical check on the seminal fluid during his subsequent watch for the medical reports.

Fortunately they were too busy checking exact co-ordinates, bringing systems up and running, and programming for an orbital insertion burn to do more than note off at a tangent these newly exposed raw souls of theirs. Undoubtedly Dr Albrecht had anticipated the psychological problem. NASA seemed to have foreseen that it would be best to maintain stasis till the latest possible moment. The time of mental transition should be that much more rapid, and automatic. Perhaps it had been simulated in long-stay sea-labs.

Mars swelled from a world, to part of a world only: a window segment; and the TV pick-ups perched atop the *Flagstaff* module out ahead were overwhelmed with world. While they could still see the north pole they had gazed by turns at the shining, black-sedimented whorls where thin bands of darkness and broad swathes of ice-cream wound round one another in a laminated vortex of storm dust and ice uncurling from the current permanent cap – tilted away from the Sun at perihelion right now, as the south pole would itself tilt in another fifty thousand years, in default of Man's steadying hand. Now was the time to warm the wintry pole, forcing the climate over the threshold in one catastrophic flip to permanent spring ten thousand years ahead of time. Then the trans-Mars coast ended; the time of the burn came, and they flew at the Martian horizon, not seeing it, bound up in instruments.

'*Frontiersman* in predicted Mars orbit, affirm,' Jim Weaver grinned finally. They all laughed, and shook hands from their seats.

Five minutes afterwards radio congratulations poured at them and the unfamiliar business of publicity took over for an hour, two hours, while they competed at finding fresh ways of describing craters, deserts, rifts, pimple eruptions higher than Mount Everest ...

The great volcano Olympus swelled from the surrounding lava plain, soaring up from two-kilometre-high perimeter cliffs in feathery waves to a summit pocked with collapsed caldera vent holes, which even from this distance was more than Hima-

126

layan. In afternoon sunlight the volcano glared brilliantly, sweating light. Then the vastest hillside in the Solar System fell away as they soared eastwards across volcanic plains towards gently rolling hills with ripple dunes, channels and levees, sure sign of drainage northwards from the equatorial highlands ...

'Jim, I'm sorry but we have a major change of plan,' Spike Thorne's voice came firmly, full of angry apology. 'We want you to stay in Mars orbit, Jim, along with *Warming Pan*. We've had a long conference about this one. Believe me it wasn't an easy decision to reach and this isn't an easy instruction to give you—'

'You want me to stay up here doing goddam housekeeping!' exploded Weaver, depressing the SEND switch with a stab of his finger while Thorne was still busy speaking. 'Are you joking, Spike?'

'Listen, Jim,' soothed Oates. He reached over to Jim Weaver's seat and flipped the SEND switch off again gently. Weaver made a flickering, fly-chasing gesture at Oates' hand, avoiding touching flesh, however. Oates and Silverman had conspired behind his back to get down on the sodomistic surface together! His face froze. No, that was idiotic! He breathed deeply and silently; composed himself; sat at brace in his seat.

When he was a kid they caught flies in their fists on summer days. All the kids did it, cupping the flies then crushing them. Dirty black hairy bodies, strawberry blood, orange goo. They wiped the muck off their hands on the lawns. Jim was always best at catching flies. Fine reflexes! He never failed. The only trouble was, his hand would never crush them. It always kept a pocket of air around the buzzing dirty thing. He took to pitching the fly to the ground instead, stunning it long enough to stamp it to death with his sneakers. In fact he made quite a thing of catching and pitching flies. The other kids admired his way with them. Their own efforts seemed caveman-style. His, technological – his hand the perfect clean tool ... What absurdities to think about while Mars was rushing by! Oh yes, Wally's hand, fluttering into his own personal space ...

Thorne's voice was still talking to them.

'. . . it's just too dangerous to risk landing all of you together. We daren't risk three. Because of those soil samples that the *Zayits* probe brought back with it and the effect they had. We finally managed to get hold of some of the soil – something to work on. Too late! The labs couldn't turn up anything. Whatever was active in it was dead, the whole sample was contaminated by earth micro-organisms. But we're sure the effect was real—' Thorne spoke in a confiding yet strangely elusive way; as though he no longer believed he was quite talking to anyone real. Or . . . as though he was concealing something – because Houston no longer fully trusted them. Why hadn't they told them about getting soil samples before? Still smarting at the rawness of their reuniting, the three men felt a hollowness, a cold emptiness. They glanced at one another, full of a sudden pity, a terror. They needed each other. But the moment of rapport faded. Each in his own way, they armoured themselves against the hurt.

'The damnable thing about it all is the breakdown of any information from Bolivia. About what caused this illness. What its full effects are – apart from the coma, the brain inflammation, the "double vision" business, becoming Incas and Gods. The rebellion's still in full swing. We were damned lucky to get any soil sample at all, under the circumstances. Completely fortuitous.' Thorne was *rambling*; but his words were stilted too. He was lying about something. They weren't in Houston's confidence.

'. . . since we know about the medical problem we can't risk you all on the surface together. One man just has to stay in orbit to start up *Warming Pan* in the event of any . . . well, four point failure, any way-out accident. We decided it has to be you, Jim. I'll give you a chance to come back at me now. I imagine you're pretty disappointed. Over.'

Weaver stared expressionlessly at the SEND switch. Then he swung his hand down and flipped it, cupping his fingers round it to make a fist of air. Obviously they wanted him to stay up here because he was the perfect reliable tool. Wasn't that exactly why *he* should be down on the surface? He knew how to keep himself free from contamination if anyone did.

'*Frontiersman* to Houston. I always thought that in times of danger a commander's place was with his ship?' He spoke tightly and vehemently as though chanting regulations. 'A commander doesn't stay in a safe place and lose his crew. He doesn't even let them get into situations where they make mistakes like that. The only sane and proper course is for me to land. For obvious reasons I need our scientist with me to find out what this bug is on the ground. Equally obvious is that Wally is the one to unfold *Warming Pan* and jockey it into the right configuration. That's why we're here. Wally has to be left in the safe place while Gene and I are put at risk. Negative, Houston. I don't see your logic. Over.'

Opening his fist then, he smiled shyly at the other two.

Silverman was staring ostentatiously out at Cerberus and the fretted hummocky land to the south, dotted with mosaics of mesas presumably left by landslips when ice decayed beneath the surface. He would land, whoever he landed with.

Oates was studying the cavorting of fish, still stirred by the earlier retro fire from *Flagstaff*, seven minutes of gravity; though he could only see the fish tank by craning his neck.

These fish had been specially bred in Earth orbit to accustom them to zero gravity swimming. Their water was slightly more pressurized and oxygenated than a normal Earth environment. Catching them involved suction tubing rather than open nets, or the whole torus would soon have filled with globs of water; but now Oates imagined himself pumping globs of air into their tank till these globs congealed in fat-beaded necklaces coiling through stiff water. Milly-Kim too wore beautiful necklaces of huge white plastic beads ... Their tank would become a tangled maze of necklaces of air, necklaces of water, while the harried fish looped the loop to stay in their element. How much air would it take before the water exploded into mist? Before climate catastrophe? Loss of flight control, gasping dying fishes?

His view of the fish tank was cut in half by the curve of the torus. His view of Mars was cut by a window, and again by the bulge of the hydrogen tank outside. Views were all cut in half by rims, horizons. No view was a whole. Air and Water, Dream and Waking. Two poles of a sand-glass. Milly-Kim stood just round the rim of his life from Kathy and the kids:

mutually invisible one to the other. But he wouldn't be cut off from the sands of Mars, damn it! Not by anyone.

'I'll tell you what they're going to say, Jim. That I'm the pilot, and that what you're talking about is landing on the first alien world without a pilot. Surface gravity's point three eight, remember! You might let yourself bounce a bit on the Moon. Not on Mars, baby!'

'You're wrong, Wally. *Warming Pan* is the vital part of the mission, not landing. Pilot's place is with the Pan. We've got our priorities mixed. Always said so, didn't I?'

'Did you? Well, you're trained to handle *Warming Pan* just as well as me. We're mutually redundant, right? Gene can even pilot us, at a pinch.'

'Whether or not we've got our priorities mixed,' interrupted Silverman diplomatically, 'we have to land now that we know about this illness. Future colonists will be far more directly exposed to Martian soil than us. Farmers can't sterilize their boots every time they step indoors—'

'Houston to *Frontiersman*, Charles Klein here, Jim. I realize you're the commander on the spot and I do know we can't run this mission from Houston. I appreciate all your points, but even so this is an order. Frankly we see Wally as having a lower chance if he has to start up *Warming Pan* on his own with the two of you down there – in trouble, out of contact – precisely because he *isn't* commander. We're afraid of a psychological block with Wally on his own – purely subconscious; but enough to mess up the deployment of *Warming Pan*. We don't see that with you, Jim. Be fair, if the worst comes to the worst and two men are sick on the surface who else can carry out a decision to change orbits and deploy? Only you. That's where command responsibility really bites. You've only seventeen days for the whole exploration, rendezvous, orbit change and deployment before you catch the launch window for Earth. You can't hang around with that schedule. And it's essential too that *Frontiersman* returns to Earth. You have to show that a round trip of this order is on. We trust you to return solo if – God forbid – you have to make a tough decision. We feel Wally would find this decision – not to mention the journey back – much tougher. My God, we want to think on the bright side, not in gloomy terms! This is the brightest adventure yet in space! But we daren't take risks. The Russians rely on machines and robots. We're relying on people, human individuals. Individuals like you, Jim. Over.'

'Bullshit,' swore Weaver; then he relaxed, and even laughed. 'You know, fellows, I feel in a very cynical mood right now?'

'It's a natural reaction,' soothed Oates, admiring Klein's sleight of hand while hating him for the put-down of himself. Yet this put-down was the very reason why he was best suited to fly down to the surface. So he could hardly argue with *that*. 'I'm none too happy at those remarks myself. You may imagine.'

Silverman watched night-time Mars looming. The previous division into a light world and a dark void reversed. Now the world died into darkness and the only light came from the void and its stars.

Weaver pushed the SEND switch.

'*Frontiersman* to Houston. Roger, I'll supervise the housekeeping. Affirm. Rely on me.'

'It is a far far better thing you do now,' quoted Silverman briskly.

'*Shut up!*' snarled Weaver.

In Houston, Thorne grumbled, 'So I've let the cat out of the bag publicly about the soil now. Much good may that do! I tell you, that really went against the grain. I hate this politics.'

'Inskip's courier did say it was essential,' Albrecht reminded gently.

'Yes, that NASA publicly acknowledge we got a soil sample from somewhere. So now we hand it over primly to the Soviets with apologies and what's left of *Zayits*. "All that survived the Inca rampage," unquote. "We had to find out about it for the safety of our spacemen, urgently, by whatever means. It took a long time. Tests had to be exhaustive." I *know*. Their intelligence service will quite understand, because they have enough trouble penetrating Bolivia themselves, covertly, diplomatically or any way. We're actually doing them a service, they might as well hush the matter up . . . Thrown off the scent. I tell you, it'll rebound. It's not worth it in the long run.'

'Not even for the whole of Mars? Inskip's man did say the Russians had wind we were up to something. So if we persuade them that it was just a matter of our scooping some soil and spacecraft wreckage from the midst of the rebellion—'

'Then we still have a chance to grab the Inca, without the Bolivians being alerted by some comradely tip-off which gives the Russians a toe-hold there in future. I know. How logical, how straightforward.'

'But suppose the Inca himself heard of our . . . ambition, and was warned, and so evaded us?'

'That's not it, Doctor, I swear it. Inskip wants the Inca for his own reasons, way beyond any desire to help us. A king in exile, to pit against that People's Revolution. It's *that* he doesn't want the Russians to latch on to! We're being *used*. The space programme is. Our astronauts are too, even though they're eighty million klicks away. And I'm instrumental in using them.'

'Oh hardly. You exaggerate. It really is vital we examine the Inca medically—'

'There's barely time to. What's keeping Inskip? He doesn't care about us, only about goddam South American politics. America's back yard isn't space, to him!'

'I disagree. He knows exactly how important Mars is, just as well as we do. The investment. The humiliation if the expedition fails. We really do need the Inca, to know about the effects of Mars on men under Earthlike climate conditions that'll apply after *Warming Pan*. Our astronauts can't tell us that! Inskip is simply killing two birds with one stone.'

'Unfortunate choice of phrase, Doctor!'

The descent to the northerly end of Mangala Vallis, five degrees south of the Martian equator, eleven hundred kilometres south-west of Olympus, passed smoothly and predictably.

The wide valley appeared braided with dried-out silt as though a mighty river had coursed along it once, carving out bars, levees and isles like long gobs of falling glue. The valley ambled downhill from the heavily pocked, scarred uplands of the South to where the land fell away into the 'dry ocean' of the North, from which Olympus and the other volcanoes arose: Hawaiis from a drained Pacific.

Braided silt beds pricked with craters. It had been a while since water flowed here; since an atmosphere burnt up incoming meteorites and comets.

Cro-Magnon times ... when Man roamed Europe in beast-pelts hunting for aurochs. Not so long ago! Silverman speculated what a big thing it must have been for prehistoric Man when Mars turned red, as they flew down. Seeing the God of War wink his red eye for the first time in many aeons: what cultural effect did *that* have?

'Does it have to look so crumbly?' muttered Oates. 'All I want is a good clearcut crater ... Ah, that's my baby—'

On a firm wedge of flat land between broad dry channels a tiny crater had been punched. It sat there with moderately eroded bowl and rim, a dark fan-shaped splotchy streak like smoke blowing from a chimney showing which way local gales blew following the annual dust storms, stirring and sweeping finer, brighter particles away.

He studied the lay-out of the fan intently, reconstructing the wind vortex, zones of stillness where the dust must lie thickest, solider zones downwind. Then he brought the landing module down smartly downwind of the crater, right of centre of the wind stream. They jarred and settled fifteen or twenty centimetres, but with less than a two-degree tilt.

'We've landed,' radioed Wally. 'This is Flagstaff Base, Mars—'

Next day was a fine Martian day: still, clear and bright, the sky a delicate pink verging on lilac at the zenith. By noon the temperature rose to forty below.

The two men set up a TV camera on a tripod and filmed each other beside *Flagstaff*, and the adjacent flag. The very next sandstorm would blow the flag down but that didn't matter one bit, because the next violent storm would be Man's own doing: the predictable aftermath of *Warming Pan*, before the atmosphere sought a denser new stability – until rain could fall and lightning flicker and the sky be blue again.

The area where they had landed seemed quite dead, yet

they set out the microbiology kits, left them to do their work and set off at a Martian lope along the soft desiccated valley.

Lee sides of scattered rocks bore dingy brittle brown scabs a centimetre or more in diameter. When they raised their ultra-violet visors to examine them in natural light, these sparkled faintly as if laced with tiny crystal facets. Hard to say whether this was a kind of lichen or not. After holographing *in situ* they tagged and bagged the smaller stones. Further along, a sparkling pebble which Oates stood on buckled and cracked apart like a shell. Kneeling, he prised it open, discovering a dry honeycomb latticework. The pebble itself stuck in the soil on a tapering spike. Other honeycomb pebbles were similarly implanted in sun-trap areas which the wind swept clean.

'It's been a plant,' beamed Silverman. 'Even if it's only a husk now. Might still be dormant, though.' They dug into the brown dirt and bagged soil round it. Returning for a small mechanical digger, they rolled it along on its rubber wheels and started cutting into a dense drift banked up against a low eroded cliff. Taking turns they cut five metres inward, begin-ning to shift material blanketed and insulated for millennia by the cliff's contours. One of the team always stayed well clear with a hand shovel to dig his partner out – although there would be no life or death urgency about this, simply inconvenience: a man couldn't stifle inside a suit. Careful not to let the walls of their trench exceed sixty degrees, they quit work to watch the walls whenever vibrations of the digger brought scurries of dirt down the slopes.

It was then that the accident happened.

Neither budgeted for an empty pocket inside this drift which seemed so solid: for a hard-crusted bubble from which the trapped ice must long ago have evaporated.

Silverman was operating the digger. Suddenly the digger cut into the empty pocket, which curved down beneath his feet. The bubble collapsed, dirt slid in to fill it up. His feet slid too. The blades of the digger raced as his left foot tangled with them. He howled. The machine cut off automatically, but one blade had sliced through this thick thermal boot.

Oates ran into the trench to haul him clear.

'Don't pull me! My boot's still stuck in the damn digger.'

134

Oates scrambled past and scooped soil away. Quickly freeing the boot he pasted an adhesive strip across the tear.

'But did it *cut* you, Gene? I can only see damage to the boot. Here, I'll help you up. Let's get back. Leave all this stuff here—'

'Cut? I don't know. My foot hurts like hell.' Silverman tested his one-thirds weight on it.

'Let's get back!'

As they neared *Flagstaff*, he'd found his stride again, though the foot still ached. Ignoring the microbiology kits they climbed into the airlock, decontaminating as well as they could with an antiseptic spray. They passed through and undressed.

Silverman's capillary-cooled understocking bore a four centimetre gash in it, iced with rime of frozen water, blood, brown grit. Pressing his palm on it to thaw the rime, he unrolled the stocking.

A saucer of flesh had bruised and swollen. The actual wound was not particularly deep, but it oozed blood in the warmth of the module.

'Kitchen accident . . .'

Oates bathed Silverman's foot and poured iodine in the cut, then dressed it. He doled out four tablets of Meperedine to Silverman . . .

Next sunrise, Silverman did not wake up.

Shake him as he might, Oates could not wake him. Silverman's brow, and whole head, burned. Pulse and heartbeat were barely perceptible. Arms were so stiff that Oates had difficulty tugging his hand off the bed to take his pulse.

THIRTEEN

'We're losing, Angelina. What a farce our Inca Empire is – three towns and fifty villages. Chickens in a back yard! We haven't grown fast enough.'

Julio and Angelina were sitting in the drawing room of the evicted prefect of San Rafael. Sunlight filtered through the filigree wrought iron of glass doors to the balcony above a neat garden of flowering shrubs, box hedges and mosaic-paved pools with a fleeing nymph for a fountain. Water tinkled from her lips midway between whimpering and laughter. Stained glass lozenges in flanking windows restored isles of rose and azure and amber to the faded carpet. The room's design was mock-Moorish: an Alhambra of red and black brick archways. Chairs were either gilded and knobbled with carving, or else soft and shapeless like dead sheep. They chose to sit on the gilt chairs, perching awkwardly, their toes barely reaching the carpet.

Over the marble fireplace hung a grand painting in a stiff style of a rampart of massive stones, down which Indian defenders were casting themselves to their deaths. Already some condors feasted on the corpses below. But if the bodies were stiff, the bevelled polygons of stone blocks were lovingly dwelt on – with a fine sense of the flow of masonry. Beside this hung the smokey portrait of some bearded long-nosed man in black with a white ruffled collar and ruffled sleeves – some conquistador from whom this prefect of the People's Revolution perhaps proudly claimed descent, as if this fact made him a more committed native of the land ...

'If only we could build such a rampart,' mused Julio. 'But the world wraps us round, in all directions. There's no isolation. That's how I knew we had to expand. To push. The whole Andes has to be that wall.'

A message of defiance was hidden in the loving rendition of those wonderfully sculptured stones – even while the painter portrayed for Spanish masters the suicide of the Inca defenders, dashing themselves vehemently to death. But the bodies

136

were frail sticks. If only one could make a masonry of people ...

The workers of San Rafael had reacted with only mild enthusiasm, initially, to the agricultural laws of the new Inca. On the other hand the sight of their former superiors toiling to restore old Inca terraces in ravines outside the town, grumbling and aching at the labour, appealed to them. They relished this reversal. There was still enough anger, resentment and surly pride of centuries. Then, too, the elevation of traditional clan headman, *mallkus* and Aymara *jilikatas*, to real authority appealed; and sustained Julio's power. Approved, too, were the closing of the churches and restoration of worship of the Apu and Auki spirits and of the few surviving *huaca* shrines in the area. Superstition had always survived, dressed up as fiesta, and in the home as domestic fetishes. Thus it was simple to transform the calendar of church festivities back into the old Inca ritual calendar. Once again the Great Ripening could follow the Small Ripening, the Sun Festival follow Harvest Song, the Great Purification follow Earthly purification, the Festival of Waters follow the Queen's Feast. Curers and magicians danced once more with alabaster amulets and necklaces of teeth. A priest who barred their way, excommunicating them with a cross, was taken out of town and buried alive in the fields to fertilize them and cancel his curse. Paradoxically, there was more resentment at this murder among the town's criminals than among the law-abiding. Who else but Catholic Action ever brought any food into the jail before? Thieves, loiterers and the lazy were now being whipped out to work on the terraces by the new Inca law, where they found common cause with erstwhile high society which used to put them in prison.

Yet people grew uneasy as the Inca's soldiers confiscated and destroyed all radios they could find. Were the radio slanders true? Then the soldiers entered homes and took away all the books and magazines and newspapers to burn in the plaza, and the Inca made a speech telling them eloquently how they should learn to use their own memories. He showed them how to knot coloured strings. He set work quotas, and a personal

137

example – by labouring all day long in the fields, one day, alongside his queen. And day by day life grew more barren and straitened. Slowly people realized that such a thing as news had once existed, however marginally relevant it had always seemed. Such a thing as Travel had once existed – albeit only for a hundred kilometres to work in the mines. Soon, too, speech seemed far less free. The Inca explained that speech divides Men from Beasts. It has a sacred function. People must learn the meaning of their own minds through words – not gabble like geese.

He proclaimed that everyone was equal: that everyone was *puric*, a worker. A hundred *purics* should be responsible to an overseer, a *camayoc*; every hundred *camayocs* to the trio of lieutenants in his three main towns. This was purely a convenient way of counting, he explained. The headmen mattered more. (Yet even the People's Government had never dared organize its population so meticulously.)

Inca Julio decreed three market days a month, where people could hear what his plans were; and three feast days too for the people's amusement, after each market day. On market days themselves no alcohol would be available. People should listen to him or his spokesmen talk, and learn the nature of the world. Because he was *Rimac*, the Great Speaker, and there was so much they must learn about themselves without fuddling their senses …

'We should never have tried to win this way, Julio. It's only an accident that it happened to us. That we cracked the shells of our old selves. It could have happened to anyone else in Apusquiy.'

'Except, they were all poisoned and burnt!'

'They were trying to help. That doctor told you, when you closed the hospital.'

'But I didn't close it, I changed it.'

'You closed it as a *modern* hospital.'

'Well, I gave it to the curers. A curer cured you.'

'No, he only stopped me being wrongly treated.'

'Well?'

'Just that Spanish medicine has its uses.'

'*Coya*, the hospital would have run out of those in a few weeks. We can't found the Inca State and ask our enemies for drugs. We have to be what we were before. Anyway the curers have quinine and cocaine and herbs. They're no fools.'

'Yes,' she sighed, 'the world does wrap us round, crushingly. We mustn't be angry with each other. Or with the world. It's our only one.'

An outer door opened, and slammed. Voices conferred urgently.

His eyes shone hungrily.

'Yes indeed. Our Inca world.'

She already read the decision coming, in his face, however.

'We may have to use Alvaro's advice, Angelina. To go to that safe place over the border. Not because of San Rafael. We're secure here. But the miners. Our Empire's failing, there—'

' "Our" Empire?'

'People really are struggling for us,' he reproached. 'They're giving their lives right now. For the Inca cause. For these mountains, for the plain. They really do want the old ways. Dignity. They want it so ... so ...'

'So savagely?'

'Yes, there's bloodshed. We have to be ready to move out, now that we've shown the way. We'll found our ideal community in the mountains of Chile, where Alvaro promised us shelter. Everyone will look to it in admiration.'

'And how will they see it?' she asked gently. 'Do you think they'll let us rule our little world an hour longer than it suits them? I'm just repeating your own words. The bombers will come.'

'The last Incas founded a place in the hills that nobody ever discovered.'

'The searchers hunted on horseback, not from aircraft – or machines far out in space that they say can photograph a blade of grass. Anyway, the last Incas died out behind their stone walls. They were too good at building them. They cut their connexion with life. They didn't dare let it wrap them round.'

'Better that, than letting a prison wrap you round! And a rope, your neck! When we're overwhelmed here, Angelina, I'll have shown what could be done – and we'll still be there in the mountains with our Inca child. He'll give birth to himself, as we have.'

The anteroom door slammed again as someone left in haste.

'I must talk to Christobal about trucks. Just as a precaution—' Sliding from the gilded chair Julio crossed the light-drenched carpet to the door.

Angelina remained, thinking of Incas seated on golden thrones; wondering what they had really thought. She wasn't bored, alone. There was no boredom or loneliness now that her thoughts gestured to themselves in a theatre of memory dolls before her eyes. Nowadays it was as though her two eyes had drifted out of focus responding to two separate depths of reality – yet were still perfectly in focus.

Outside the filigree window the nymph giggled and whimpered. But as she listened to its voice – and her memories raced upon a mountainside – the water supply to the fountain finally quit. The nymph's throat gurgled and she choked, dry-throated.

'Well, Christobal?' Julio glanced at the newly delivered knotted strings laid out in a multicoloured spider's web on his secretary's desk. He read them as rapidly as must the first Inca, who invented this means of coding information: ideally, a simple thinking machine as much as a record of fact – a web representing the world with resistance, capacitance, connectivity, indicating not merely what was the case, but also what to do about it.

Christobal Pinco still had difficulty with the strings. He ran his fingers over the quipu like a blind man telling beads, losing his way, backtracking. Hardly surprising! The Inca interpreters – the *Amautas* – had to pass through many years' apprenticeship before they were fully proficient; and no White Face had ever learnt what an Inca quipu really was in all the hundreds of years since the conquest.

'Things aren't well,' frowned Christobal, though Julio already saw it in the strings. 'We've just lost Aracayo to the False Government. Our miners fought well enough for two days and two nights. Then it was all over. They lost heart. You see, the False Government promised them a new mine. A vast new reef of tin has been found by surveyors. American space machines saw it from up in the sky. They can slave underground again. For double wages—'

'And a halving of the value of the money, I suppose! That's how money governments behave. But not governments of land. You can't devalue land. Is this really true, though, that America told the False Government where to look for tin? Who's lying? The False Government, or America?'

'Does it matter?'

It mattered. Because ... if the foreign friends who dropped Alvaro and his horde of weapons and promised Julio Capac sanctuary were the friends of those who gave the False Government the perfect bribe to fool the miners of Aracayo: then they wanted to *force* him to choose sanctuary. Staring into the quipu he was suddenly less aware of the strings than of the gaps between them – all the empty space he knew nothing about. Really, his vision of the world was such a partial thing. Its sheer intensity fooled him into thinking that it was all there was to know. He cursed, understanding how the web of his knowledge had been spun in a particular place, at a particular angle.

Really, this quipu from Aracayo was too clumsily made. No time to learn properly. Even though he spent hours teaching apprentice *Amautas* to knot string. Should he have used writing and radios? No! He had to show the Inca Way, from the start.

Reading the strings, he saw the Aracayo mine re-opening. People emerging. Five survivors.

'When the shooting was over the False Government persuaded the miners to dig a way into the mine again,' added Christobal helpfully, having heard it by word of mouth from the recent courier. 'They lowered a listening machine down an air shaft. And heard people alive.'

'Corpse eaters.'

'They fed on death, yes. Now they're bent on Death; yours, particularly. The wife of the man you shot was among them – badly crippled.'

'Yes, I see.' The strings made sense now. Perhaps they'd never been meant by the old Incas to store so much information, but had only been for counting men and grain. But they *could* be made to do more!

In time.

There was no time.

'Her survival changed the miners' minds most of all. They swung from love of you, to hatred – like a rubber band wound round a bobbin, twisting the bobbin suddenly.'

Beneath the dance of the memory dolls and their mind landscape lay an even deeper level: a geometry of life that he'd tried to picture in these miserable, simple quipus – so that what happened and *how* it happened should be the same. (Or at least converge.) The root-fibres of human words reflected this deep shaping: all the folds, ellipses, forkings, gradients, cusps and waves; all the inflections in the fabric of the world – the thoughts that the world thought of itself. But only approximately. Indefinitely. Evasively, as yet. Indeed, the world wrapped you round, wherever you were – and revealed itself through you! There'd once been a secret speech of the high Incas. Surely it was made of these shapes beneath the ordinary words.

To rediscover that!

He was only beginning to learn! Time ...

No time

'I want six trucks, Christobal. One loaded with oil and petrol for the other five. One with food and seeds and blankets and everything we need to live in the mountains of Chile. Whoever will come with us can ride the other four. Have heavy guns mounted on all of them except the petrol truck. We'll set off across the salt pans to Chile ... tomorrow night. Tell those we trust.'

Which was the more important? Inca Strength and a tiny war in a half-known country? Or the shapes of the world that shaped a man so that he could be reborn during his own life, and know these shapes!

'We're going to run away, Inca?'

Julio smiled wanly. He had found something worth more than any Inca Empire. More than any idiot dream of farming tin from the hills.

'Human people are all children, Christobal,' he said calmly.

Even as he said it he saw how irrelevant it seemed to his secretary. 'And yet it's given to us to grow up and see what we are. This is what the Sun gave me when I was reborn.'

'I'll make arrangements,' Christobal nodded stiffly. 'I still believe you. Because you came back to life, a God.'

A God with clay feet.

FOURTEEN

'God, it's the worst,' muttered Dr Albrecht when he arrived, roused from sleep at three in the morning, at Mission Control and heard Weaver's report played back on tape.

'Do you want a rewind?' Spike Thorne asked.

He shook his head.

'No need. So far as I can judge the symptoms are the same as the Inca sickness. Well that definitely ties it to Mars. I suppose we should be grateful to our Intelligence friends.'

'We'd be more grateful if they had any intelligence for us, damn it. I already called Inskip's office. They told me not to talk over the telephone. Shit, what's a telephone for? You'd think they were so sorry about ever having bugged a phone that they regard the use of them even in an emergency as a federal offence! He got in touch himself ten minutes before you arrived. Wouldn't even let me précis the situation. Just said he'd fly down personally. Be here in about three hours. Meanwhile you'd better talk to Jim. He's worried, you can imagine. Klein'll be here. Public relations hitch, too! There was supposed to be a telecast at noon tomorrow via *Frontiersman*. We'll have to cancel that . . .'

Thorne switched the recorder to fast forward and spun the tape through to remove the spool. When it came to replaying it the tape would have to be wound all the way back again.

Panic, thought Albrecht. He didn't comment on Thorne's oversight; but did make a mental note to himself to route each decision of his own for the next few hours through a private censor filter, for scrutiny.

Taking an elevator up to the Control Room, they walked down to the second row of desks in the trench. The night shift of flight controllers, Shift Scarlet, were busier than Albrecht expected, since this was no mechanical emergency and *Frontiersman* was in a stable orbit with *Flagstaff* parked securely on the surface.

'What's up, Spike?'

'They're plotting a return and rendezvous for Wally, flying solo.'

'Has he requested that?'

'No. Obviously not. Wally wouldn't want to abort the surface studies—'

'Especially after Charles's psychological patter,' frowned Albrecht.

'I told them to go ahead anyway, just in case. So far there's only one man sick.'

'A sick man's best treated on the surface under some gravity. I wouldn't like to put a man in a coma through the strain of lift-off . . .'

Thorne consulted his watch. (Which in itself was another curious action. At least two clocks were visible from where they sat, slaved from the cesium-atomic master clock downstairs. Even if Thorne's watch *was* spot on, it was no atomic clock. It even took longer to see your own watch than to look at the wall. But Thorne had taken the decision for Shift Scarlet to set up this escape lift-off on his own account; he was feeling defensive, reflected Albrecht.)

'Jim will be coming out from behind Mars in about twelve minutes. So you can start talking in another seven.'

'I don't particularly want to speak to Jim yet—'

'Don't want to!'

'What I mean, Spike . . .' But then Charles Klein arrived. He assessed the situation with a glance. (And then another glance, to confirm that this *was* the situation.)

'Did you order this, Spike?'

'It's just a contingency . . . I haven't mentioned it to Jim.'

'Thank Heaven for that. Well, we're not rushing anyone into space. Don't you see why, Spike – do you really not see? Silverman's contaminated. Wally has to see that illness through on the surface right till it's time for *Warming Pan*. That's precisely why we told Jim to stay up there, and I want you to be reinforcing this message, as delicately as you can – not wasting people's time and energy, including your own, on escape dramas. Tell Scarlet to bow out of that one, will you?'

Thorne carried out Klein's instructions without even the moment's hesitation one might have reasonably expected (as though he had only been pulling one way – in a lift-off direction – the more rapidly to rebound). He looked distinctly relieved. His gesture of conscience had been quashed, as he'd known it must be. He was glad, both for the gesture and for the quashing.

'Spike already phoned that man Inskip, Charles. He's flying in. I'll talk to Jim in a couple of minutes, but I won't record anything for relay to Wally till Inskip arrives. He may—' Albrecht opened his hands invoking a *something*. I'll ask for three-hourly reports on Gene's condition – excluding Wally's sleep time, of course.'

'Three-hourly? And how long did it take the Inca to wake up: a whole week? Suppose it's the same . . . In and out of the airlock, decontaminating all the time? That really cuts into the man-hours we have left on the surface. Oates may as well be sitting by a sick-bed staring out of the window! Exhausting, unproductive and demoralizing. No, assuming no change in Gene in the next six hours, Oates will have to get on with the research work normally. Make it six-hourly reports, Doctor – with a mike rigged by Gene's pillow. It's the only sensible way.'

'You can speak to Jim in one minute from now,' said Thorne, staring up at the wall clock. '*Mark*—'

Albrecht regarded the microphone dubiously. Inaction seemed indecent. An adolescent heroic voice in him clamoured for some kind of emergency operation – nature albeit unknown – by remote control. The voice was talking nonsense;

just as the voice that prompted Thorne to set Shift Scarlet on alert was. Charles Klein's was the voice of sanity.

'Houston to *Frontiersman*. We have Dr Albrecht here to talk to you, Jim—'

A green light winked on.

'This is Albrecht, Jim. I'm terribly distressed to hear this news about Gene. So far there's no miracle treatment we know of, except time. That's the one essential thing we do know from what happened in Bolivia. All treatments turned out fatal. The two survivors had no treatment at all. No drugs, no efforts to relieve the cerebrospinal pressure, no intravenous drips, nothing. Left absolutely alone, they recovered. Will you make this very clear to Wally? *No course* of treatment is the best course. He mustn't interfere. Not even to try to give Gene water. Just let whatever it is work its way through Gene's system. I don't think it matters that Gene took some pain-killers before he turned in; that was *before* onset. Ask him to report on Gene's status once every six hours. Otherwise, to carry on as normal on his own. There'll be a number of seemingly lethal metabolic changes. Believe me, he must do nothing—'

Inskip's plane was delayed. He didn't arrive till four hours after Albrecht had spoken to Weaver. When he did come, Inskip, Albrecht, Klein and Thorne closeted themselves once more in the conference room. Without comment Spike Thorne slipped the spool that he'd played to Albrecht on to the tape recorder and pressed the PLAY switch; but there was silence, apart from the faint hum of blank tape passing the pick-up heads …

'Damn it, what's wrong now?'

'Rewind it, Spike,' Albrecht murmured. It might have been comic if the situation had not been so serious. Albrecht found himself wondering about mistakes in general, and particularly the error on Mars. Would it have occurred if the astronauts hadn't been split up for safety? Would it have occurred if they hadn't been made to feel potentially unreliable, hence vulnerable? Like kids who'd already learned to walk put back into reins and stumbling on account of the reins? The accident happened to the only member of the trio whose performance hadn't in some way been subverted by Charles Klein. A perverse form of compensation? Who knew what psychological support systems had grown up between the three men, thus isolated?

Thorne rewound the tape vexedly, flipped it and played it through.

'That's awful.' Inskip shook his head. (Commiserating? Chiding?) 'That's exactly why I came to you in the first place, isn't it? Tragic that it had to happen so soon.' (Yes, *chiding* them. He couldn't be by everybody's side.)

'Where's your news?' Thorne demanded. 'We learned nothing at all from your *Zayits* wreckage or the soil. It was about fifty per cent Bolivian graveyard according to your report! Nicely riddled with Earth Bugs.'

'Steady, Mr Thorne. The treatment reports were valuable *negatively*, weren't they?' Inskip felt in key now. The world and his predictions meshed. A smooth purring filled his head. He remembered someone remarking to him once, in a time of economic gloom, that what the universities really produced, GNP-wise, with all their fancy courses was *negative unemployment*; the comment stuck in his mind as a useful nostrum.

'That's true,' adjudicated Albrecht. 'We've passed on the message not to try any form of treatment. You may have saved Silverman's life.'

'Excuse my impatience,' apologized Thorne tetchily, 'but we need more. We need your Inca. Blood samples. A full medical report on him. Where is it?'

'There, alas, we're having difficulties. It takes slightly longer than we budgeted. The Inca's still in control of the heart of his tinpot empire. I can tell you in strictest confidence that the Bolivian authorities have already squashed its sides in – and our man is in charge of the operation. Exactly as we wanted it. Unhappily we lost the agent sent in to contact the Inca personally. Our people saw him rendezvous. Only, he never radioed back. Not a word. They did use his guns though.'

'To kill him?'

'No idea. That's one of the things we'll just have to find out when our army man gets to him.'

'How soon?'

'Before the week's out.'

'That's no use, man. Silverman is sick right now. Send your troops in faster.'

A rueful look.

'They're not our troops, are they? That's just it. Surprised at you, Mr Thorne, when you were so reluctant before. We run a very discreet organization nowadays. And you see the sort of difficulties we meet? People are so-o reluctant to co-operate, then they slap us in the face as soon as we don't deliver their goods on time.'

'There'll soon be no point in bringing the damned Inca out!'

'Oh, we have other good reasons for bringing him out.' Inskip dismissed these reasons with a hitch of the shoulders. *I told you so*, Thorne glowered at Albrecht.

'When you say "before the week's out" do you mean this weekend, or in the next seven days?' he demanded.

'We'll do it as soon as we can.'

'What sort of answer's that?'

'Bolivia isn't our country, Mr Thorne. We aren't almighty, don't pretend to be.'

'Damn it, would any of this have happened!' Albrecht surmised that Thorne too was wondering whether in some perverse way they had actually caused the accident themselves. Whether Inskip had caused it with his warning. Whether Thorne had caused it by letting himself be used politically and not levelling with the astronauts one hundred percent.

'Very likely it would, Spike. Only, far worse. Three men involved. At least this way Jim's well out of it. The real sorrow is having Gene out of action. Fine pilot that he is, Wally makes a very .. middling scientist.'

Charles Klein nodded. 'Whereas, the other way round, Gene could have got on with some very meaningful research, particularly on this stuff in the soil.'

'Still, he couldn't have blasted off to rejoin *Frontiersman*?' queried Inskip. 'Assuming the worst case, that Oates woke up mentally unbalanced? Perhaps this is a case of count your blessings.'

For just a moment, Klein looked very angry. 'Silverman is

perfectly capable of lifting off, Mr Inskip! Do you think we didn't train for that? Suppose Oates had a fatal accident on Mars? And Weaver too, since we were going to send all three men down originally. Do you seriously think we could have had one survivor sitting on the surface not knowing how to return? Judging on the performance of your vanished agent I'd say you people have something to learn about non-expendability.'

'My apologies,' breezed Inskip. 'Of course you're right. Well, item two on the agenda is the Soviet reaction. Painful as the main situation is, I think we must cover this too right now. This accident really validates our borrowing of the Russians' soil ... It did turn out vital to find out as much as we could as soon as we could. I heard the tape of your first message to *Frontiersman*, Spike. You handled that neatly enough. We've handed over the soil now, and the full lab reports on it and bits of the *Zayits* craft. We couriered it off to our opposite numbers in Helsinki, neutral territory.'

'Just bits? I hope you haven't kept any for souvenirs.'

'Negative, Spike. We melted the rest down, buried it.'

'Will you stop calling me Spike?'

Inskip registered the snub without rancour, manifestly pitying Thorne for his touchiness. 'Obviously we couldn't hand the whole craft back, or the operation would have seemed far too smooth on our part. Besides, the Bolivians could have got annoyed. We've explained to the People's Government that we had to blow cover because of the accident; but in such a way as not to implicate them in any "deal".'

Thorne looked scathing. 'None of my business, really, but aren't you playing into their hands just a bit? Aren't you giving them a trump card they can play when you eventually play your Inca? They can blow the whole *Zayits* deal wide open, now that you've told the Russians positively otherwise.'

'There's that risk. We rate it low. We don't compute the current Bolivian government being around for very much longer. Anyway, how do you mean "eventually" play our Inca? We already played him. We armed him. He seriously sapped the strength and solidarity of the Bolivians.'

'A king in exile, obviously.'

'God, *no*. That's just what we can't let happen, Spike. Sorry ... Look, your two Incas have to fall into our hands very privately indeed. Once out, they *never* make a come-back. The worst thing happening to the world right now is ethnic balkanization. Cries for an independent Mohawk nation, Free Cree, *Québec Libre*, Artic for the Eskimos ... not to mention the whole Black Separatist movement here in the States. These are awful spectres, that could tear the States and Canada apart at the seams. A genuine Indian God-King would send sympathetic ripples all the way from Arizona to Alaska. No, it's unthinkable. Once grabbed, we keep our Incas very much on ice. In one of our "farms". All comforts, even the right climate. Somewhere high up in the Rockies. I guess I've said too much about that ... but I want to allay any fears you have on their account. Now, any threats from the Bolivians to blow the deal – supposing they do hang on, of course – we simply counter with the threat to re-equip the Inca. Not that we ever will. Too risky geopolitically, as I say. Still, that's the only way we'd ever play the card: by keeping it in our hands. So the whole situation's tied up and secure. Even the Russians won't kick up now, in view of what's happening on Mars – which, being public knowledge, we naturally keep them largely posted on. Right? We only committed a justifiable misdemeanour in their eyes, no crime.' Inskip rubbed his hands, looked brightly at the three men.

'It may be all tied up,' retorted Thorne, 'apart from one disaster on Mars and the matter of two missing Incas ...'

FIFTEEN

The Salar of Uyuni is over twenty-five thousand square kilometres of salt crust overlaying vast interlocking water caverns:

a gargantuan salt-water reservoir useless to beast or man. Its surface is blinding white, a smooth arctic icecap dappled with shallow pools so saturated in salts that they sprout miniature crystal forests and coral reefs. These pools seem tropic in their exuberance of tiny forms – antlers, pyramids, rhombs and polyhedra – but it is a blanched sterile exuberance. No water flea can live in such pools. Their temperature is zero, the water itself too saline to freeze. Nature carves for nothing, practising forms as though otherwise in that vast blank of the Salar it might forget. Sterility reigns.

Under that crust mysterious desolate caverns coil like intestines from one part of the Salar to another between salt ribs and humpbacked hidden mounds: sufficient water for whales to swim in. Dead water.

The crust varies between a metre and two metres thick, with no way of knowing whether a spur of land or a water cavern is below. Occasionally trucks vanish into these caverns when a thinner zone fractures under their weight. Their drivers sometimes scramble clear in time and wander about the blank Salar till they go blind, or freeze, or starve – or are picked up, by chance.

Mirages shimmer. Salt devils dance about.

A convoy consisting of Julio's command jeep and six trucks drove out on the Salar at dawn, where it was a hundred kilometres wide. Panicked by the roar of their motors a herd of vicuna scampered out on to the salt flats ahead of them, outdistancing the speeding trucks before curving back in a wide arc towards the *tola* thickets where they had been grazing.

An hour later, and they were almost in the centre of the Salar, when the lookout in the rear truck fired a shot.

They stared back; and saw an aircraft flying in low across the Salar from behind them; already close – emerging from the Sun, white furnace octopus, coronal pulse melting their eyes as they searched. Upon the blinding light, a bar of black danced in and out. Julio wondered could it be the same aircraft that had parachuted Alvaro and the map. But no, its wings were smaller, and it had propellers, not jets. It was one of those ancient passenger planes that he'd been ferried in once, while a soldier.

'Shall we shoot at it, Inca?' Two shots from their jeep would signal an outburst of fire.

Once more Julio was a soldier, inside the plane as it bucked through the air pockets of the Andes. (This wasn't a war plane. No guns poked out of its nose or wings; no bomb doors opened from its belly. People were its cargo; soldiers. And freight in the unpressurized rear.)

'No, wait.' He swung round. Ahead, the image of the plane skidded down on to the salt to disgorge troops who fanned out, firing at the approaching vehicles. (But how easily their convoy would split up and circle round the troops, and away, while hammering the exposed figures with their own fire.) Another image of the plane skidded down on to the salt and crashed right through into the water caverns. (This was far more probable.) It couldn't land. Nor shoot nor bomb. But only fly over them.

A moment later, and it did fly over. But the rear cargo door was missing. A hole gaped. Figures hung inside strapped to the walls: in miners' helmets and goggles, and oxygen masks. Stiffly they tossed out tiny bundles.

'Swerve!' screamed Julio. 'Shoot, Christobal!'

The first clump of dynamite hit the salt fifty metres ahead, thunder and flash sending a snowstorm skywards as Baltasar slewed the wheel aside; while Christobal fired up through the billow. As all the gunners opened fire the first truck peeled off to the right; the second to the left, and so for the third and fourth. But already the salt was falling back showing the way clear; and the supply truck and petrol truck drivers took their more heavily burdened vehicles straight on through.

Standing in the racing jeep Julio waved them furiously away from his image of the loaded plane crashing through the crust, the great vent it had made. Vainly. Salt crust cracked around the two trucks, sinking them to their axles: where they rested awhile as the two drivers and single roof-top gunner who first saw the plane jumped away, wading and hopping. One driver sank through sludge quicksand. A salt slab turned head over heels, shutting the other, tumbled driver under its lid. Only the gunner escaped on to firm salt and sprinted after the nearest truck, which slowed and stopped for him. The two wallowing trucks hung a moment longer, plugging the wounds their own weight made; then together both sank from sight. All the fuel. The seeds. The blankets.

The plane was swinging round and flying towards the scattered convoy at right angles to their course. Machine guns fired from the truck tops, but already the drivers were swerving, ruining the gunners' aim. And that lumbering antique plane was piloted with a hatred that lent it a hawklike pounce and precision. It crossed their paths dropping its excrement on them. More dynamite boomed *TUNRÚN* in a terrible voice. More salt plumed; and spray.

And then the huge lid of the world was opening for the riders in the jeep. A slab of crust had broken free all round them. They were upon it; and it was tipping. Baltasar braked, appalled. Christobal whimpered as he stared behind the slowly rising jeep at the water depths awaiting: liquid almost as transparent as air – except that deep down the light was squeezed out of it by a stiff vagueness.

'Drive forward, Baltasar! Drive at the sky, drive *up*!' Julio pressed Baltasar's left hand into the wheel, to become the wheel; and squashed his right hand around the gear stick, making it the gear stick.

And Baltasar drove blindly up the rising lid of the world above their heads – racing the engine in low gear against the slope. As they clawed past pivot point the lid stopped rising and slowly began settling back. Sky sank back towards horizon.

Yet the closing lid would dip as deep below the horizon on the downswing. (Already Julio saw how they drove headlong downhill into water depths, the lid rising back over them as they sank down, down ... But he also saw them crossing the lid's edge on to firm salt in a bound just before the lid dipped down; their jeep jumped off the sinking ramp, four wheels airborne. Two images, equally strong.)

'Drive at the edge, Baltasar! Drive exactly as fast as I say. When I say slow, go slower *whatever you think*. When I say fast, *huayra-hina* – quick as the wind!'

Baltasar obeyed automatically. Fear had snatched his *coraje* away: and it was a good thing. The wheel turned his hands, the pedals pushed his feet.

'Now *slow*.'

Dipping lower, misleading slowly, with massive inertia, the lid squeezed a salt mist from underwater effervescently. Two fists up from the horizontal, judged Julio, *now* ...

'—Now! *Huayra-hina!*'

The jeep roared forward in first gear, to little avail.

'Change up!' screamed Julio.

Gearstick and clutch pedal forced Baltasar's hand and foot to change them. Then the jeep raced indeed.

The edge had cracked jaggedly, irregularly in a circuit of large jutting cogs. To interlock with the corresponding gaps below? Cog passing through cog? Not if the salt disc had rotated even a little during its rise and fall; those teeth would crash across other teeth, then, momentarily stemming the plunge till the impact ground its way through and snapped them ... and between each overlapping pair of teeth: holes, snares.

The disc might easily have rotated ... Toothed wheels of salt turned before his eyes: wheels of a giant watch, timing Death. Catching the wheel himself Julio swung it to head the jeep out along the broadest tooth.

'Now *fly*!' (As the jeep reached the edge; as the salt slab crunched into teeth of the opposing crust – spray pluming through the tooth gaps.) And the jeep flew: as well as any boulder in an avalanche. While the lid finally crushed its way vastly underwater, wallowing and awash, it bounded on to the mainland. (Cracks already zigzagging after it.) The crash tossed Baltasar Quispe into the steering wheel; there was bubbling, coughing blood. Something beneath the jeep broke too: wheels, axles. The vehicle slumped sideways while still skidding, though it did not turn over.

To his astonishment Julio found that he wasn't in the jeep at all; he was metres away, sliding to a halt on scraped stinging hands. He finally scrambled up, trembling with shock.

Baltasar ... llama, chest-broken by a miner's axe. His bloody, bloody heart still pumping, emptying him out ...

Christobal's head had hit something and he sat rocking back and forth nursing it, though there was little blood: something soft, then. Seats, Angelina.

'Angelina—'

Christobal reacted to Julio's call and was lifting Angelina up as Julio reached the jeep; she was stunned, but conscious.

He stood on the jeep and stared round the Salar. (Nothing to be done for Baltasar.) At first he saw nothing but the white plain. A buckled, pockmarked, groaning whiteness, bereft of life, equipment, Empire. But no, one truck was scuttling eastwards. Running away? No again. His heart quickened as he realized that the truck was circling round; from a long way off.

Closer by, across the rifted crust, a second truck lay toppled on its side leprous with salt, soldiers hunching behind it with their weapons. The aircraft! (The miners's plane – only they would have used dynamite so skilfully and devilishly!) It was circling way out of range of any guns. Watching. No, it wouldn't land; the pilot had seen the salt crust snap.

'One truck's left . . . And two truckloads of people. We'll have to walk to meet it, they daren't drive this close—'

'Baltasar?' blinked Angelina, wondering what she saw in the front seat.

'There's nothing we can do for him, *Coya*. He's . . . empty. We have to reach the truck. Then there are those men over at the other truck – how can we reach them? They'll all have to cross the broken salt on foot.'

'Who would do that?' Christobal protested.

'How can I leave them? We can reach them by driving right round all the cracks.'

'And the plane only needs to drop more dynamite—'

'No, they've used it all! Why else are they holding off?'

Angelina's ankle was wrenched. Not broken, she insisted. They supported her, hobbling across the salt field towards the now waiting truck. A long hobble. They could have come closer!

'We've lost, Inca,' remarked the driver bitterly. Yet he had driven back. Courage overcame his fear. That remark was only *susto*. Julio still stayed *Inca*.

'I saw the way you escaped from the salt island,' said the driver. (Julio still had *luck*. Safer to be with him, than without him.)

'We must drive right round the holes and cracks to pick the others up.'

'Ages, to do it safely. Anyway—' The driver nodded at the circling aircraft.

'They've no more dynamite – or they couldn't stop themselves using it on us now, don't you see? There's blood in their nostrils like a maddened bull's. It's safe.'

'If we pick them up will we get to Chile ... Inca?'

'Where else?' snapped Julio wearily. Wheels of salt still turned before his eyes. An ocean hung above his head as he sank through chilling embalming liquid. His lungs filled with it. His body froze. He clutched Angelina to him, shivering, and she clung to him; but toughly, holding him together.

'Drive! Find a way round.'

They picked up nine men (three crippled), three women and a boy. Then they were on the wrong side of the broken salt again with an overcrowded truck. Heading west finally towards the mountains, they had the aircraft keeping them distant company with their truck as the hub of its wide circle.

An hour later, the snow peaks had freed themselves entirely from the salt; a solid rock wall humped between these two whitenesses. No shadows to drive into now; the Sun hung overhead. No one else knew how to drive. The driver rubbed his eyes.

'I'm going blind. I can't see our tracks in the mirror. What do I drive towards?'

'Keep on going.'

'Am I still driving ahead?'

'Yes, yes.'

Far ahead spread the grey contrast of *tola* scrub – the end of the Salar. But now that no more water caverns lay beneath the crust, there was progressively firmer soil for a foundation. The aircraft circled one last time, then glided down to land on the last stiff stretch of crust before the bushes. Soldiers jumped down ahead, fanning out – as he had seen! Men in miners' gear ran to the open cargo hatch to pull their frozen comrades free; they had to haul them out, so stiff were they with cold.

'Our truck's faster,' reassured Julio as they swung south

to parallel the edge of the Salar. He even summoned a laugh. 'They can't follow us in their plane on the ground, can they?'

Some shots chased after them, missing the fleeing truck. Shrubs grew waist-deep, dense and wiry, on and on. No tracks led into them.

'They headed us off from the right way out,' mumbled the driver. 'That's why they landed there. I was going the right way after all! I didn't believe it. I was! You saw the marker stones, didn't you?'

'Hush,' soothed Angelina. 'You've done so well. Can't you drive through the *tola* without a road? Make one?'

The driver tried.

He drove the overloaded truck into the thickets, ploughing through, uprooting, dragging branches along. Twigs wrapped themselves round the wheels, catching between mudguards and tyres, scraping, squealing. Yet they made progress.

A broad open river of earth ran through the bushes, surface cracked and crazed, pitted with stones. Dry rivers often made good roads. Unfortunately this one ran the wrong way, north and south. Hunting a gap in the bushes on the far side they drove across.

Halfway over the earth subsided and the truck ploughed into stiff black mud to its axles. Racing the engine in reverse only splattered mud about while the wheels dug deeper ruts.

When the driver and Julio got out their feet sank ankle deep. An underground well must be feeding this treacle. Then why no bushes? Julio stuck his finger in the mud and tasted it. *Salt.* Water leaching from the Salar caverns away into the scrublands ...

'We can still dig out. Tear up bushes, make a raft to drive on. It's only soft in the centre. Hurry, hurry. Lighten the truck—'

However, they were still digging mud and laying *tola* half-an-hour later when the soldiers reached them. Shrubs made excellent cover. At the shrill of a whistle, soldiers and armed miners stood up all around them covering every man and woman.

A loudhailer deafened them.

'Don't fight! We only want your Inca, not you *campesinos*. Give up, and we'll let you all go back home!'

They kept their word, after a fashion. They took Julio Capac and Angelina away with them, tied with ropes, and left the others to find their own way home a hundred kilometres across the Salar, after first wrecking the truck's engine with a final stick of dynamite.

SIXTEEN

Wally Oates was tidying the module and packing, feeling disappointed at the little he had achieved with Gene out of action as he stowed away double-sealed samples of soil and 'lichen' stones and possible 'pebble plants'. Lift-off and rendezvous were due next day as per the original schedule which stayed unaltered. As Silverman's illness had started so rapidly and as Oates remained healthy throughout it seemed perfectly safe for him to transfer to *Frontiersman* and deploy *Warming Pan* himself.

As he worked, Silverman awoke.

'Backwards, then forwards,' croaked Silverman dryly.

Oates swung round, dropping a film pack.

'Christ, you gave me a shock. Do you feel okay?'

'Backwards and forwards!' Silverman cackled, frogs in his throat.

'Are you really okay, Gene?'

Oates peered nervously. To be shut up in a tiny space module with a delirious guy! Backwards and forwards? What did Gene think he was in, a rowing boat?

'Don't worry, Wally, I'm perfectly sane. Just elliptical! And thirsty as a desert. Will you fix me something hot? Then do rub me down, that would help.'

Tearing the tab off a can of quik-soup, Oates held it to the other man's lips. Silverman sucked the soup noisily, flexing his arms and legs, making his joints crackle.

'Pummel me back into shape now. Make this a massage parlour – while I tell you all about this so-called illness.'

Dubiously Wally Oates kneaded and pounded Silverman who lay back grinning sybaritically at his masseur, whilst revelling in a hard, prominent erection. Noticing the drift of Oates' eyes, Silverman smirked unashamedly.

'You must excuse me – but sex and thought are rather similar, that's all! Did you know, thinking's a permanent orgasm inside the head?'

'Can't say I did.'

'A rippling field of gratifying wave-fronts! I enjoy thinking so very much now, Wally. How long's it been?'

'Oh, that. Seven days.'

'All that time I've been travelling backwards down the past so I could leap right forward into the future. My memories have been realigning themselves, reorganizing my head for me. All the shapes of past experience. It's those shapes that count, Wally . . . I suspect the human brain contains all possible memories of states a human brain can experience—'

'Sure, Gene.' (Pummel. Slap.)

'All the branches of all the trees we can be perched on. Only, all branches bar one get shoved down and suppressed by the fact of living! That's the real difference between dreams and memories. Our life experiences attract the actualities into existence – out of the pool. But we dream all the possible forms of Being—'

'Does that feel better yet?' (Tickle. Thud.)

'Landscapes we've never seen. Having wings and flying. Meeting kangaroos that speak. Whatever! These saturate our heads. Dreams permutate the possible forms of Being: the genetic forms—'

'Don't excite yourself, Gene.' (Punch. Wobble.) 'Look, I don't know all that much about massage. I mean, I'm mainly guessing . . . from what I remember of massage here and there. Mainly there! Penang . . .' (Milly-Kim massaged him very

159

nicely with her slim black Asian hands; but Milly-Kim was perpetually 'over there': around the torus of his life, from home. Kathy's hands didn't have the experience, the lickerish lubricious skill, the lubrication.) 'I might be beating you up ... mass of bruises.'

'But if we dream all these genetic forms when we're awake, we're deluded. Hallucinating. All the potential forms of Being have to be repressed and squeezed down – so that we can walk and talk and function smoothly.'

'So I'd better quit.' (Hands off.) 'This isn't a sauna, it's a spacecraft. Look, are you really all right?' (Can you count backwards from a hundred please? Can you divide seven into twenty-two up to the first few dozen decimal places to keep your mind on the tracks?)

'I'm right as rain. I'm telling you this because it's ... like an orgasm, understanding it. The sheer emission of the words to flesh out the thoughts is a ... sort of sexual emission that never drains you. Well, detumescence at day's end, perhaps! We have to return to the fountain of forms. Thoughts and memories are basically all geometries, Wally. While I slept I've been shown the forms of Being behind my life's memories.'

'I must call Jim and tell him you've waked up.'

'But you can't tell him what it means to *wake up*!' chortled Silverman.

'I can report the fact.'

'Can you? All the facts in the world join together geometrically. "God ever geometrizes", someone said! We never actually *saw* this with our eyes, because we couldn't. Our minds are a suitcase with a single window. Ideas are only present, on condition of the absence of all other possible ideas. No two ideas can occupy the same quantum of mindspace. That's the rule. *Was*, till now. But the plan says that they *shall*—'

'For God's sake calm down, will you?'

'But it's ecstasy to tell another fellow human being this. This is no delirium. I'm saner than I've ever been. Much wholer. Shall I tell you what consciousness is, Wally? Or rather, what it's always been till now? Each thought in our minds is the arc of a circle. There are so many, many arcs: as many as the thoughts that our minds can possibly think. And these all co-exist in n-space – a super-space that no thought alone can record by itself. These thousands of arcs of mind perpetually rotate through one another – forming a simple, plausible, single space. We call it consciousness. Whenever we try to chase a thought – to set another thought on its heels, to see the *full picture* – the arc we're chasing gets squeezed down and away to another part of mental superspace. Far away from the space occupied by the other hunting thought. "Consciousness" still exists. We're still the same conscious "whole" because the great circles all still cohere in that one same simple space – the field of mind. But the rest of the arc we were seeking has been squeezed right out of this space, by the very fact of our hunting it with another arc.

'Mind's a hyperstructure, Wally. We have to exist in a simple-structure world. Hell, that's true of Physics. You can only *explain* how electrons behave by using six-space, multi-dimensional space. But the electrons and the atoms all still appear to exist inside one single three-dimensional world—'

'Please! Help me just a little, will you? We have to take off tomorrow. I have to radio Jim. Jim must radio Earth.'

'Just hear me out, I'm nearly done. You don't break off making love before climax if you've any sense or you get prostate trouble, right?'

'What has that to do with it!' (That blatant erection.)

'As I said, thinking's sexy. Well, I see a power in these forms in the n-space supporting the visible universe, Wally – a dynamic. A drive! I swear it's coded into us to move towards being able to see all this. I was watching nightfall over Mars before we landed. As Mars blanked out the rest of the Galaxy grew bright with stars. Something was teasing me ... I dreamt that scene through again while I slept and this time I understood the question it was posing. The nature of light! Of information. What is light exactly? Is there "light" while it's in transit, from star to eye? No: in transit it can't be seen. It doesn't impinge. It's something else, then; call it a jiggled wave. On arrival it becomes what we think of as "light" – when it's seen by the eye of the observer, translated by the brain behind the eye. But in that very same moment it vanishes. Can't travel on! Further possibilities exhausted, except inside the brain. Does light in some strange way *need* to be "seen"? That's why light has to be both a wave and a particle at one and the same time! That's why light must always have a double nature, a double rationale. Putting it flippantly, a Universe has to be seen, to be believed!'

'There must be one hell of a lot of light going to waste, then. Falling on barren soil all over the place! I'm really surprised at you, Gene. What a load of unscientific drek.'

'No, the dream was using light as a ... way of showing me something essential.'

'It could hardly have used darkness, could it?'

'It's really an analogy: light, the eye, the brain. Language isn't really designed for talking about six-space or *n* dimensions – except in metaphor, analogy, leaps of association. Math can, in a specialized way. But we can't *talk* mathematically. Oh to meet a race that could! A race of musicians, at the same time. Music can analogize what I'm talking about: but *inexplicably*. The "space" of music is formalized emotional space ... I was learning about the Universe. Why life evolves. Where to. What's the evolution of this strange phenomenon *life* about, after all?'

'Does it have to be about something?'

'*Yes*. Mutations aren't just random. They can't be because mutations move towards ... genetic niches – geometrical niches, niches of structure, as surely as birds and beasts fill up all possible ecological niches. Mutations have been moving us towards this act of seeing all the time. That's what light is a metaphor for: seeing. That's why the dream used light as its emblem.'

'The way I remember my high school biology, mutations are supposed to be mostly recessive.'

'Exactly! They get pushed down, till the pool's saturated. Till the time is ripe. *Then* they erupt. In a Big Change. I'm talking about the Big Leaps, not about modifying the shape of a toenail or an eyelash. The change from No Language to Language: the interface between the two. A change of that order. I'm sure this *Seeing* is waiting in us all. It's the next great leap. But the programme can only be carried out after we've been born and grown up – because Seeing has to have something to see: real memories of real events as its scaffold. We have to have rebirth in our lives. This is what I was trying to get through to Jim when we first heard about the Inca – but he couldn't take it in. My God, do you think this was an illness? This is the next step, Wally. It must have been saturating Humanity for thousands of years. Of course, children will have to go on being born ordinarily—'

'That's nice to know. Just how do you *know*, incidentally?'

'Kids will be born the same. They'll grow up and mature and become men and women. But they'll still all really be pupae, larvae – just as we've all been, up till now. We're the ultimate type of neoteny, Wally: the persistence of the larval form into adult life. We breed in juvenile form. We live our lives in juvenile form. We die in juvenile form. That's going to end.'

'You seem privy to some mighty fine revelations. Do me a favour, Gene. Distrust them, will you?'

Silverman looked puzzled; passed a hand over his face as though brushing cobwebs.

But I do see the shapes of things, Wally. I see the geometrical forms moving through the Universe attracting matter and life and thought into existence – right now, before my eyes. My "light" dream was just part of this … This is all *within* the brain, of course. There's nothing *out there*, when I say geometries – even though I'm seeing them: formalized memories, interacting geometrically – in shape equations, in energy transformations …

'I mean, what is seeing anyway? It's a model inside the brain. We have word models that break up and capsulate our tolerably shared experience of "out there". But words are mainly arbitrary sounds – even if the unfolding of the grammar system and the *conceptual* roots of words observe the same topological shaping modes, the same archetypal morphologies as – oh, the unfolding, crimping and bifurcating of cells in the embryo, or the birth of a bubble in water or the diadem of a splash, or the behaviour of spiral galaxies for that matter … What happens when the brain "sees" the world? A topological model of filtered reality is produced in the n-space within, by interacting, interfering electro-chemical wavefronts What happens when I *see* the forms that constrain and sustain the thought-system? The *n*-space within bifurcates in a shape-catastrophe, like a cell dividing, reduplicating, but not disconnecting – because there's still "status" or "gradient" information interfacing between the two cells. And I have access to additional "virtual" space, that can coexist with the field of mind. I don't mean that I'm developing a double brain or anything! I mean that out of one model – of the world around me, in my brain – is being generalized a secondary model of the topology relationships permeating the first model: using memory as the "virtual" building blocks, because you can *remember* and see the real world at the same time. It's happened in open brain surgery, before – as a strange aberration ... I'll bet that some of the so-called "unused" dormant brain area is accepting this programme – and is meant to. I'm ... controlling the process, too. I can summon it up – like alpha waves, only here it's the memory illusions—'

However, Oates had stopped listening several moments before.

'*Flagstaff* to *Frontiersman*,' he radioed unhappily. 'Do you read me? Over.'

'Loud and clear, Wally. You're late. Over.'

'Thank God, Jim. Gene's woken up. He's a real bundle of energy. Talking nineteen to the dozen about how he knows what evolution is all about and how he's the next evolutionary step upwards. Do you get my point, Jim? Gene's fine, only now we have some sort of superman on our hands, that's why I'm late, he can't stop talking about it, claims it's sexy. Over.'

A long pause; till Oates thought he had lost Weaver round the bulge of Mars. Then, leadenly:

'I see.'

Chuckling, Silverman reached for the microphone.

'Hi there, Jim. Wally thinks I'm nuts. I don't blame him. He can't see what I can. You can tell Houston I know all about what afflicts that Inca of theirs. He's gone through the same process as I have. He can see the geometry underlying the world so now he's building himself an empire to express it. Of course he has to make do with his own memories! Those

164

must be fairly unscientific ones. I was explaining to Wally how I know that our kids will go on being born just as at present — with the big change coming later on in life, because you need the knowledge of life to work with first. You need to have one set of real memories to be able to handle the welling up of the archetypes—'

'*Flagstaff!* Now hear me. I'll be passing out of radio range in five minutes. This positively isn't the time to discuss evolution or whatever else you dreamt. Welcome back to the real world, you old Rip Van Winkle, but for Christ's sake clear your head of dreams. You can't dream you way into orbit—'

'But this isn't a dream. I'm experiencing it, dammit – in real time!' At last Silverman's erection limpened. (A waking-up erection. That was all.)

'—You'll have to help Wally all you can: if only by shutting up! Now, I want you both well rested. You're *both* to take sleeping pills tonight, understand?'

SEVENTEEN

As the far small Sun sank, a mauve sky deepened to un-compromising jet black, pincushioned by stars whose light hardly wavered. It was soon very dark and isolated. The sense of being locked up in a suitcase with a chattering maniac oppressed Oates so much that he switched on the outside floodlights and stared out at the meteorology kits he had deployed, wondering if he had anchored them firmly enough to withstand the coming hurricanes. He hadn't drilled too energetically, to avoid another accident. Still they ought to hold.

They had talked with Weaver twice more before sunset, when Weaver repeated his order to take sleeping tablets and signed off for the night.

Silverman merely laughed merrily and went on telling Wally about the things that Wally could not see. There was a geometrical structure outside space-time, which programmed space-time, he announced. He told Wally again how a man could think two things at once without jamming his mental switchboard by using a doubling of awareness, by duplicating the streams of consciousness: the same effect as in open-brain surgery, he re-emphasized, when the surgeon's probing reactivates old memories as solid as the sense of being on the operating table – as though that made his account less, instead of more, pathological. He could harness this consciously, he boasted; only instead of simply remembering he was using the memory stream as a way of commenting on the ongoing thoughts themselves; on their shapes, their geometries. (He spoke half to Wally and half into the tape recorder, erasing a long-play cassette of Wally's descriptions of the desert; but Wally was past caring.)

The act of grasping prey in space (he dictated, by way of Wally's ears, into the machine), the acts of emitting, cutting, crossing, fastening, rejecting, electing, stirring, sending, giving, but most of all *capturing*: these were the basic mechanical shapes of thought. All these he could see in overlay: in a hyped-up movie by Piet Mondrian depth-imposed on the representative art of the real world.

Art? Human imagination? Why, that existed at root because all life was predatory in one way or another. A predator had to think itself into the form of the prey to be caught – whether this be a rabbit or an apple. A predator had to become the thing it pursued before it could catch it bodily. *Ego*, the sense of self, was born when the hunter suddenly expelled his image of the prey, in a mental flip, to capture it solidly *out there* and feed. In this sudden discharge, the *Cognito* – the 'I think' of life – was born *orgasmically*. For what was an orgasm but the sudden expulsion of genetic forms from the self? He was still telling Wally Oates all this, obsessively, the best part of an hour later.

'Gene,' sighed Oates at last, 'why should something Martian affect a human being in this way? Have you stopped to ask yourself that?'

Silverman switched off the recorder. Obviously he hadn't asked himself.

'Now look, you've been affected by some Martian substance. Bug, virus or whatever it is. But it has to have some function *on Mars*, damn it! Okay, so it's changed your way of seeing things. Ditto for that Inca in the Andes. You two see the world in a different way since it infiltrated you—'

'I wouldn't use that word,' smirked Silverman. 'This isn't anything malign. I'm not taken over by some mind parasite. I'd know it if I was.'

'Of course, Gene.'

'This is something that's all programmed into Man. Dormant. Latent. Waiting for the trigger, the catalyst. There must have been eruptions of this in human history already. Premature ones. Single remarkable individuals here and there, labelled visionaries or mystics. The potential's probably been saturating us since the dawn of civilization. Look at Egyptian mummies. Mistaken homage to the future of Man based on a few rare incidents that did take place? Why not? We've misunderstood Evolution.' His hand slipped back to the recorder, switching on again. 'Mutations aren't random apart from deformities and malfunctions. In the long run life has its own "subconscious" yearnings. It has metabolic desires pushing it in certain directions. Genetic "errors" aren't mistakes any more than slips of the tongue are! They're what we're really trying to say, deep down!'

The floodlit shadow of the atmosphere analyser upon dormant barren Mars resembled a praying mantis ready to leap: sag-belly and folded saw-blade arms ...

'What's more, evolution *can* move in leaps and bounds. Changes don't need to take a million years. Once the genetic pool's supersaturated with certain "functional" errors – then, flip! They all cohere. They express themselves. A new level of creature can be born.'

'Drek. Apes didn't turn into people overnight.'

'Oh, and how do you think an ape ever gave birth to a baby with a humanoid brain? It would have stuck in the pelvis. Apeman had to be saturated with a hundred recessive gene-changes in a hundred different locations. Changes for skull size, pelvis size, hormone balance, the whole works – till flip! The New. We're ready for the New now, Wally. The human race is. This really dwarfs the mechanical splitting of the atom into insignificance – because it will show us *why* atoms are, and how. Why life is, and how. What thought itself is! All the underlying geometries.'

Oates yawned, exhausted by the other man's constant prattle, and in a state of shock from it. He'd have to dope up with amphetamines tomorrow and loathed the idea because of the depression which would hit him afterwards. He looked away from Silverman at black Mars as long as possible, excluding the other man from his visual space to keep his stress level down – even if he couldn't exclude the noise.

The cassette was full; it clicked itself off automatically.

'Will you answer one simple idiot's question? Whatever put you in that coma and hyped you up, what the hell *is its role on Mars*? Why's it here in the soil at all, eh? If you can't answer that, please shut up, because you're not thinking straight.'

'Okay, we'd been bagging soil samples. Did you bring them back? Are they still here?'

'Sure. Sealed and stowed away. Houston told me to get outside and do some work while you were sick.' He yawned again helplessly, his body trying to put him to sleep to save him from Silverman's infestation of him. Silverman patted him on the shoulder, breathing in his ear. Oates expected him to start singing a cosmic aria any moment.

'Big day tomorrow! Time to dole out the sleeping pills, right, Wally?'

Oates was quite clear in his own mind that the barbiturates were for Silverman alone. Jim had just ordered them for both men to be tactful. However, Silverman now watched imp-ishly while Oates located the tube of pills. Ostentatiously Oates knocked out four into his hand, intending to palm two of them. Just so long as Gene took his! But Silverman made sure that Oates took his own two pills, standing over him aggressively till he saw him gulp them down. Did he think

168

they were poison?

Silverman apparently swallowed his pills too; then he lay down quickly on his bunk and doused all the lights.

'Sweet dreams,' he chuckled in the darkness.

As soon as the noise of Oates' breathing modulated to light snoring Silverman switched on a pencil torch and slipped from his bunk. Silently he undogged the storage bay and searched through the tagged bags of dirt.

A crazy risk. But he had to do it. This was more important than *Warming Pan*.

He watched geometries moving through the Universe underneath the fabric of the Universe: archetypal forms bringing a Universe into being, of such a type that it must tend to perceive itself, to establish the grounds of its own being. A Universe which must tend to generate life from non-life; thought from non-thought. Which must somehow think itself into being. Swept along exhilaratingly on this tide of creative forms, he moved towards something which, as yet, eluded him ...

Martian soil lost its effect on people after a while, apparently.

One man coming back from Mars with a relevation was a lunatic. Two men coming back from Mars of the same mind were radiantly sane.

He couldn't rely on the Inca, though he surged with love for him in his sudden alienness – for he was an alien, he was Future Man. Future Man is an alien. You don't need to go to Sirius to find an alien; the aliens are inside. That's no reason not to go to Sirius or anywhere else, though! Fuck the stay-at-home brigade, he thought.

He found the 'accident' bag, so tagged, and carried it to Oates' side. Then he tested a scalpel blade against his own skin; its touch brought a line of blood, with hardly any pain. He slit the bag.

Oates' limbs should be stiff after his week's work on Mars; his mind should have the memory of jabs of muscle pain. A dream would rationalize.

Slitting the sleeping sack, Silverman exposed a bare hairy

thigh. Smoothing the hairs, he dipped his scalpel into the bag of soil, then sliced along the skin.

Blood oozed and mingled with dirt. He sprinkled more dirt on the wound. Grunting in his sleep, Oates half-turned.

Silverman waited for five minutes, torch extinguished, before he switched it on again and made another gentle cut, on Oates' exposed buttocks ...

He was aware of a certain purely prankish element inside himself prompting him to play this very dangerous joke upon Wally Oates, as a devastating trick that would march all Wally's mental Go-stones right off the board into a game with a wholly new dimension added; for which Wally could only be duly grateful afterwards. Oates had the bouncy resilience to cope with the new increment of thought and vision – whereas Jim Weaver, locked in suburban religiosity as in a strait jacket, might well crack up. Yet the prankish, trickster streak was of far less consequence than the sheer pragmatic need for two separate individuals to bear witness to Man's own innate capacity for mental evolution of this order *independent* of Martian soil. Wally would understand the essentially *human* nature of the experience, once he woke up. It was independent of Mars, viruses, soil. Yet, without Mars, it could be limited to rare genetic eruptions for many years yet. A neolithic shaman here, an Egyptian pharaoh there, a pre-Pizarro Andean Indian or two. They were all contemporaries, evolutionarily. Humanity could hardly afford to wait another few thousand years for the full programme to express itself, in order to learn to think!

Still, people might say that instead of one sick, Mars-bugged individual they simply had two now ...

This must be guarded against – quite scientifically, above and beyond the ringing authenticity of Silverman's and Oates' reports. He must answer Wally's question of what exactly the soil substance did *on Mars*, so that he could show that the Martian stuff potentiated what already lay dormant in Mankind anyway, on account of the *structure* of its Martian role, which was to ... what? That, he must find out.

For this, he must stay here on the surface untimely long;

which also demanded that he infect Oates. No other way. The logic appeared impeccable. The trickster in him was amused at the double *coup*; the scientist enthralled; the visionary intoxicated.

By morning Wally Oates lay in a stiff coma, hardly breathing, limbs chilly and head burning. Silverman paid scant attention to the symptoms; the little he paid, only out of curiosity, not having been present at his own illness. When the radio beeped he switched on promptly.

'Gene here, Jim. Bad news. Wally's got it now. He split a bag of dirt and cut himself. He's out of action – in a coma. Just like me. Over.'

'You bastard!'

Silverman swivelled the TV camera he had set up to show Oates' bunk. Silverman himself had shaved, spruced up and trimmed his hair. He moved round the bunk, showing the band-aid he had pasted on Oates' thigh.

'Here's where he cut himself. He got worried about the weight distribution in the storage bay. He was fretting and it stopped him getting to sleep. But your pills must have made him woozy. Your sleeping pills, Jim. He tripped.'

'Why didn't you call me as soon as it happened?'

'What, wake you up in the middle of the night because he scratched himself? He went to sleep normally enough.'

'You did it. You're crazy.'

'Well, that'll make two of us insane when he wakes up, so don't expect a majority vote on sanity to go your way. Meanwhile I'll ignore the insults. But try not to leap to conclusions.'

'You have done it! *Why?* Today is supposed to be lift-off day. Don't you realize how near we are to the end of launch window for Earth?'

'Of course. Nine days. Wally will be in the coma for seven, same as me. Now you listen for a change, Jim. Wally was going to deploy *Warming Pan* but now you'll have to deploy it yourself or there won't be time. You're perfectly able to do it, as Klein kindly pointed out. You can deploy between now and our rendezvous with you. We'll be okay on the ground. The effects won't be rough immediately.'

'But I have to change orbits. I can't come back to this orbit to pick you up *and* launch for Earth too—'

'You have to move into a new orbit to launch for Earth. We can meet up. We have enough fuel on board. 59 percent left. Wally was quite miserly setting us down. There's no logic to say we *must* rendezvous before *Warming Pan* is deployed. Thermal storms generally start in the Noachis area then they spread westwards – slowly for the first few days. We're round the other side. There'll be plenty of warning. Earth can see if you can't. A storm's perfectly visible from home: a great bright streak—'

'That's normal weather, when the south pole melts.'

'Right. And we're starting a storm to blow back dust upon the north pole, remember – not equatorially! Sure, storms'll spread, but there's plenty of time to get clear.'

'Not if one starts right on top of you!'

'Can't start near the equator, Jim. I'm the expert.'

'But we'll waste fuel meeting up afterwards—'

'Not much.'

'Enough to stop us correcting our course en route for Earth. We'll have no fuel for tweaking up our trajectory. It's cutting it too fine.'

'So long as our exit trajectory's reasonably accurate. Houston have got six months to get a ship out to intercept us – refuel us, evacuate us, whatever costs less. No real problem. Just requires a rethink.'

'Quit fooling around. Tell me the truth for God's sake. What so you want to stay on the surface *for*?'

'Well now, Wally asked me that very interesting question before he had his unfortunate accident. We know now that this Martian dirt affects human beings. But what the devil does it affect on Mars? I intend running the experiments I ought to have been running but for illness. I'll simulate the conditions we expect after the climate changes – outside but under cover. That's the kind of information we really need to know if we're ever planning to live here.'

'I've got to talk to Houston . . . I'm passing out of range . . .'

'Get them to check the change of plan on their computers. Tell them our fuel position. They'll confirm it's okay if you can't make a simple change of plan yourself.'

When Weaver called again Silverman was already suited up outside *Flagstaff* assembling his kit for a Martian greenhouse.

It took shape before his eyes before he even started: a ghost around which he had to reorganize the outer world, to bring it into harmony with his vision. With spars, hoops, acrylic sheeting and thin-gauge steel cannibalized from *Flagstaff* without harming its basic minimum integrity as a craft, he traced over the mental ghost.

It took the form of a Fuller dome: a geodesic tensegrity sphere of apparently loose spars pulling one against another by a system of cords, its flimsy appearance belying its strength. The velcro-sealed airlock pouch from one of the expedition's unused Martian tents would let him crawl in and out without much loss of pressure; the pouch could not resist vacuum, but there were six millibars of carbon dioxide outside it, a sufficient atmosphere. The dome would be one-third buried in the Martian soil and one-third full of Martian soil.

It was light work. The blueprint hung before his eyes. He whistled as he traced over it.

A voice interrupted.

'Gene? Gene—?

'I've talked to Houston. Naturally they're very distressed about Wally. But they're giving your plan a run through the computers.'

'Of course they are. There's always an economical way to do things.' Silverman carried on building up his vision.

'What are you doing? Don't just shut up, Gene, it's lonely up here. You were chattering away before. Damn it, I'm concerned. I'm sorry I said those things to you—'

'Think nothing of it. I'm building a Martian greenhouse. A Fuller dome. Nature's very economical, you know. It always packs shapes in the most economical way like a Fuller dome. Take the human mouth. It eats, it breathes, it speaks. So many different roles all converging and wrapping around each other, making Humanity possible. Then there's this Martian Activator substance – that's what I'm naming it. It pulls things together in the human brain. Quite a necessary substance for us! The human race settling in this environment is bound to change on account of the Activator. Of course, it has to happen on Earth, sooner or later. We're primed for it. But what does the Activator activate on Mars? As Wally said, it must do something locally.'

'Suppose this Activator does activate something,' said Weaver cautiously. 'Leaving aside the tautology! They say one man's meat is another man's poison, don't they? They're damned right. Alkaloids play a biological role in plants back home. All they really do to people is drive them out of their minds. Interfere with the brain transmitters, right? But people think they're having revelations when they dope themselves up. Ultimate reality. All that. So they talk as though the junk's been put in the plants specially for *us* to find – so we can see God. Whereas the stuff just poisons us, in a sly convincing way. Like alcohol or tobacco, for that matter. God didn't put them on Earth particularly so we could get drunk and smoke! We're the dopes—'

Silverman whistled as Weaver faded out of range.

EIGHTEEN

Silverman's dome was complete now: pressurized with a presumed post-glacial Martian atmosphere, mainly carbon dioxide with modest oxygen, generous nitrogen and water vapour. Inside was pleasantly warm, though Silverman could only tell so from the thermometer. He could have survived inside his dome by now, with an oxygen mask and perhaps some extra heating. But he kept his helmet on to avoid contaminating the experiment. He had built a plastic pool in one corner, and splashed water out of it now and then on to the ever-thirsty soil. Hunting on hands and knees, he stared at the ground through a magnifying glass, occasionally scooping soil on to a slide to examine under a microscope.

Gritty like dog turd, and much the same colour.

'*Frontiersman* to *Flagstaff*. I jettisoned Met Satellite One in this present orbit to double as a radio relay. Houston will watch the weather via it. And Mount Palomar ... It's queer, Charles Klein almost seems to condone your staying down there now, *even at risk,* to work on the soil. I thought they'd just bluntly order you up. I don't understand it ... Well, I'm going to shift orbits in fifteen minutes. It'll be another two to three hours before I start deploying *Warming Pan.* How's Wally?'

'Fine. No change.'

'That's fine?'

'It means he's going through the process as per plan.'

'What plan? What process?' Weaver sighed.

'The genetic plan – for bringing the archetypes up from the pool into consciousness, of course! How's our Inca? Any news?'

'None that I've heard.'

'Good for him! And a steady hand to you too. Warm Mars well for me.'

'You'll be ready to lift off if we see storms?'

'Don't worry, I'll be out of my greenhouse in no time at all.'

'I really hope you mean it.'

Stooping to the soil, Silverman tongued his radio off to concentrate in silence.

Inside this little bubble the climate was clement: Mars as it had been twelve thousand years before ...

He remembered someone asking about Martian fleas and caterpillars in the Fuller Concert Dome years ago. What type of complex life could adapt to a life cycle of airless, waterless winters twenty thousand years long? He had poured scorn on the notion.

Yet something complex had adapted – something which

thrived all over Mars then switched itself off, dismantled itself and disappeared. Something more complex than the bacteria currently multiplying in the dirt.

While the Sun was sinking and the sky darkening to black chocolate, he held his torch beam aslant across the dampened and aerated soil. Through the magnifying glass he thought he saw a faint stippling of darker dots. But his eyes ached – and his body too, from kneeling motionless so long. Perhaps they were just shadows of larger bits of grit. The mind sought patterns; it linked up the random dots of craters on Mars and named them canals ...

Unclenching his body, he squirmed out of the dome and hobbled back to the ampler interior of *Flagstaff*.

While he ate, alongside comatose Oates, Weaver's voice talked to Houston and to the whole Earth telling how he had successfully deployed Humanity's *Warming Pan*; finally Silverman cut the exuberant voice off.

He was remembering some verse by the poet Yeats which Renata had enthused about when he met her; a verse that seemed to describe perfectly her untouchable tactiles, those ghost bodies yearning from grotesquerie towards ideal perfection ... Bodies whose perfection only existed in the mind, and had to die out of sight. The poem seemed devastatingly appropriate now, on Mars. Its mummy-cloth. Its floating images. Its Hades' bobbin: the netherworld, the understructure of space-time unwinding threads that wove towards ... the superhuman. Silverman repeated the poem to himself meditating about it. Death-in-life, and life-in-death ... Yeats was quoting a saying of Heraclitus, two and a half thousand years old: to the effect that Men and Gods die each other's life, and live each other's death. That same Greek philosopher, innocent of the solid mechanical bodies of Euclidean space which stamped out solid mechanical Western Science, had thought that existence unwound from a Hades' bobbin – an underworldly *logos*. The Word. The Form that assures unity and stability for any object in the Universe. Silverman watched geometric forms moving through the Universe, attracting it into Being by their movement. They

176

flowed, but never really solidified. All was in slow motion, nothing truly held still. A struggle of forms forever went on: attracting, capturing, grasping, cleaving, emitting ... Renata's sculptural forms – elbowing, thrusting and inter-penetrating one another to occupy a space and achieve some temporary structural stability – were intuitively right. Exactly right.

> 'They told me, Heraclitus,
> they told me you were dead,
> they gave me bitter news to hear
> and bitter tears to shed—'

he murmured.

All the scientists had told him that. All the Euclidean matter-manipulators said so. But they lied. Heraclitus wasn't dead. The ancient Greek was right in his great intuitions about the nature of the Universe. Everything flows ... His own mistake was to suppose that Martian life must needs be as fixed and permanent as Earth life to survive through the twenty-thousand-year winter.

As he drifted off to sleep, he understood at last what he should see next day, in the dome ...

'Main storm's blowing up nicely, but there's one round Alba Patera too,' Weaver's voice warned.

'That's a long way north.' Silverman slid through the pocket airlock.

'But the temperature difference is showing already. There's sign of another hurricane forming at latitude 60 north, longitude 240.'

'Way round the other side.' He velcroed the bubble shut behind him and was wrapped in birth-caul like a new-born calf.

'There's already a lot of dust injected into the atmosphere south of the cap. The storms will grow—'

'In a day or so.' Silverman clove the bubble and knelt to see the soil through his lens.

Yes.

Tiny dots, evenly spaced and as yet invisible to the naked eye, stippled it.

'But this isn't a slow spring Sun-thaw. It's sudden concentrated heat. Think of a lens focusing the Sun's rays on a sheet of paper. It suddenly flares up.'

Silverman considered his magnifying glass. However, it couldn't do that kind of harm. No, it wouldn't burn his experiment up. Relaxing as well as he could, he watched the dots; saw them growing, joining, patterning themselves out rapidly in a ghostly grid superimposed on the reality. He was back in college again, in the biology laboratory, watching a colony of social amoebas.

'I see the pattern, Jim.'

'So do I, a hurricane pattern.'

'No, not that—'

At first the micro-organisms on the agar dish were spread out evenly, feeding on bacteria, looking like a negative photograph of faint stars in some undistinguished sector of the Galaxy: with no discernible constellations, no special pattern legible in the stippling of specks. Then, as food grew scarcer they began streaming together. Half-a-dozen cells selected themselves as founders, and drew these streams towards them. They became first magnitude stars, black giants, splotches. More and more social cells streamed in to the central mass till the mass became a crawling, migrating slug thousands of times larger than the founder cell. How did a cell ever 'choose' to become a founder? Initially, it was the same as the rest. Tiny. Indistinguishable. Identical.

Yet it did. It formed this long thin worm, this *grex*, as the biologists called it, which crawled off across the micro-world.

And after crawling for a while, this grex rose up in the air. Stiffening itself with cellulose fibres, it formed a tall thin tower with a sphere-head balanced on the top. A fruiting body. In this tower every cell now knew its special place. Each cell became a specialist in place, as the overall geometry of the creature gave its separate individuals, now mere units, a role and a function in a more complex body ...

'So I want you ready for lift-off by this evening.'

'They'll be aggregating by this evening. Clumping and

crawling about. I don't think that'll be the end of it by any means ... Maybe my little greenhouse is too small, but out in the open desert when it rains and there's air – I wonder. Superclumps? Clumps of superclumps? Ever more complex structures!'

'What are you talking about?'

'The Martian pattern has to be the social amoeba, Jim. The slime mould. It's quite untypical on Earth. Even so, it does occur in miniature in this one species. Here, it could be typical on the large scale. How else can you break down a complex beast and store its building blocks in spore form for twenty thousand years? The Activator substance guarantees they'll clump and repattern themselves into more complex life, which in turn excretes the chemical.'

'*Met One*'s passing out of range ...'

'The Activator is a biochemical trigger for organization. That's how it repatterned me. It's the perfect patterning catalyst – wherever there's potential for higher order structures. We must have that potential in the wiring of our own brains, handed down genetically. Building up through the centuries ...That's the only explanation.'

In the actual Martian dirt, underlying his ghost vision, he watched the first irregularly spaced black spots forming collection points. Streaming was starting already. Miniature, microscopic streaming ...

A breeze sprang up from the east by the evening. Content with his day's observations, Silverman promised to lift off the next morning and updated the computer.

He had seen the tiny clumps on his greenhouse floor pull together – quite visible now to the naked eye. They must have eaten most of the available bacteria. Presumably the bacteria would replenish their stocks while the predators were otherwise engaged. On the terrestrial model, the clumps should then have built towers, fruited and perished, commencing the cycle over again with new spores. To his delight this did not happen. There was no fruiting and no collapse ... Instead, the grexes crawled towards one another, conglomerating into double grexes half the width of a fingernail.

Those grexes which failed to conglomerate in time soon became food for the larger grexes.

On the terrestrial model, recalled Silverman, a chemical called Acrasin triggered the crawling together; while an inhibitory gas kept the fruiting bodies separate once formed. Here, some similar inhibitory factor must keep the newly-formed scavenging double grexes distinct from their fellows while the numerous single grexes were being scavenged ...

After the scavenging, the Attractor substance operated again; well-nourished double grexes began to stream in turn towards a new founder.

They clumped; and fused with it.

But they (or rather *it*) did nothing.

It squatted there like an amputated finger joint, apparently paralysed.

Simply not enough double grexes in his greenhouse for the next stage! Thus the abortive superclump stagnated on the soil.

'No need to stay down here any longer, Jim,' he radioed cheerfully. 'I've found out as much as I can. Of course it's still only guesswork as to how large or complex this sort of life can grow. The really neat trick is the way the grexes which don't grow big enough become food for those that do. As soon as the majority of minigrexes are used up, feeding stops and aggregation restarts. After which you have a food supply of proportionately larger supergrexes which didn't quite make it. A whole hierarchy of thresholds is built into the system, but it's a beautifully neat one at heart. And complexity increases as the ladder is climbed.'

'The 64 dollar question being where the ladder stops—'

'How soon mind and consciousness set in.'

'You're not serious.'

'Why not? How sophisticated a being is the system aiming for? Considering the effect of the Activator catalyst on the human brain I'd say it could be quite a complex thinking creature.'

'An intelligent one? As intelligent as a chicken, or what?'

'How do I know? It's the perfect adaption to this oscillating climate. Complete basic simplicity and standardization, coupled with a programmed drive towards complexity.'

'So this is the process I've started up with *Warming Pan*? Martians? They're going to be very ... aggressive, aren't they? I mean ... this constant cannibalism.'

'Not necessarily. I wouldn't call it cannibalism. Right now it's no more of an aggressive process than the human foetus building itself up from a single cell. No less an aggressive process either! A lot of incorporation of other living matter has gone into your own biological history, Jim, before consciousness set in. Heraclitus once said that "War is universal; and everything comes into existence by strife." But that doesn't make you personally a savage. That isn't what Heraclitus meant.'

'Who? Frankly I don't like the sound of it. It's too ... violent. Humans don't eat the immature members of the species.'

'Ah yes, but the grexes that lose the race aren't immature members. They're not babies who never got a chance. They're just what bricks are to a house. They don't have any meaning in isolation, outside the higher system.'

'You're reading an awful lot into a blob of reinforced slime the size of your fingernail. Why should it become any higher?'

'Because I see the pattern. Right before my eyes. The geometry of it. I've been pulled over a sort of grex-threshold myself.'

Outside in the pitchy night the breeze strengthened silently while the stars grew dimmer from lightweight dust particles diffusing throughout the upper atmosphere. Dust on the sunlit side of the world cycloned high into the thin air soaking up the Sun's rays, thus heating the air to feed the mechanism of the hurricane: which swirled more dust aloft, heating and accelerating winds still further ...

A tearing thud tipped Silverman out of sleep.

The wind was ripping a hundred linen sheets in half outside, however the thudding was *Flagstaff* itself, rising and thumping back again like a lino carpet undercut by gusts.

Quickly he floodlit the night; and saw a desert rushing through the darkness, bringing thicker darkness with it. The rising storm was scudding under the cone of *Flagstaff* between the landing legs and engine nozzle, picking the module up and setting it down again in a slow tapping pulse, measuring the heartbeat of the storm. His tiny geodesic dome, one-third anchored in the Martian soil, looked blessedly integral by comparison.

The radio howled at him. If there was any voice there, it was drowned.

Paperboard Fuller domes built by the Peace Corps had gone through hurricanes in Puerto Rico; and the Defence Department's early warning radomes stood up to the full violence of Arctic winter after Arctic winter ...

'My God, I'm sorry, Wally,' he avowed, and began dressing Oates, forcing the stiffened limbs into the Mars suit, a troublesome task even when the suit has zippers all the way down body, arms and legs.

NINETEEN

Aracayo Plaza was crowded with miners, lacking a mine. A crippled woman presided from a chair set on the rubble of a wrecked wall. It was time for the fiesta of revenge.

A residue of some forty Government soldiers commanded by Colonel Vasco Pomona Garcia maintained a discreet presence; yet there was little that they could do to pull the sting from the revenge. These were their People again; they had made promises. Amongst which were a new rich vein of tin in another mountainside not too distant; relocation grants; aid and amnesty. Finally, revenge against the upstart Inca who had led the miners astray, wrecked their livelihood, murdered their finest Union leader.

The town had been lightly bombarded in the initial confrontation with Pomona's troops, before the rebellious miners saw sense; now it blended with the general wreckage of the mountainside even more. Craters and mounds of tailings had moved into and through the dwelling places. A mauled town needed to strike back. At whom else, but at the Inca?'

Thank God that woman had still been alive inside the mine, mused Pomona. Her survival made things so much easier. A creature of rage and strength, her finger now stabbed the sky, resurrecting her husband's leadership.

La Paz wanted the Inca dead too. Though not directly at Government hands; at the hands of an enraged populace, convened in a People's Court ...

The majority of Pomona's troops were still busy pacifying San Rafael and a dozen outlying *campesino* villages; he should really be with them, re-establishing sound government.

He dared not leave the Inca and his Queen.

Or they would start torturing them. (This undoubted fact provided an excellent excuse for Pomona to stay in Aracayo personally; an excuse which his subordinates had readily swallowed.)

How he despised them: peasants and miners alike! Their sloth and violence appalled him. Yet how well he hid his fear and disgust.

Pomona wore a black bushy beard in wry condescension to revolutionary hirsutism. Equally, it was a defiant sign of his European heritage in this beardless Indian land. A shaven upper lip emphasized the lugubriousness of a large sallow oval face: the face of someone who had emerged from mental encapsulation in the bourgeoisie and could not afford to laugh a hearty revolutionary laugh lest it seem a sneer. The face of a prisoner of conscience, though the conscience that he was prisoner of was someone else's conscience in another land, another America, North not South. For the Sleeper had finally been awakened: by the simple word BOLSHOY. At long last he could leave and be well rewarded, safe from the madness of the People.

So long as he brought an Inca out with him. One of those whose brains had gone sick.

But it was taking so long! By now it was well over a week since the Inca and his Queen were brought to this dismal bombarded place. If his own men guarded the two of them in improvised cells, equally the armed miners guarded *his* men, to see that promises were kept and People's Justice done. That crippled woman's friends had been out hunting in the mountains for the fate she decreed for him. Pomona still didn't know what it was.

'You'll find out on Fiesta Day,' the woman had told him. 'Fiesta of Liberation, right? We need a fiesta, don't we, to thank you all properly!'

'He mustn't die dirtily,' Pomona had insisted – emphasizing his death as much as the cleanliness of it. She should understand that the one depended on the other.

The courier had only told him to rescue an Inca, not specifying man or woman, so it could as easily be the woman Angelina that he saved. While they were busy killing her man. Especially then. It would make her trust him, co-operate in her own kidnapping.

His soldiers were bringing Julio Capac out into the square now, as instructed, and Angelina too, whom they marched over to Pomona, sitting there in his jeep. Pomona's nursemaid had babbled Aymara at him in the cradle. Angelina Sonco could speak enough Aymara to follow him speaking it.

That first night spent in her barracks cell, she had stunk to high heaven! She'd smeared herself with her own excrement to stop anyone from raping her. She was carrying a child. A baby Inca.

So much the better. A political heir – two Incas in one!

Overcoming his disgust, he'd talked to her, explaining how his soldiers had orders to guard her against precisely this sort of outrage. Obviously this was in the Indian character. He recalled a particularly insanitary episode some time during the Conquest when a captured Inca princess resorted to the same expedient over and over again. A sense of heritage, pedigree, history came to his rescue and deodorized her behaviour somewhat. He finally persuaded her upon his word of honour that dirtying herself was unnecessary. So she already trusted him, a little.

'They're going to kill him,' he confided from the driving seat. 'Because he killed that cripple's husband. It will all be legal. This is a properly constituted People's Court. Nothing I can do about it.'

'Nothing – with all these soldiers?'

'People's soldiers. They'll get around to you too. At least I can save you from that. I already stopped anyone from assaulting you, didn't I? I gave my word of honour and I kept it.'

'I suppose you did.'

'Well, I promise to get you away from here. When the moment comes.'

'Moment? What are they going to do?'

'I don't know, honestly I don't.'

At least no makeshift crosses were erected on their slagheaps; nor any in evidence for the Inca to drag uphill with a crown of barbed wire to some miners' Calvary. Even if the Inca called himself a God it wasn't that.

'They waited a week. I don't know why. I give you my word.'

She watched a lying face pretending to be what it was not. Master pretending to be Servant. Yet he seemed to be telling the truth about this. For some reason he desperately wanted to save her.

The trial lasted a mere twenty minutes, during which the crippled woman harangued Julio Capac in jargonized automatic Spanish accusing him of murder, sabotage, counter-revolution, blasphemy.

Blasphemy? Pomona wondered. What a strange revolutionary accusation. Perhaps they simply hated the idea that anybody should rise above other men, whether God or Aristocrat. A witness testified that Julio Capac personally killed the union leader in cold blood, then ordered the firing of anti-tank rockets into the mine, where people were. The Inca was officially sentenced to death.

Then pitch-torches blazed around the plaza, sending

shadows leaping and cavorting in a *diablada*. Three miners wearing gloves and goggles carried out a large packing case and set it in a clear space in the middle of the crowd, then tore the lid off. A great wing unfurled and beat against their faces. Another wing unfurled, and they staggered about, padded, goggled and helmeted as they were, barely restraining the condor. Two miners rushed Julio beneath the bird, tore his poncho off, tied his wrists with ropes to outspread wings. They fastened trailing ropes to his ankles; on the end of each a stick of dynamite with a curling fuse cord. Then they pushed him free, in an arena of people.

As the bird tried to beat aloft, wrenching Julio's arms up and down in a parody of flight, he staggered to his feet. Scaly claws raked his spine, and he ducked his head down as the bird's red raw head reared from his shoulders. Briefly Julio seemed to wear the bird's living head as his own, before its beak descended on his neck.

It was a huge bird. The hugest. *Mallku*. It had taken seven days to snare this one, with nets and llama entrails.

Julio ran about for a while as senseless as any goaded bull while his persecutors jeered and pushed flaming torches at him and the terrified bird. Blood ran from his neck and rake-marks down his spine. The two ankle ropes zigzagged their unlit dynamite behind him like snakes with fangs planted in his heels.

But then, wonderfully, he stood still. He raised his head and looked round coolly. The panic discord between Man and Bird calmed in a pause of clarity. Bird and Man surveyed their mutual enemies. The condor's head rested along the crown of Julio's black hair as though indeed belonging there.

A second head. A second mind.

Then Julio Capac screamed a song at them all, turning slowly, his human eyes beady bright in the torchlight, the condor's eyes glittering.

> *'Condor of the heights!*
> Mallku *condor,*
> *Only carry me to your heights!'*

he sang
186

> *'Beat wings for me,*
> *Only let me be Bird!*
>
> *'Tear my carrion*
> *For your meal,*
> *Only bear me away!*
> *'Wind-quick,*
> *Fire-fierce,*
> Huayra-hina,
> Nina-hina,
> *Eat my flesh*
> *To feed your wings!'*

Undulatingly he began to beat his arms.

> *'Beat wings,*
> *Leap up,*
> Wat'akk!'

he cried.

> *'Leap!'*

Arms and wings beat in unison. Bird muscles and man muscles strained to the same task of escape. The bird's red head lay along his head. And he sprang.

He rose in the air. A flying man. Creature of feathered arms.

The wind of wings whipped the people's torchlight into their faces.

This was the greatest *mallku condor*; Julio a small light-weight man. It could bear him – just. For a while. If Man and Bird both flapped its wings perfectly.

'Angelina,' urged Pomona, 'climb in now.' Entranced, she obeyed. Julio had become a God, indeed! Pomona's hand closed on the ignition.

Then the cripple cried out from her rubble throne, breaking the mesmerism which Julio's flight had brought upon the crowd; she signalled at the strings still hanging down, dangling their fuses. And men and women danced out with their blazing torches, leaped to be the first to light a fuse. Starting the engine, Pomona signed discreetly to his men to clear a way to the rear.

But Julio was too high above them now. Seven metres. Eight metres. Rising level with the barrack roofs. Were either of the fuses lit? Nobody could see. Firelight splashed about the square. Those could as easily be stars up there as sputtering fuse-braids. Still gazing upwards, willing the blast upon their heads, the crowd shrank back to the walls.

And still Julio Capac escaped . . . Surely a man could not fly a bird so long, however superhuman his fear of death made him! His heart must burst – and his shoulders be torn, dragging the bird back down. As Pomona drove away Angelina's last sight of Julio was a dark flapping shape in the sky.

The plaza sky flashed bright and boomed with thunder.

TUNRÚN, TUNRÚN!

And Pomona put his foot down.

Then for a long time, there was only the empty plain: silent lawns of *ichu*, bare soil, pebbles and beaten dirt sparkling with reflected starlight.

Angelina sat numbly for an hour, two hours, letting Pomona drive her away from the scene of Julio's martyrdom towards wherever he chose, which seemed to be: towards nowhere, towards the middle of emptiness. The vision of Julio taking flight, only to explode, recurred vividly in afterimage after after-image, alternating with her own earlier vision of the human being in the sky riding on a condor's back, raw nerves riding a bird vehicle whose wingbeats rewove those nerves into new patterns. Julio had tried to fly the condor, physically; of course he failed. Because it was too late, yet was his only way out of the trap he had built round himself with his dreams of conquest and glory. Power was the trap. He was dead because he was only an ignorant man, flooded with sudden understanding. He believed that all his ignorance was washed away; instead it formed the cornerstone of his understanding. God *is* born out of Man, thought Angelina, yet Man's ignorance still invades God; because memory is the only language which the new understanding can use – the only way that life can send a message to itself about itself. Memory is the language of life, just as the endless moment of present experience is its breath ...

Finally she roused herself, dimming the alternating pictures and turning her attention to Pomona.

'You've fled from your own soldiers, Colonel. Where are we two going, alone?'

'Nowhere in this wretched country, I promise you.' Momentarily his lugubrious face achieved a smile.

'To Chile?'

'Only for a day or two. I'm afraid I can't tell you your final destination. But it will be far away, and very safe. You shall have your Inca baby in the greatest security. He'll be well cherished; you too.'

'He or she.'

'That's true!' Pomona laughed. Switching on the jeep radio, he spoke into it rapidly in Spanish telling their position in terms of so many kilometres due west of Aracayo. The radio acknowledged him curtly.

'We're days and days late,' he mused, 'but they'll still meet us. They keep their promises. They'll fly us to safety, freedom, happiness—' He hesitated; if he had made them sound like eloping lovers, his voice still told her that they weren't both going to share these three promised gifts. Of the three, she was only going to know the first, conceivably (which was entirely up to herself) the third too.

The Moon had not risen yet. When it did, it would only be as a thin sickle moon. As Pomona drove he checked his direction by the stars, by the girdle of the Milky Way.

'Odd,' he remarked, pointing ahead at the curve of the world where night and light met the ground. A planet had risen, disc perceptible, brightness unwavering. Not a star. 'Mars. It must be Mars. Because there's Venus over there, much brighter. And Jupiter too. But Mars is a red world ... I wouldn't say that world was really red, would you? Maybe there's a cloud in the way.'

'There's no cloud.'

She watched the strange planet rising for a while; till they arrived at a perfectly straight roadway cutting from north to south, quite bare in both directions, its surface, unlike any other wilderness roads, thinly metalled. Though the metal had cracked and cratered it still provided quite a firm smooth surface, and shone with brighter star-sheen than the plain.

'Pan-American Highway,' Pomona commented, swinging the jeep on to it and braking, pointing north. 'Aid for development. Years ago. Before the Revolution.' He stared behind the jeep, southwards towards the horizon. When the next terse radio message came, without ceasing staring south he groped for the light switch and began rhythmically flicking their main beams on and off. Finally he left them switched on, illuminating the road.

Angelina recognized the silhouette of the long-winged jet as it flew in darkly along the line of the road from the south. It passed barely a hundred metres over their heads, descending on to the northward cone of light. Pomona restarted the engine and drove after the braking jet, to abandon the jeep behind it with its lights full on, to brighten their take-off.

TWENTY

Wally Oates swam up through the chlorinated Hickory Lake. And awoke. An indeterminate time had passed. Cool brown dirt pressed his face. Weak sunlight and bars of shadows dappled the dirt. He breathed stale dizzy air.

He lay inside the Dark Room, his body no heavier than a boy's; however the room was bright and he could see all round.

Oxygen tanks lay on the soil. Packets of food concentrates. A plastic jerrican. Spars and struts, pulling and pushing against each other, held a small geodesic dome together around him. The sky above looked strangely dark blue, with grey wraiths of cloud boiling about in an upper atmosphere in turmoil. Yet what was strange about blue sky, however dark the blue? It was strange that it was any shade of blue at all . . .

Red rains crossed the landscape . . . or rusty mists . . . dust devils, hard to see . . .

A Sun only half its proper size. Yet its reflections shone a few small silver pools, that were wrong too.

I'm on Mars. After the thaw.

The scene rippled, and he saw a flag planted in the desert beside the burnished cone of a landing module called *Flagstaff*. The desert was unreal. The flag wasn't really there; nor *Flagstaff* either. Two scenes superimposed, one wet, one dry, with the contours of the terrain melding them together. The effect was stereoscopic: in time rather than in space. He'd been abandoned: in a pocket of past or future Martian time! The present had vanished along with his spacecraft and his friend . . .

Wedged between oxygen tanks and food packs, he noticed a tape recorder and squirmed numbly towards it. A cassette was already in it. He switched it on.

A thin banshee wail rose and fell. An anxious voice tried to talk it down.

'Gene here, Wally. You've just woken up from your Inca trance. I'm afraid I was responsible. You'll notice some cuts on your thighs and backside. I rubbed some soil in. Initiation rite! Shall I say sorry? Do you really want me to say sorry now?'

But Oates was hardly listening.

A young girl stood in the illuminated Dark Room, her hair jet black and long; her skin black too, her face oriental. A split-skirt *cheongsam* printed with yellow roses clung wetly to her childish limbs. She smiled wistfully at him but she said nothing. Instead, she began to dance some Korean folk dance.

'—So the hurricane is on us and I can't lift off. I don't know if *Flagstaff* will pull through in one piece. It isn't anchored down and it's already banging about. I rigged my Martian greenhouse as a survival hut for one man. Appearances notwithstanding it's the better structure to be in in a storm. Still, if you are hearing me, you'll know all about *appearances* by now?'

She was trying to tell him things by the movements of her body. He relaxed and studied her gesture-talk. The meaning was in the shape alone: the way it hung together. Her wordlessness evoked a sort of sexlessness. Curious, since hitherto he'd associated the wordless domain with sex. Sighs, bird-like cries – but always verbal darkness. Words were missing – firm graspable bodies of things. But her body was not to be grasped in lieu of them. Her body was the expression of itself alone, rather than a sexual focus for him. Rather than being a locus for inexpressible, alienated desires, it signified the shaping wholeness of itself, which every contour, step and gesture voiced. He saw the entirety of her, looped back through time from Los Angeles to a Korean childhood; and loved her fully. Yet his love for her wasn't exactly his acknowledgment of the integrity of that other person there – because, in fact, *she was himself.*

She was his own wholeness, separated from him.

She was the wholeness, and separatedness, of the Self. And it was he who thought her into being, over there. He shaped her – even as she stood free from him.

Her hands held the sand glass destined for her: both cones full of shining sand. The sand flowed continually through itself, from top to bottom and from bottom to top. Neither cone ever emptied. Both were always full, and the sand grains flowed through one another from glass cusp into glass cusp – cusps very like Milly-Kim's own hidden, water-moulded breasts. Thus the sand flowed within itself, never still, the pressing of sand down to the base permanently squeezing sand back into the top, while the sand squeezed to the top pressed the sand down from there.

Wally was one cusp of the sand glass; Milly-Kim the other. Between these two cusps his thoughts flowed ceaselessly, fleeing as they formed, forming as they fled.

Milly-Kim *was* Wally, though she couldn't say what she was thinking of him ... yet.

But she could show him that, in beautiful and loving gestures.

'—I know what the Martians must be, Wally. Maybe it takes years or decades of streaming and aggregating to grexes and supergrexes, to move all the way up the rungs of the ladder back to really complex beings. Everything has to be relearnt by them afresh, every Martian summer. Maybe this isn't too harsh, if the process leading up from simple to complex is present as their whole environment, their very way of life. If aggregating goes on all around them all the time, perpetually generating fresh individuals out of simpler units, which are also alternatively food. A magnificent morphogenetic landscape, this – right there in the outside world! The "aware" Martian at the end of this process, presuming there is one, is born out of countless shockwaves of life capturing itself and grasping itself – food on the one hand, hierarchy of form on the other!'

Milly-Kim faded back into twin Marses oscillating between death and life, airless desert and damp soil, black space and blue sky.

Oates turned the tap of the oxygen tank higher; and breathed clarity. How much oxygen was left? And how much in the Martian atmosphere? Could he concentrate it? A breathing mask? A CO_2 filter? Men would be back in a few years if *Warming Pan* went on working. They would have to be to service the *Pan* or the climate could collapse catastrophically again. All that investment lost!

'—Martian life must be a very Inca-like system, ironically – in the biological sense rather than the social. If my history serves me those Incas organized society in a pyramid style, politically. But they were really the same people at the bottom as well as at the top. Not so here! Micro-organisms at the base, intelligence at the peak! It will feel like a very strange society to us. Culture and intelligence perpetually emerging out of raw nature, all around. Maybe it'll feel like an evil one. I hope not. It's truer. Well, more naked—'

Food? A few weeks' supply.

Could he live off the land? Eating slugs for years, slugs that would be bound to make him retch if they were edible at all. *If* they had enough minerals and vitamins. *If* they weren't laced with poison. *If* his body could process them. Maybe he could fix up some equipment to process them. Prospects of survival ranged from the vile to the improbable. Still, he might as well start to colonize the planet, in anticipation . . .

Aching, he got up. Extra height let him see over a rim of land beyond which the future river lay with one or two rainfall pools already moistening it. Would a flash flood rage down from the highlands soon?

Flagstaff lay on its side in the river bed where it had finally rolled. An explosion in the engine or fuel tanks had torn the base apart. The ascent cabin where Gene had sheltered was split wide.

'—But we need them, Wally, I see the human race coming to Mars to be . . . baptized, in the soil. Good luck.'

Milly-Kim reappeared. And Wally Oates wept for his lost friend, and his found self.

TWENTY-ONE

There were no Grex generations to begin with. An amoeba which splits and splits again possesses an infinite time line so long as one survivor survives. So it was, in reverse, for the grex that fused with other grexes to form a supergrex, which paused and fed on subgrexes, incorporating them as food, before streaming towards other supergrexes, not to feed now but to fuse with them, and further specialize, sophisticate itself. To begin with there were no generations; but there were levels – each level divided from the one below by the abrupt, catastrophic flip from feeding to fusing.

Grex-levels: a grex-23 fuses with other grex-23s, and becomes a different kind of being, a grex-24. In the end, will there only be a small, highly dispersed band of supergrexes on the world? Which then, for lack of food, are at last forced to rise up in fruiting columns and cast their spores to the winds, starting the cycle all over again?

No. With increase in mass comes increased complexity. Out of cellular instinct comes motivation. Out of the upward switchback of feeding/fusion, incorporation/corporation, there dawns with the leap from one complexity level to the next grex awareness, intelligence held in tension between the poles of social streaming and of egoistic feeding. Social resonance of a different order becomes possible between the separate egos of supergrexes – distinct from simple chemical resonance leading to fusion, or the other resonance between food and feeder. These two forces now balance one another. Locked in an adulthood which will eventually culminate in death and dissolution, setting off this grex generation from subsequent generations, communication is now born ...

Excreta of spores from which new simple cells can grow are laid down all along in a grex's travels; cells feeding on bacteria, streaming to a grex, feeding and streaming from a grex-1 to a grex-2, upwards – too tiny, from the sporulating supergrex's point of view, to feed upon, large enough to climb the ladder, though, to become food for adults, till these adults reach their span of life and new generation adults at last succeed them. Though some second generation pre-adults achieve adulthood notwithstanding the predation. Thus generations both leap-frog one another and coincide in community ...

Grex-46 is a hollow, a basin wanting food.

Grex-46 hunts by scent, tastes the attractor wind and the soil slime-line of a Grex-45. Grex-46's locomotion is more sophisticated. Melded lower-grex cells have specialized to soft cellulose cartilage pre-limbs that thrust it through the damp alluvial dirt, contracting, stretching, pulsing.

Grex-46 holds a hollow, Grex-45 will fill it.

Overtaking Grex-45, it overwhelms the lesser worm; incorporates Grex-45 into its body. This fills the empty basin of its belly, cancelling the hollow. Grex-46 contained its prey-image of Grex-45 within itself until it ate – a memory of the several Grex-45s from which Grex-46 itself had conglomerated, melded, restructured itself.

So it sees its own earlier self-image, and captures it; eats it. The release of hunger-tension and the shock of annihilating its own false-image throws it into a new state of expectation where its own grex level is itself a hollow; which must be filled, not by food this time but by its own real-image, by Grex-46s that roam around it. Failing which, it must be food itself.

Predation yields to vulnerability; the anticipation of being prey.

Consequently it constitutes itself a collection point, a founder, and calls with its scents across the landscape to any other Grex-46s, at once to incorporate them and to be incorporated. It will be a prey; yet not prey. Itself and other grexes must mutually digest one another now in the fusing.

Other Grex-46s flow to it slowly throughout the warm night. When there are five Grex-46s clumping together, they inhibit the area around them; fusion begins.

They fold themselves; incorporate themselves. They leave behind the level of their being. *It* leaves *it* behind. Cells and organs melt and flow and respecialize, repattern.

In the morning, Grex-47 rises up towards the Sun in a squat tower-body, with a reorganized nervous system rising to a neutral dome with an optic strip. Sight overrides scent, and it sees the landscape of its own genetic history spread around it, flatly. Correspondence is perfect. Vulnerable lower-grexes are laid bare. Though it does not see itself anywhere – because itself is everywhere. The world is without real dimensions, yet. It extends nowhere, except back into itself. The outside space maps back into its own body. The hollows, basins, channels are all hollows, basins and channels within itself; processes of capturing, attracting, melding are its own process of organization. The Sun is merely a mode of light by which it sees. The Sun is its own organ of vision.

And then it sees the domed tower of another Grex-47. *Itself* – distanced from it!

196

Not itself! Another – in its own self-image!

It stands frozen in adulthood, alienated, realizing the existence of another being equal to it out there in the world. The World becomes Object and Subject. Itself – and the World.

And already the dawn of this consciousness of Self and Others is receding far within, becoming implicit. Flowing along on its single fused body-foot, now that there is a visual attractor to head towards, it slides towards the second Grex-47, discovering en route that locomotion changes the appearance of the world. It flows now, not to feed, nor to mix either, but to *send*: the image of events. (On the way, it shrinks down to feed on a minor grex, but then erects itself again; the memory of the other Grex-47 remains clear and imperative.)

Its optic strip distends, forming a lattice of receptive and emissive cells. Receptive cells receive the pattern of the world in honeycomb form; while emissive cells duplicate this pattern in honeycomb points of light, reprinting the world, reduplicating. Grex-47 tests out other patterns against the world while it flows and the world alters shape progressively.

Its light organ moves down slowly towards the other's head, sinking and growing dimmer. Perhaps that is not its own private organ.

Soon it displays the geometry of the other Grex-47, in a statement of identity, and describes the process of how it came to be Grex-47 itself, calling upon the forms it has embodied. But the other Grex-47 returns a strange pattern, with no genetic prototype. An architecture without innate significance. Twisting itself around, aware of subject and Object, Grex-47 looks for the origin of the other Grex-47's vision in the flatly rumpling otherness behind it.

It sees a four-ways forked column progressing towards these two Grexes by raising one horn off the earth, swinging it forward, planting it; raising, swinging and planting the second horn. Turn by turn.

By this means the jointed column progresses, growing larger, towering up. Its upper horns (which point downward) also swing to counterbalance it. But the tip of one upper horn splits into five pods, while the tip of the other folds up to grip a small weak light-organ. This light-organ blinks on and off.

It must only have this single cell to emit, and to receive. Meanwhile, the Grex's own former light-organ is sinking down into the darkness, being replaced by multitudes of little lights, above and all around, all weaker than the approaching light. They wink far more rapidly than the Column, light waxing and waning with no exact dark-gaps.

But the Column blinks long and short, in succession.

It comes closer, till almost *here*; and stands twice the height of Grex-47. Abruptly it sags and folds itself, sinking as though to feed, becoming the same height as Grex-47. Emitters on Grex-47's optic strip quickly compose the figures associated in its neutral bulb with Capture and Incorporation; while its scent buds emit an inhibitor chemical. Obeying the inhibitor, the folded Column does not proceed to eat the Grex or its companion. Its light-organ blinks *ON ... OFF* (for a long time); *ON ... ON ... OFF* (for another long time); *ON ... ON ... ON ... OFF ...* Grex-47 searches its hoard of forms.

And its emitters compose a simple triangle.

ON

ON   ON

ON   ON   ON

Slowly it deforms the sides of the triangle into curves, as though the triangle is drawn on a flattened sphere, discovering new shapes all the time. The trick amuses it, suggests developments, and it deforms the triangle still further till the apex meets the base line and two cones are wrenched apart. It plays with these forms, twisting and elaborating two cones side by side ...

Still on his knees, Wally Oates switched the flashlight off and contemplated the geometries of the Grex. Finally, he rose and trudged back towards Silverman's dome which was refurbished and mechanized now with improvised scrap from *Flagstaff*: air and energy systems, a food homogenizer-detoxifier rigged from the bio-assay kits.

He didn't know whether to bless or curse the Grex with

its blinking shapes. Bless – for this was company, of a sort; though what 'company' could you expect from a Being as land-scaped as the Grex: a being for whom awareness was primarily of morphogenetic forms present as its real environment, then only secondarily of the world that it mapped itself on to, the canvas beneath the paint?

Or curse: because their growth system, their means to-wards a mature organized Grex, which had so radically affected his thinking through chemical infection, was perhaps now demonstrably a matter of sheer physical organization against a hostile natural background – and this cast a great deal of doubt upon the ... inevitability versus the gratuitousness of his vision.

He wasn't afraid of hallucination: of confusing reality with the secondary 'pictures'; because there was control over these pictures. Unlike self-shaping dreams, they could be shaped and transformed within certain specific bounds which he was still discovering. Surely there was no danger there. But what did they really tell him about the world out there: the universe which Gene felt so confident they modelled, or repre-sented to him? If a model – the world understood in the human brain – only models itself on to another (memory) model in-side the *same thought system*, what then?

Milly-Kim walked with him as he made his way back to the dome; she walked unprotected against the thin carbon dioxide laden air; this time she spoke aloud.

She said, 'A Universe is stranger than your betrayer friend thought it was, at the end. It's all there is – including all the contradictions. Certainly humans will be affected in many dif-ferent ways if they come here. Connections will connect. But what will they connect? Only what is there already. You're probably dying, you know?'

'Yes, I know.' (Did he actually speak those words aloud? *Those* words?)

'You can't really feed on alien slugs no matter how well you rig biology kits.'

'People will come.'

'Will they really come, when Jim Weaver reports what hap-pened? All this way, to see if it happens again?'

'Some time they'll come. The Russians . . . Venus . . . It's inevitable.' (How far away the dome still seemed, as though the distance was growing greater, not less.) 'I wish I could touch you. I wish I could sleep with you tonight.'

'I sleep within you all the time. The miracle is that I ever wake up. You can't expect miracles.'

'How do you mean, I *can't* expect them, if I *can* expect them too – if you wake up?' Dark loom of the dome at last. Starlight silhouetting her black body, which was darker than the rest of night. Was she naked for him?

'Alas, that's the trouble with miracles. They swallow themselves like snakes. Twist away just as you touch them.'

'You won't twist away,' he pleaded. 'Not now. You're too dark to be wearing anything . . . dressed . . . hidden.' Darker than the dome. A darker gap in the dark dome; a portal he must enter. The velcro-pouch airlock parted like a dress unzipping; but she was already against it, undressed, as he reached his hand to part the pouch. Had he already parted it, or not? The more present she became to him and the more certain he was that the very next moment would bring the touch of her, the very next moment he would enter her, the darker grew her presence.

'Do you understand now? Do you grasp it?' she teased, her words laughing with him rather than at him.

Cracking his helmet open, he mixed his breath with hers. She joined him then, and slowly he slept, sinking beneath the dark lake waters with Milly-Kim.

Epilogue

The Torus was empty; emptier than the great doughnut hole in its midst where *Flagstaff* had once been stabled upside down. However strenuously or wide-eyed he walked or swam around it, to fill the emptiness with his own activity of his own voice or the memories of lost friends, the emptiness fled before him, unseen and unseeable – always around the other side of the hollow annulus – likewise dogging his heels, pursuing him. If he could see emptiness, it would not be empty. He had torn the doors of the three privacy cubicles and 'The Can' wide open and kept them that way from the day when he found an item of graffiti on the wall of 'The Can'. Presumably he had written it himself and forgotten about it. It said simply (right above the suction toilet): *It is a far far better thing you do now*—

Which was perfectly true; for he kept his sanity intact, even though his feet ached with his constant prowling around this toroidal basement, still four months away from Earth, in the void. If only there was gravity, and the exercise bicycle had wheels, he could have cycled round the torus – ever faster, building up a crazy speed: a charged particle, without a target, without any atom to split ... He discarded the idea of varying his route by trudging round the ceiling, refusing to turn the world on its head, for sanity's sake, so as not to forget which way was up, which down.

Eighty days into the transearth coast, Houston radioed:

'—We're not too happy about the configuration of *Warming Pan*. The stability ...We don't think it's aligned exactly enough ... We think it might degrade in a year, on present telemetry. But we're working on it. We think we can nudge its computer by radio ... alter the configuration slightly. It might work. So don't worry, Jim. You did a fine job, against odds.'

Why couldn't they have waited to tell him that till he got back? They waited long enough to tell them (who was *them*? – to tell *him*) about the Martian illness. What did they expect him to do: open his honourable belly like some Japanese, to atone? Commander Weaver must stay with his ship; and with his sanity.

Against odds? Who sets those odds? You people did when you let Silverman stay on the surface. You over-rode my authority because you were so damned greedy to know about the soil. You should have lied about the orbits or the fuel consumption or something – anything to get them back up there with me! You'd abort a mission on the Moon, but Mars is too far, eh? At least now you know one thing about the soil. Your colonists are going to need sanity-filters to live on Mars

However, he didn't say any of this aloud, into the radio. He knew he could shoulder the extra responsibility – of Houston's neglect to back up the man on the spot one hundred percent. He felt like another Lloyd Bucher captaining a second *Pueblo*; only there were no North Koreans swarming there in outer space ... His thoughts drifted to vistas of welcome: ticker-tape scattering down upon the limousine he rode through downtown Cleveland, banners outside Lakewood Senior High greeting their very own Martian alumnus, who had never set foot on Mars. He never could explain to the assembled school-kids that if *he* had set foot on that dirty soil, this mess would never have happened. He would keep quiet. Had Lloyd Bucher cracked? History ... He found that he couldn't remember. No, Houston didn't want him to open his belly. They were just pre-paring him, steeling him. The first steel swords, he remembered from an anecdote told by a West Point instructor, were quenched by sticking them into the bodies of slaves; after a while someone had the bright idea that a bucket of water might do just as well ... Was he some such slave? If so, the aim of the exercise was only to toughen him, not the sword.

On the eighty-fifth day Houston admitted that all was not well with the Russians. Sounding anxious and stilted, Spike Thorne promised, 'We'll lick the problem of the soil, Jim, I'm sure. We have some other leads, even if Gene didn't ... get any. But listen to this, the Russians launched the first stage of their Venus terraforming programme today, some months ahead of schedule according to them. Four identical Venus orbiters – robot biology labs to breed the algae they've tailored. They're following them up with more algae factories in about six months' time and an automatic orbiter to supervise the first algae drones and measure dispersal effects. In about three years they say they'll send a manned orbiter, to monitor progress. Capacity: six men, three women – they're not cluttered up with any landing module. We were once almost promised a seat on any large manned orbiter they sent. They say we can't have one now. It's their way of paying us back for the way we got hold of the Inca ... the Inca soil, I mean. *Zayits*, damn it! Their official reason is the fiasco with *Flagstaff*. Jim, it's so important you bring *Frontiersman* back perfectly, you see that, don't you?'

'Do you think I'm blind?'

The Sun rose and set a hundred times a day, transiting the self-dimming windows; and Weaver stared inwards towards the Sun, towards Earth and Venus. Inwards, but not inward.

Panther Science Fiction – A Selection from the World's Best S.F. List

More Great Science Fiction Books from Panther

DOUBLE STAR	Robert A. Heinlein	50p	☐
BEYOND THIS HORIZON	Robert A. Heinlein	40p	☐
STRANGE RELATIONS	Philip José Farmer	35p	☐
THE DISPOSSESSED	Ursula K. Le Guin	75p	☐
THE LEFT HAND OF DARKNESS			
	Ursula K. Le Guin	50p	☐
CITY OF ILLUSIONS	Ursula K. Le Guin	50p	☐
THE LATHE OF HEAVEN	Ursula K. Le Guin	35p	☐
THE FREDERIK POHL OMNIBUS	Frederik Pohl	40p	☐
THE WONDER EFFECT			
	Frederik Pohl & C. M. Kornbluth	40p	☐

The Classic LENSMAN series

TRIPLANETARY	E. E. 'Doc' Smith	50p	☐
FIRST LENSMAN	E. E. 'Doc' Smith	50p	☐
GALACTIC PATROL	E. E. 'Doc' Smith	50p	☐
GREY LENSMAN	E. E. 'Doc' Smith	50p	☐
SECOND STAGE LENSMEN	E. E. 'Doc' Smith	50p	☐
CHILDREN OF THE LENS	E. E. 'Doc' Smith	50p	☐
MASTERS OF THE VORTEX	E. E. 'Doc' Smith	50p	☐

The Classic SKYLARK series

THE SKYLARK OF SPACE	E. E. 'Doc' Smith	40p	☐
SKYLARK THREE	E. E. 'Doc' Smith	50p	☐
SKYLARK OF VALERON	E. E. 'Doc' Smith	50p	☐
SKYLARK DUQUESNE	E. E. 'Doc' Smith	50p	☐
THE IRON DREAM	Norman Spinrad	50p	☐
SLAN	A. E. van Vogt	40p	☐
MOONBEAST	A. E. van Vogt	40p	☐
THE VOYAGE OF THE SPACE BEAGLE			
	A. E. van Vogt	50p	☐
THE BOOK OF PTATH	A. E. van Vogt	40p	☐
THE WAR AGAINST THE RULL	A. E. van Vogt	40p	☐
AWAY AND BEYOND	A. E. van Vogt	35p	☐
DESTINATION: UNIVERSE!	A. E. van Vogt	30p	☐
LORD OF LIGHT	Roger Zelazny	40p	☐

All-action Fiction from Panther

Bestselling British Fiction in Panther Books

GIRL, 20	Kingsley Amis	40p	☐
I WANT IT NOW	Kingsley Amis	60p	☐
THE GREEN MAN	Kingsley Amis	30p	☐
THE RIVERSIDE VILLAS MURDER			
	Kingsley Amis	50p	☐
THAT UNCERTAIN FEELING	Kingsley Amis	50p	☐
BEST SUMMER JOB	Patrick Skene Catling	60p	☐
FREDDY HILL	Patrick Skene Catling	35p	☐
THE CATALOGUE	Patrick Skene Catling	35p	☐
THE SURROGATE	Patrick Skene Catling	40p	☐
GEORGY GIRL	Margaret Forster	25p	☐
THE FRENCH LIEUTENANT'S WOMAN			
	John Fowles	75p	☐
THE COLLECTOR	John Fowles	60p	☐
THE SHY YOUNG MAN	Douglas Hayes	40p	☐
THE WAR OF '39	Douglas Hayes	30p	☐
TOMORROW THE APRICOTS	Douglas Hayes	35p	☐
A PLAYER'S HIDE	Douglas Hayes	35p	☐
THE GOLDEN NOTEBOOK	Doris Lessing	£1.00	☐
BRIEFING FOR A DESCENT INTO HELL			
	Doris Lessing	60p	☐

All these books are available at your local bookshop or newsagent, or can be ordered direct from the publisher. Just tick the titles you want and fill in the form below.

Name ....

Address ....

....

Write to Panther Cash Sales, PO Box 11, Falmouth, Cornwall TR10 9EN

Please enclose remittance to the value of the cover price plus:

UK: 18p for the first book plus 8p per copy for each additional book ordered to a maximum charge of 66p

BFPO and EIRE: 18p for the first book plus 8p per copy for the next 6 books, thereafter 3p per book

OVERSEAS: 20p for first book and 10p for each additional book

Granada Publishing reserve the right to show new retail prices on covers, which may differ from those previously advertised in the text or elsewhere.